# Sweet Twins For My Brother's Best Friend

An Enemies To Lovers Romance
Claire Kirby

Copyright © 2024 by Claire Kirby

All rights reserved.

No portion of this book may be reproduced in any form without written permission from the publisher or author, except as permitted by U.S. copyright law.

# Contents

1. Chapter One   1
2. Chapter Two   9
3. Chapter Three   20
4. Chapter Four   31
5. Chapter Five   41
6. Chapter Six   50
7. Chapter Seven   57
8. Chapter Eight   65
9. Chapter Nine   73
10. Chapter Ten   81
11. Chapter Eleven   92
12. Chapter Twelve   98
13. Chapter Thirteen   103
14. Chapter Fourteen   109
15. Chapter Fifteen   113
16. Chapter Sixteen   129
17. Chapter Seventeen   134
18. Chapter Eighteen   144

| | | |
|---|---|---|
| | Chapter Nineteen | 149 |
| | Chapter Twenty | 155 |
| 21. | Chapter Twenty One | 161 |
| 22. | Chapter Twenty Two | 166 |
| 23. | Chapter Twenty Three | 173 |
| 24. | Chapter Twenty Four | 180 |
| 25. | Chapter Twenty Five | 188 |
| 26. | Chapter Twenty Six | 194 |
| 27. | Chapter Twenty Seven | 203 |
| 28. | Chapter Twenty Eight | 210 |
| 29. | Chapter Twenty Nine | 219 |
| 30. | Chapter Thirty | 225 |
| 31. | Chapter Thirty One | 231 |
| 32. | Chapter Thirty Two | 238 |
| 33. | Chapter Thirty Three | 243 |
| 34. | Chapter Thirty Four | 250 |
| 35. | Chapter Thirty Five | 262 |
| 36. | Chapter Thirty Six | 267 |
| 37. | Chapter Thirty Seven | 275 |
| 38. | Chapter Thirty Eight | 280 |
| 39. | Chapter Thirty Nine | 287 |
| 40. | Chapter Forty | 291 |
| 41. | Chapter Forty One | 297 |

| | | |
|---|---|---|
| 42. | Chapter Forty Two | 305 |
| 43. | Chapter Forty Three | 310 |
| 44. | Chapter Forty Four | 316 |
| 45. | Chapter Forty Five | 324 |
| 46. | Chapter Forty Six | 330 |
| 47. | Chapter Forty Seven | 340 |
| 48. | Chapter Forty Eight | 348 |
| 49. | Chapter Forty Nine | 355 |
| 50. | Chapter Fifty | 369 |
| 51. | Chapter Fifty One | 377 |
| | Also By Claire Kirby | 383 |

# Chapter One

## Hannah

I hear myself gasp.

As Chris walks into my new CPA office, I'm totally unprepared for the shivers of desire that go through me, causing me to flush and stammer as I greet him.

I've known him for years as my brother's best friend. I never thought I'd actually be attracted to him. My eyes feel glued to his slightly open lips until my gaze wanders down his body over his broad shoulders and achingly smooth skin.

I swallow hard, embarrassed to find that I'm literally salivating. I glance up at Chris' eyes and think that maybe I see him lick his lips for half a second before he meets my stare.

"Are you okay?" my brother, Tyler, asks me, trailing behind Chris with a drink carrier of coffee cups in his hand. He ducks under Chris' arm to get inside the office.

"Did you have to hold the door like that, you monkey?" Tyler asks him, grimacing as he sets the drinks down on my desk.

"I'm – I'm fine," I tell him, tapping the bottom of my pen against my desk as I try to make myself look away from Chris. Something about the lighting, maybe, or the fact that his tank top is stretched snugly across his torso and is practically a rag that barely covers his bulging, sweaty muscles – I seem powerless to stop staring at him.

"What are you two doing?" I ask in an attempt to make my drifting eyes seem normal. I point at the cups in Tyler's hand. "Did you bring me some coffee?"

"No, Ma'am, these are all for Lucy, yes, they are, yes, they are!" Tyler's voice rises up a few octaves as he plucks the smallest cup from the carrier and removes the lid to show a cup full of whipped cream. He squats down and holds it out to Lucy, my golden retriever, who lies sleeping like an angel beside my desk. Her nose twitches as the smell of dairy makes its way into her dreams. I picture her dreaming of a cartoon scene, where she's floating towards the animated airy pixels of the scent.

"Please, Tyler, don't. Last time it gave her the runs," I protest, but Lucy's long, purple tongue is already lolling out of her mouth, her big brown eyes slowly opening like the broken shades of an old house.

"Great, thanks, Ty," I sigh in exasperation as Tyler turns his one available palm up in a gesture of unarticulated confusion.

"Give him a break, Handy, he was so excited to bring Lucy a treat," Chris says defensively, pulling a cup out and setting it in front of me. "Here, drink your coffee and cheer up. Jesus."

Squinting, I squeeze the lid off the coffee to let it cool down. "Don't call me that," I warn through gritted teeth, lowering my hand to pull Lucy's tail through my hand and feel her smooth, silky fur. I remember now why I've never liked this cocky jerk, even if he is my brother's best friend since college.

"What? Handy? Why not? Tyler does."

"Tyler's my brother."

"We're practically siblings, too, Handy, come on. I've known you almost as long as he has." Chris sits at the other side of my desk and crosses a leg over his other ankle. He winks at me and sips his drink.

"Even if that were true, which it's not, Tyler calls me Handy. You cannot call me Handy. You are not my brother." I shoot daggers at Chris, my earlier lapse in judgment long-gone and replaced with the annoyance that Chris always stirs up in me.

'Handy' is a nickname Tyler gave me when I was just a little kid, a play off partly on my name and partly because I was always so helpful. What started as something cute, helping my dad with changing the oil in the car or mowing the lawn, turned into something else when Chris got his hands on the nickname.

Chris took something cute from my family life and started calling me Handy when I went off to college. He did it in a way that implied something rather smutty; something probably obvious to everyone except me.

It's as if he knew I was a virgin and was embarrassed about it, probably because I walked around as if I had 'virgin' written on my forehead. I think he therefore thought it would be funny to imply the exact opposite.

Young and fresh and incredibly vulnerable, I fell for it a few times, thinking he was simply calling me 'Handy' the way my brother did.

But that was before he gave himself away one year, really laying it on thick at Thanksgiving when I brought a boy home for the holiday.

I've thought of him as an arrogant prick ever since and can hardly stand to be in the same room with him. I wouldn't put up with him at all, under any circumstances, if he weren't Tyler's best friend.

Now, as a 25-year-old virgin, well, the nickname has only gotten progressively more ironic and painful over the years, though I have no idea if he's aware of my virginal status or not.

I mean, he can't be. How could he?

"What's the difference?" he asks, smiling coyly from behind his coffee cup, revealing a dimple in his left cheek that deepens as he holds in a laugh.

"All right, all right. Chris, you're not really helping your case here," Tyler warns from the floor.

He's sunk onto the floor completely and pulled Lucy's big head into his lap, where she can lazily lap at the bottom of the cup without having to move at all.

"What case? What are you two talking about?" I look from Tyler to Chris and see Chris slouch a little.

I can feel my green eyes sparkling with excitement as I realize that Chris needs something from me.

He sees my realization and shakes his head slightly, sighing.

"Oh, do you need financial advice, Christopher? From little ole me?"

"Don't sell yourself short, Hannah, I would never call you little," Chris jabs. I roll my eyes.

Maybe that insult would have worked in high school when I was incredibly insecure, but now at 25, I know that being tall is beautiful and most women envy me my stature.

Of course, when I am trying on jeans in a department store fitting room and subsequently piling them back into the sales woman's arms because they don't go down past my ankles, I usually hear the refrain about how men simply love tall women.

"And a redhead to boot," they gush. "You must be beating them off with a stick!"

I'm always tempted to ask where these men are, but I just smile and thank them.

Most girls are told the same lie I was told as a kid: that maybe I was being bullied now, but just wait! I'd grow into a beautiful woman and men would be all over me!

Yeah, right. Well, I'm still waiting.

"Great, well, how about you both get the fuck out of here so I can get some work done? You know, some people in Los

Angeles actually have need of my financial acumen and want my advice.

"You may not believe that, but I do have a lot of work to do and I am just starting to build this business, so...it was nice catching up with you as always but I've gotta get back to work." I stand up to emphasize my point, waving my hands in an upward motion towards Chris.

"Hey, I make money! I'm an orthopedic surgeon, for heaven's sake. And I take your advice a lot, so don't give me that."

Tyler protests from the floor, laughing as I shoo Chris toward the door and close it, leaving him standing outside.

"Come on, Ty. Play time's over. I've got a mountain of work here."

"Come on, let him in!" he laughs.

In response, Lucy pricks her ears back and forth.

"Sorry," he tells her, quieting down. Lucy lifts her large head and whines while looking at Chris through the window.

"Let him in. He needs your help. Please, Handy?" he implores.

I stand with my hands on my hips, still in front of the door but facing Tyler, who pulls Lucy's long, floppy ears through his hands.

I sigh and turn to face the mirrored door. Chris checks his hair in the two way mirror, and I roll my eyes.

"Fine." I open the door and let Chris back in.

"Christopher," I begin as he straightens and drops his hands to his sides.

"Hannah," Chris responds in an equally serious tone.

"I will let you in and help you if you apologize, beg for my help, tell me you've always been jealous of me —"

"—done," he says, pushing his way further into the office.

I stop him before he can come in, "and promise to never call me Handy again."

Chris twists his lips which, mere moments ago, I had felt were juicy and luscious, and cocks his head at me, his stare boring through me with his bright blue eyes.

"If that's really what you want."

"It is. Obviously."

"End of an era," he sighs. He swivels himself around and crouches down on one knee.

"Hannah, I am deeply sorry for hurting you and acting the way I have. I guess I'm just really insensitive."

He shrugs, looking down at the clay tile floor.

"And hell, I guess I am a little jealous of you. You're so good with numbers," he looks up at me and grips my hand, sending an electric jolt through my body that I ignore as he continues, "And all I'm good at is, well, toning my body – and helping others tone theirs, of course."

He looks up at me from under his ridiculously long eyelashes. I tap my toes, and gesture for him to continue.

"But that's no excuse, and I know that. At the end of the day, I really, really need your help. Will you do me the honor of helping me, even though I don't deserve it? Please...Hannah?"

I glance over at Tyler, who shrugs from the floor. Good natured Tyler, who never seems to see the bad in anyone, even Chris. I peel my hand out of his.

"Sure." I curl my lip and sit back down behind my desk. "But not for free. You can afford me and I'm not letting you off cheap."

I wave my hand at the seat he had been sitting in earlier and pull out a notebook, a file of contracts, and a calculator. "So, Mr. Stephens, let's talk money."

# Chapter Two
## Christopher

Tyler stands up, awkwardly forcing Lucy out of his lap by scooping her up and swirling her around on the tile. "Well, that's my cue."

I grin, watching him walk around Hannah's desk to kiss her forehead. I've always found it hilarious how differently they feel about money.

Tyler can't talk about money at all. He finds it deeply uncomfortable. I pray for his future wife.

Hannah looks up at him sternly and jokes, "We'll get to your finances next."

"Sorry I couldn't get you that discount, Chris," Tyler tells me, dropping his hand on my shoulder thickly, "but also, if you think about it, it's really your own fault."

"I know." I try to look properly wounded, then wrap my hand around his wrist and draw him down like I'm going to kiss him.

He dodges me expertly and heads for the door. "All right, all right, cut it out."

In the doorway, Tyler points at Hannah, who points back. For a moment, they look like a scene out of ET.

"Good luck," is all he says before disappearing out the door.

"Good luck," she says confidently. "Psh. We don't need luck. We got this. So tell me about your vision for your business, Chris."

She tucks the end of her pen in her mouth, pulling down her bottom lip, while she cocks her head at me, her green eyes large and unblinking. I haven't seen her since a couple of years ago when I attended a Jackson family Christmas party.

She seemed less confident then, hunched and quiet, but now behind her own desk of her own business she's definitely come into her own.

I can feel my short tighten slightly when her tongue peeks out as she taps her pen while waiting for my answer.

"Sure, well, you know, I own a chain of fitness centers around LA and I am thinking of expanding further. I'm just not sure I can afford it and need expert advice."

"OK. I think Tyler has mentioned that from time to time. I think he said that he sometimes refers his post-surgical patients to you for physical therapy while they recuperate." she tells me, looking down at her notebook and writing something down.

I blink at her. "Yes, that's true. And, on occasion, I refer clients who have ortho complaints to Tyler so he can check them out medically and determine whether they need surgical intervention."

She shrugs. "Yeah, that sounds familiar, but I'm not too clear on the details."

Ever since I made the Forbes '30 under 30'...God, that was 6 years ago...there seems to be a woman lurking around every corner, usually acting as if she doesn't know who I am – until she eventually slips up and reveals that she recognizes me from the article.

"Well, as I say, your brother and I refer clients to each other," I point out awkwardly, uncrossing my ankle from my knee and crossing the other.

"You assume everyone knows all about you, Chris, and what you do?"

"I think you should, at least."

"Why? Because you and Tyler are friends? You came to me. You showed up with coffee asking for my help, even though I haven't talked to you in a few years. Back then, I thought you were arrogant and full of yourself, and I don't see that you've changed appreciably in the interim."

I turn my hands up to the sky and leave my mouth open, surprised by the anger I feel coming from her. "I didn't mean to upset you."

She lets out a wry laugh. "Upset me? Again, Chris, I don't care enough about you to be upset. I'm just pointing out that not everyone knows your every move or is intimately familiar with either you or your business."

"I'm your client."

"Well, I'll look you up on LinkedIn later, how about that?" she spits out, her hand moving furiously on her paper.

"Okay...sorry, I guess."

I wince as soon as I say it – "I guess" – but it's too late to take it back.

I should have just said sorry. I am always assuming people, at least people in LA, do know who I am and what I do and maybe that is obnoxious.

But, to be fair...well, look, I have been to Hannah's and Tyler's parents' for various holidays and dinners. There's no blessed way that Hannah doesn't know exactly what I do – and probably how many gyms I now own. I can't for the life of me understand why she's pulling this attitude with me.

Unless...no. It couldn't be. Although...she is protesting a bit too much. Where's all this coming from?

Her eyes shoot up at the same time as I wince, and I see her irises follow the path of my cringe. I must have looked apologetic enough because she nods to herself and says, "OK. Let's move on. Go ahead and tell me your plans for the fitness centers."

"I want an empire, basically."

"I always tell clients how important it is to have realistic goals," she jokes.

She glances up from her paper for a second, her eyes sparkling, before continuing to scribble something down on her notepad as I talk.

"I'm serious. I mean, I'm already pretty successful, but I'd like to open up some more fitness centers outside of California, too. I'm terrified of making the wrong move, expanding too quickly, and losing it all. I've heard that's a big danger when you don't expand with a financially sound business plan in place."

It's the truth. I haven't told anyone, not even Tyler, but my dad went to prison for tax evasion when I was younger. He missed a chunk of my childhood.

I never thought I'd have a successful business, let alone be considering expanding it interstate, and I'm afraid of doing anything wrong and running afoul of the law. 'Like father, like son' and all that. I know enough to know I need good, solid financial guidance.

For a moment, I consider telling Hannah all of that. Something about her gentle eyes and the smattering of freckles across the tiny slope of her nose makes her seem innocent, trustworthy.

But while I'm still considering it, she asks, "Which fitness centers are yours? I'm not sure Tyler ever mentioned the name to me and I've only recently come back to LA from school, so I'm a bit out of the loop."

"CHOICE Fitness," I answer, peeling a dog hair off my shorts that somehow appeared, despite my not having touched Lucy even once.

Hannah opens her mouth wide. "You're kidding! No shit?" I shrug, and she leans forward a little, so that her breasts push together over the desk.

I look at them for a beat before glancing back up at her face, ashamed. "Wow, Chris, congratulations."

She sits back again but continues to smile at me with amazement. "I've heard of those, yeah. I have a couple of friends who work out there."

I can't help but laugh a little. "Yeah, I mean, half of LA works out there."

Hannah's eyes drop back down to her paper. "And yet so humble, too."

Her face reads like someone who's so done with me that a pang shoots through me.

I don't want her to be done with me. I try to think of something to get back the moment she was impressed with me.

"Thanks, though, Hannah. You know, I worked hard for what I have, and I just want to do the right thing here, you know? Expand in the right way, create jobs for people, help folks keep healthy and fit. Do some good, you know?"

Hannah lifts her chin so that her lips pout in understanding.

"Totally. I get it."

She leans back and looks me over for a few seconds, looking completely relaxed. She looks over at Lucy and smiles at her in a way that incites her to stand and come over to her.

Hannah chuckles and pats Lucy with her palm.

"Well, at least I think I have a better understanding of what's motivating you."

"That's good. See, I know how to set up and run a gym or fitness center. But I'm not a numbers guy. I don't know how to interpret them for the most part, and putting them together into some sort of business plan is pretty much beyond me. My last CPA did that for me but he died recently and I don't like the guy who took over the business. The fact that you are getting yourself set up as a CPA is perfect timing for me."

I watch her face disappear behind her desk as she nuzzles the top of Lucy's head. Involuntarily, like scratching an itch or dancing to a beat, I feel myself smile at her happiness. Something about watching a good woman with a big dog...I'm a simple man. I like simple things.

She appears again and smiles a smaller smile than the one she favored Lucy with.

"Thanks for saying that, Chris. Listen, here's a list of the financial records I'll need you to gather up so we can have a serious discussion about what you'd like to do and what the business can afford. Once you get all that info together, give me a call and we'll set up a time to draw up some plans for your continued expansion. Here's my card. Email's right there."

She slides a thick card across the shiny, lacquered top of her desk.

"So impersonal, Hannah. I could have just asked Tyler for your number," I say, flashing her my best winning smile, the smile that has half of the women in LA tearing out my picture from the Forbes magazine.

Hannah looks at me with something like curiosity, perhaps mixed with sarcasm. She lifts her lips in an emotionless smile as though it's hung by string, though her eyes twinkle at me under long, blonde eyelashes.

She taps her desk with her pen, rat tat tat, and runs her tongue over her top teeth. "No, this is good." She points at the card.

Is this flirting? Are we flirting?

I think we are, but I'm not sure when it started, except that she's gorgeous, there's no denying that. Her almond-shaped eyes seem to take up half her face under delicate, wispy bangs, a smattering of freckles across her nose and cheeks, and a beautiful head of voluminous red hair.

I clear my throat, embarrassed by the realization dawning on me.

I pull on the legs of my shorts, attempting to hide the growing erection I'm developing because I'm staring too hard at Hannah's body.

I pick up her card, turn it over, and smack it against the desk, smiling awkwardly.

"Well, hey, I will definitely email you soon then, after I get everything together. Thanks, Hannah. And you'll share your notes with me next time we meet?" I slap my knees and stand to my feet, pointing at her notepad.

"My notes?"

"Yeah, the notes you've been writing this whole time?" I chuckle. "What, are they secret? You're not a therapist, so I'm pretty sure you can share your notes with me, can't you?" I scratch at my neck and rest my grip on the collar of my tank, stretching it out even further.

Hannah's smile leaks slowly from the corners of her mouth as it spreads across her face, pushing her cheeks up and showing a wide smile of brilliantly white teeth.

She scrunches her nose like a rabbit and lets out a small giggle, one of surprise and delight.

"Ah, my notes. Here, I'll give them to you now." She rips off the top page, scribbles something quickly, then hands it to me.

Now I'm the one filled with surprise and delight because in blue ink she's sketched out a startingly realistic portrait of me, smiling.

"Hannah, you did this in like… less than 10 minutes."

"Ah, see, you are a numbers guy!"

When I don't move, frozen to the spot and staring at the picture, she lets out a chuckle. "Go on. I signed it for you, don't worry."

"You have real talent, Hannah!"

"Shucks." Hannah rolls her eyes but twists a small smile in her cheek. "I'll see you soon, Chris," she says in a quiet voice, gathering all her hair in one hand and twisting it into a spiral that shines in the light of her office windows.

"Yeah," I murmur and walk towards the door. Lucy patters over to me and leans against the side of my leg.

"Well, hello," I tell her and crouch down into a squat to pat her side.

Hannah smiles at the interaction. "I pat her just like that. Everyone always says it's too hard, but I swear she loves it."

"Of course she does." I look Lucy in her eyes and say, "She's tough" in the voice that people always affect when talking to animals. In response, she jumps up and licks at my face, nearly knocking me out of my precarious stance.

"Oh! Lucy, no! Sorry, she's not really a jumper. She must really like you."

"That's okay. I like her, too. Hey, girl!"

I smooth her ears down and hold her face in my hands. I bring my nose to hers, and her wet snout is cold against my own nose.

"Hannah, I really am sorry about..."

Before I can apologize again for the stupid nickname, she waves her hand, visibly flinching. I tap the drawing on my thigh with a small nod. "Right, sorry."

I shut the glass door behind me and head for my car. Halfway down the sidewalk, I turn back to look through the windows and realize that they're mirrored.

There's no looking in, no looking back. I look at the reflection of my own face, with its curly hair, thick brows and bumped nose. I wonder how she could see me so clearly so quickly.

# Chapter Three
## Hannah

Knowing that I have no other clients for the day, I lock up, Lucy trailing behind me as I double check the locks on filing cabinets, sweep the floors, and turn off the lights.

Hearing the clack of Lucy's nails against the wood floors comforts me. It's all so mundane, and I know it'd probably be nothing special to anyone else, but this is exactly what I've worked to achieve and I will never take it for granted.

Six years of higher education, first getting my Bachelors Degree and then my Masters, allows me to relish the sensation of sitting in a comfortable rolling chair in my own office, at my own desk, in my own business, as I am bathed in sunlight with my dog by my side.

I clip Lucy's leash to her collar and try to avoid the excited tongue she laps at me as she anticipates going for a walk.

I open the front door and lock it behind us as I take her down the sidewalk to a nearby dog park. The walk is short and part of the reason I leased this particular office in the first place.

I love walking down the sidewalk in Los Angeles. It's very robust during the daylight hours, but calms considerably after 5:00 when most businesses close for the day.

I love watching all the so-called beautiful people enjoying their lives, almost as if none of them has a job.

I'm always surprised at how many people don't seem to be working in the middle of any given day, until I remember that I am out and about in the middle of the day, too. So who am I to judge?

Lucy walks directly beside me, her face turned to look up at me, her tongue hanging out. Sometimes I look at her face, full of love and trust, and I just can't believe that I am lucky enough to call her my own.

I'm so sorry she went through what she did, abandoned in a dumpster as a little puppy, but I do count myself lucky that she ended up with me, coming out of what must have been a horrific situation, still willing to love and be loved.

When I found her she was wearing a collar, but it didn't have a name or contact info. I can't imagine how anyone could have left her there.

I open the gate to the park and sit down on a park bench as I let Lucy off her lead so that she can play and roll around in the grass.

As always, she instantly rolls around on her back from side to side, filling her fur with blades of grass and pine needles.

"Go on, girl, run!" I tell her, prodding at her side with the toe of my shoe. She untwists herself and looks at me for one moment before bursting into an erratic run that zigs and zags across the park.

I pull out a medium-sized canvas from my computer bag, a thin one I bought from a secondhand art store and painted over in white, and sketch out just the idea of a painting that I'll get to later once Lucy has fallen asleep in her crate and I don't have to worry about picking small, black hairs out of the paint as I go.

I cross my ankle over my knee to balance the canvas across it and draw out the landscape in front of me, paying special attention to the perspective.

The image of Chris' awe when he viewed the portrait I drew of him pops into my head.

I quickly realize that I would gladly draw a picture of him every day if I could bring out that same look in his eyes.

"You're so focused," a man's voice says next to me, and I jerk in surprise.

"Oh, sorry, I didn't mean to scare you." I swivel my head to the man next to me -- a lanky, blonde man with an easy smile and brown eyes.

"That's okay," I respond quickly, glancing over at the man's dog, a golden doodle sitting calmly and waiting for him to throw a tennis ball. I look back up at the man.

"Sorry I jumped. You just startled me."

He laughs a little. "Like I said, you were focused."

He throws the ball hard, and his dog instantly launches into a high-speed run.

"I'm Scott, by the way." He holds out his hand to shake mine. "Better shake my hand now before it's covered in dog drool."

We shake hands, and I say quietly, "Hannah" before I retreat back into myself and my world, hunching back over my canvas.

I can feel his energy shift as he realizes we aren't going to be talking, and I feel that familiar shame creep into my cheeks, the blood heating my face the way it's always done when men talk to me.

I've never felt capable of having a comfortable conversation with any man, especially not men that I can tell find me attractive.

It's like being stuffed under a pile of blankets. I just can't seem to get comfortable. I feel hot, sweaty, and heavy. Stifled.

Something in me shuts down when confronted with my own sexuality.

I can barely put on a bathing suit without cringing. Before the energy of Scott next to me, quietly tossing the tennis ball for his dog over and over, becomes too much, I stick my still mostly-blank canvas into my bag and stand up.

"Lucy! 'mere, girl!" I call and force my shaking hands to steady enough to clip her leash on.

"Hey," Scott says, "I'm sorry if I messed up your moment or something. I didn't mean to scare you off."

His smile is crooked and it honestly reads to me like the smile of someone who hopes I'll tell him that he has it all wrong, that I've got a hair appointment I forgot about or a meeting I need to get to, but instead I shrug with one shoulder and half a smile and slip out of the park, telling Lucy what a good girl she is all the way back to the office.

I unlock the door again and let Lucy off the leash.

She scuttles to her water bowl instantly, and I follow her to the small kitchen to scrounge for some snacks, settling on a small bowl of nuts, chips and a couple of string cheeses.

Living out of the office has its pros and cons, of course.

Sometimes a friend will come over and balk at the lack of a stovetop, but the reality is that I can't remember ever using a stovetop more than once or twice a year, anyway. I never really learned to cook, aside from eggs, and even those I usually manage to burn.

I go into the back office, which I've set up as my bedroom, putting my foot firmly on the arm of the couch, so I can yank on the hide-a-bed as hard as I can to pull it fully out.

The stiff metal squeals under my fist before finally giving way and stiffly unfolding in sections.

I slick my sweaty hair back and pull it into a low ponytail before folding my legs underneath me and collapsing onto the bumpy mattress.

I pull out my canvas and try to finish the sketch I started of Lucy, but my mind wanders as I begin to draw her. I know it would stress out my family to know I live here in back of the office.

I haven't told any of them, not even Tyler. I really don't want to be nagged about it.

They think I have a quaint little apartment out in Valencia, and the only reason no one comes to visit me there is because Mom and Dad have a nice large home where we can all gather when we get together.

I go over my rehearsed answer should anyone find out the truth.

No, it's not weird, and I'm not in debt. Oh, my God. Okay, well, I'm in some debt, but no more than the average American, certainly less than the average Californian, so don't be so dramatic.

Look, I went to school for a long time in order to get this business, and now that I have it, I just want to pay off my student loans, get the business off the ground, and maybe sacrifice some creature comforts the first couple of years so that I can be on a solid financial footing before I get a place of my own.

I cringe at the phrase 'couple of years,' I can already hear them shrilly repeating, 'YEARS? Oh, Hannah, no!'

No, 'years' won't do. Gotta find a substitute for that last part. I nibble on the end of my string cheese, pulling a long mozzarella cord and letting it sit between my teeth for a second before chewing.

But anyone who has their own business would get it. Businesses are sacrifice. Real legacies are hard work. If you think you can be a legend in a comfortable two bedroom in Beverly Hills right out of school, well, you can't. You're just another face in the crowd.

I remember when Tyler was going through college, rooming with Chris, and they'd come to our house for holidays, and they'd always look so disheveled, exhausted, and grateful for a real mattress and home cooking.

Tyler would say, "The mattresses, Handy, you wouldn't believe it. We sleep in bunk beds" and then point to the two of them before they'd burst out laughing. They seemed happy, though, back in their salad days.

Chris. Now there's someone I've been avoiding thinking about. My face flushes just thinking about the memory of him being here in the office earlier.

He was flirting with me, wasn't he? Was there a moment? Not that I could date my brother's best friend if I wanted to. Not that I want to, especially since he's also my client now.

And he's so full of himself. He talks like someone who's never experienced a moment's rejection. But he has. And so publicly, too. I think it's all just a big defense mechanism.

I look down at my sketch and see that I've given Lucy five legs. I put the canvas down and lay back with my hands behind my head.

I've never been rejected either, but I've never really put myself out there.

What would that even look like? I try to picture it, closing my eyes and feeling slats of soft sun through my blinds and on my eyelids.

I could just say to Chris, "Hey, enough work. How about we do something else?" Then push aside all the paperwork, and reach over to pull him to me by the front of his shirt.

No, that's too...I don't know what that is. Too forward, I guess. Not me. I shake my head and open my eyes for a second, then close them again.

I could coyly drop a pen and when he goes to pick it up, I do, too, and our hands meet. Then the touch of my hand ignites something in him and he grips my face with his hands, seeing me in a way no man has ever seen me before.

I sigh. This is so stupid. Nothing will ever happen between me and Chris because I am incapable of reaching out. Unless he reaches out.

But since I basically can't stand him and find him too arrogant and cocky for words, even that wouldn't work. But it does conjure up some interesting thoughts...

It's late at night. We've stayed up working on his documents and financial plan. He's at the door about to leave, and he says, "Aren't you coming?" and I shake my head. "No, I sleep here." A brief look of shock crosses his face, but he quickly drops it. "Oh. Well, do you want some company?"

I slide my hand into my underwear, my breathing already heavy, and I hold my lips open, feeling cool air hit the soft, spongy skin inside.

I shrug at him. "Maybe. Are you offering?" He laughs gently and places a hand on my hip, then slides it around to my lower waist, pulling me into him. I look in shock down at his arm and then up at his face. He is smiling and unaware that I've never been touched like this…ever.

I slide my finger into my opening, feeling a wall of juices, ready and waiting for something.

I plunge my finger farther into them, coating my digit in the sticky lubricant, and follow the curved tract of my tunnel, then pull it back out achingly slowly, feeling it retract and pulse as I leave it empty.

He puts a finger on my chin and lifts my face to him as he bends down to kiss me softly, his lips two warm pillows. I moan automatically and my hands know what to do on their own as they wrap around his neck and stretch down his shoulder blades.

He wraps arms around my waist and lifts me up to slither my legs around him. His hands are under my ass, holding me up, and he mutters into my ear, "Do you have a bed you want me to take you on or can I take you right here?" and the hair on my arms stands up.

I keep my index finger inside my canal and with my thumb, I slowly increase pressure on the hood of my clit, not rubbing yet, just letting it sit on top and feel the weight of my thumb.

I spread my legs slightly and hold still, enjoying the moment. everything is just teetering on the edge. My finger is inside me. My thumb is on my clit. I hold my breath. I'm still.

Even in my fantasy, I don't know what to say.

I whine a little at the question as he holds me and nibbles on my neck. He brings me over to my desk and lowers me onto it.

"How about I take you right here?" he growls, lowering to his knees. He lifts my skirt and pulls my panties aside, revealing my pussy already wet and ready for him. It's bald and fat and swollen with a slick of wet sheen.

"Oh, you're ready, aren't you?" He looks back at the window then smiles at me. "Do you think anyone can see us? Do you care? Would you like someone to be watching us? Maybe someone is looking now."

His tongue laps at me, cleaning off my labia and thighs and drinking in my juices.

I run my fingers over my labia lips and feel how soaked I am, really. I'm coated in a sticky gloss.

I hurriedly kick my pants and underwear off and lie back down. My clit throbs with desire, and I give in to it, finally moving my finger back and forth across the delicate knob, feeling my orgasm swelling and building.

I beg him to lick inside me. "Please, please, please," I whisper, coiling my fingers through his black curls until I can't tell where his hair ends and my fingers begin.

He lets me guide his mouth closer to my opening and I feel his warm breath against it as he breathes. His tongue plunges inside and I let out a moan that turns into a scream of delight as he holds my ass to push his tongue further inside me.

I can feel his cheeks flat against my thighs. I stroke his forehead as he laps at me like I'm a delicacy. "You taste so good," he whispers, looking up at me before going in for seconds.

My orgasm explodes from me, and I let out a breathy moan as I feel the release throughout my body. I feel it most in my chest and realize I've been holding my breath.

My heart pounds in my chest and in my pussy, and I continue stroking my clit, feeling it throb beneath my fingertip.

I let off some of the pressure, only illuminating the spot with soft touches. The cum on my finger dries quickly, and I finally relax, melting into the mattress beneath me.

As a 25 year old virgin, one thing I know how to do is touch myself. I have developed a strategy that works every time. My masturbation sessions are short. My orgasms burst and typically taper off quickly, but this one was a little different.

This one was longer and came in oscillating waves, each one crashing over me more heavily than the one before.

I breathe heavily, lying on my soaked sheets, and consider whether or not I should go to the gym tonight for a shower to wash off all the sweat and cum I've accumulated. Before I can think about it too hard, I fall into a delicious sleep.

# Chapter Four
## Christopher

The next day, I wake up alone in my condo like I always do. I water my plants like I always do, one at a time, humming as I go because I read once that it was good for them, and then I make myself breakfast like I always do.

Today, it's an egg white frittata. I save the yolks for baking later. In they plop, mixing with the other yolks in the Tupperware, dropping like a rock in a lake, and then I stand over the stove, listening to nothing.

I have a pact with myself which states that, in the mornings, I can't use my phone for at least the first hour I am awake.

I stay out of the news, off social media, and away from podcasts while I shower and make breakfast. By then, usually an hour has passed and I'm ready to rejoin society and the world at large.

I walk around my condo naked, and I even cook naked, leaping back from the oil splatters as I do.

I find comfort in rituals. When rituals end, there's change, and where there's change, there's often discomfort and, occasionally, devastation.

My therapist, a nice man named Jerry with a red beard and gray hair, tells me that it's a byproduct of being left at the altar. So much changed in that one day.

I decided to go on my honeymoon alone for two glorious weeks, I felt free. I drank and danced and pretended nothing was wrong or different.

Then I got home, and my fiancée had moved out completely, leaving me nothing, not even a note. She took the ring I gave her and the puppy we'd adopted together that year. I didn't fight for either one, and I never got an explanation as to why she left me on our wedding day.

Sometimes in my sessions with Jerry, I want to ask, 'Even now? Five years later? It's still about her?' but I'm afraid he'll tell me that it always will be, so I refrain.

After I finish my frittata, I pull on some workout clothes – basketball shorts and a tank – and I fit a pair of headphones into my ears.

I turn on a motivational podcast, one where a woman talks slowly in a low voice and birds chirp behind her, and I go outside and start to run.

I've heard all sorts of takes on running. People say it makes them feel alone but in a good way, people say it stops the voices, people talk about the so-called runner's high.

When I run, none of that happens.

I simply feel. I can't think about anything. At all.

I feel the bottoms of my feet on the pavement and my toes squished against the narrow sides of my running shoes. I feel my shirt dragging across my skin and the sun on the top of my head and my lungs bursting open like hot sand against wet skin.

I run to my closest gym, 5 miles away. I arrive sweaty and exhausted, and I lean against the brick wall outside for a moment, trying to slow my breathing against the rhythmic pounding of my heart.

People pass me with strange faces like they won't be gasping for air on a treadmill in a little while.

I love what I do, and I'm happy that I've created a place where people feel safe and enjoy working out, but I wish LA wasn't so removed from...nature.

The outdoors is, in so many ways, really good for people. It nurtures us. We need to get outside more and appreciate our surroundings.

I push open the front doors of the CHOICE fitness location I frequent, the one I tend to favor for my own personal workouts, nodding at the front desk employees, pretending not to notice their whispers as I walk past them and into the men's locker room.

I know they speak quietly to each other in order to illustrate their best behavior as long as I'm in the house, and I don't take it personally since I am, after all, their boss and the owner.

I know what it's like to have the boss breathing down your neck. People are always surprised to find that I have an active hands-on relationship with my own business, which I find strange – but about right for LA.

There are too many trust fund kids with business investments that they have no real emotional or personal connection to, I guess.

But I'm not here today to workout. I'm here to gather all the financial information that Hannah asked me for.

I change out of my sticky workout clothes, shower, and change into some branded work clothes.

I could put on a button up shirt, do the whole I'm-the-boss shtick where I then stand out and tend to be approached by our clients when I'm on site.

But it embarrasses me when that happens, as I prefer to leave customer service issues to the staff, so I stick with khakis and a CHOICE tee.

In the cramped back office, I find my administrative assistant, Sarah, clacking away on a loud, hot pink keyboard. She stops for a moment when she sees me and sips on something I can see is green through clear plastic, nodding her head upwards in acknowledgement, her sleek black hair sliding to the side.

"Mm." She lets out the noise involuntarily as she pulls the straw out of her mouth and acknowledges me.

"Good morning, Boss. Didn't expect to see you here today," she says, returning her fingers to their fast little happy dance on the keyboard.

"Please, Sarah, Boss was my father. You can call me Chris," I joke, sitting on the edge of her desk. It's a small area, basically a closet really, except for the window.

I shoved her in here when we first started expanding and I realized I needed to start hiring some administrative help as well as trainers and staff to work the floor and assist the clientele.

Since then, I've been promising Sarah that when the next expansion phase begins, she will have some serious responsibilities in getting it off the ground – and I'll see to it she get an office more befitting her status in the organization. I definitely don't want to lose her – especially now that I'm preparing to broaden our horizons.

Sarah rolls her eyes at me. I don't normally use this phrase to describe people, but Sarah is what I think of as chronically professional.

I noticed after I stuck her back here, and away from the front desk, that not only was she happier, but the front office staff actually unclenched their shoulders and relaxed more as well.

Maybe they feared Sarah was a little "spy" for management? Who knows?

"Okay, Chris, what are you doing here…in that?"

She wrinkles her nose at the CHOICE shirt. I have half a mind to be offended, but I know she's a fashionista who was relieved to be able to go back to silk blouses and high neck tanks. She'd prefer me in a more tailored look since she believes the boss should look like a boss.

I consider reminding her that I am, in fact, the boss and can wear what I like and show up when I like, but I decide to cut straight to the point of my visit.

"I'm just here for the financial data for the last two quarters. I also need the current balance sheet, profit and loss statements for the last two years, tax returns for the last two years, the operating agreement, a list of the businesses licenses for each location, leases for each location, and a list of company employees. How long do you think it will take you to get all that together?"

I glance around the room at the strangely empty space. Although small, it leaves Sarah with plenty of room since she only needs a desk, a chair, a computer, a printer, a phone and a credenza.

When I was younger, years ago now, maybe a decade, I interned at a physical therapist's office with a nice man named Jonathan, and he had an entire room just for files. He had filing cabinets upon filing cabinets, big bulky metal things with peeling paint, full of folders. I wonder how long it took his team to eventually go digital.

Sarah nods. "Mhm, sure. Give me a second."

"No worries, just tell me when you're--"

"Done. They're printing now."

She smiles widely at me and sips from her drink again before going back to typing.

I take the warm, freshly-printed papers and flip through them for a moment to make sure it's everything I asked for.

"It's all there," she assures me, looking up at me and then handing me a thumb drive.

"I made you a digital copy of everything, too, in case your CPA would prefer it.

She folds her hands under her chin. She has long fingers that taper off into long square nails with rhinestones on the end. She sometimes scratches her head with them, and I can't help but think about how satisfying it looks. She catches me looking and holds out a hand.

"Do you like them?"

A little taken aback by her foray into personal matters, I smile encouragingly and peer at them closer.

"I do."

"Well, that's great to hear, because I got them done while with a potential investor, so they were billed to the company credit card."

I sigh deeply. "One day, we're going to have a real conversation, Sarah," I tease and leave the small area, holding the papers rolled up in my hand.

I look through them as I approach the front desk and call out, "Up ahead! A treasure!"

Dropping the papers, I say, "It's you guys. You're all the treasure."

Collectively, they groan, and I shrug. "Whatever. I tried."

A guest enters through the front door as I stand at the desk, and a blonde bombshell in a pair of leggings and a sports bra enters, and I welcome her in.

A spark of recognition lights up her eyes as she approaches the scanner and scans her barcode for entry. Her face fills the screen in front of me, along with her personal information.

"Have a good workout, Charlie," I tell her enthusiastically.

She offers me a friendly smile and sidles up to my side of the counter, so that she's closest to me, leaving the other two staff members looking our way with small little grins – they know what's coming,

Charlie waves me over with a subtle hand flourish. My eyebrows head for my hairline as I approach her in response to her conspiratorial motion. "Is this like an Undercover Bosses thing?" she asks me.

I whisper back, "What do you mean?"

"Aren't you Christopher Stephens? The owner?"

I return her smile. "That's right. But don't tell anyone."

I straighten up as another guest enters through the front door and I say a good morning to him as well. I glance over at Charlie and wink, placing my index finger over my lips.

***

Two hours later, on her way out, Charlie drops a scrap of paper on the desk and tells me to call her so she can take me out for drinks.

"I don't know if I should, Charlie. HR might not appreciate that," I respond honestly, fingering the corners of the paper.

"Well, it's not like you're my teacher or anything. And I'm not an employee. So I think we're good."

She's slightly sweaty, her blonde baby hairs sticking to her face, and I admire her confidence. For a woman to know she's gorgeous even after a workout is something you don't see every day.

"I know, but still." I shrug, leaving it there, letting the lame answer hang in the air.

I expect her to walk off in a huff, but instead she whispers, "I can keep more than one secret at a time."

Her tongue peeks out between her teeth a little, and her eyes flit down to my mouth. She's bold.

I give up and respond as though I will definitely call her, shoving the paper in my pocket, but knowing deep down that taking her out would go nowhere.

I haven't been able to commit to anyone since Julie, and I don't feel any closer to doing so, either.

And I don't know if I ever will be.

# Chapter Five
## Hannah

The next few days are the same as most of my days are now.

I stay busy.

I work on my art, I play with Lucy, and I go to work. I haven't taken Lucy back to that dog park since that man, Scott, talked to me. I'm too afraid I'll see him again and he'll remember me, and I won't know what to say.

I sit at my desk eating a toasted bagel with a microwaved egg on top as I read an email. It's from Tom Dougherty, a client I've been working with for a while.

He runs a nonprofit in town that provides toiletries for various organizations like food banks and foster homes, and I help him at an extremely discounted rate.

He's a bit needy, and I've learned that I can likely only manage one nonprofit at a time because they require so much auditing.

Frankly, most people at nonprofits don't know much about financial issues or how to plan or manage within their budget. They seem to run on dreams and good intentions. I think that for Christmas I might give him and his team a few dream catchers. I can't decide if that would be funny or rude.

His latest email is a request to check to see if they qualify for a grant that they're looking into. I responded that I'd get to it sometime today and get back to him within the week.

My fingers fly across the keyboard while I hold my bagel in my mouth and a little piece of egg slides off and between my 'd' and 'f' key. Groaning, I try to pick it out and another piece falls into my lap, so I stand to wipe it off and onto the floor.

Lucy gratefully runs to it and greedily licks it off, her tongue flat against the wood.

Looking around, I realize I don't have a canister of compressed air, so I pick up my laptop and shake it.

Of course, Chris picks this moment to prance in, a smile across his face and his hair sweaty again.

My shoulders droop when I notice him and, for a moment, we just stare at each other, me with a bagel in my mouth as I shake my laptop, him still in the doorway, pulling the headphones out of his ears. "Do you need help?" he finally asks.

"No, I'm good," I say, but with my mouth full it sounds more like, "Nnnmmmgd."

He steps forward and pulls the bagel out of my mouth. "Does that help?" he asks with a laugh and sets it down on my desk.

I smile awkwardly without teeth. "Thank you." I wipe crumbs off my pants. "What are you doing here? You don't have an appointment, do you? Wait, do you?"

Anxiety shoots through me as I wonder if I missed something in my calendar and I open it up, still standing.

"No, no," he assures me. "I didn't know I needed one. I need one?"

He sits down in the plush chair across from my desk. It's a wingback chair with red velvet upholstery that's seen better days, but it's all I can afford at the moment. The feet are elegant swirls of cherry-stained wood.

I shoot Chris an icy look.

Setting my laptop down, I sit back in my chair, shooing Lucy away from repeatedly licking the no longer egg-y spot on the floor.

"Well, I don't know, Chris, do people need an appointment to see you in a professional capacity?"

Grinning, he says, "Well, look, you're lucky, aren't you? You would have been stuck in bagel limbo if it weren't for me."

"Chris, I gave you my email for a reason, all right? Please use it. Do not show up here unexpected. It isn't fair to me or respectful to my schedule."

I use my firmest voice, which is admittedly not very firm, but I hope the firm words make up for it.

Admittedly, I may be laying it on thick because I feel a bit awkward right now.

Seeing Chris floods me with memories of last night's fantasy, remembering how I touched myself while thinking about him licking my pussy. Right where we are now.

I feel vulnerable and on display somehow, like he could somehow know my thoughts and is teasing me because of them. I'm afraid to look, but I sense that my nipples are hard, and I know my panties are damp.

"You know, not to be rude, but I'm sort of a high-profile client. You should count yourself lucky to have ended up with me, and you're acting instead like I'm some sort of burden."

His voice has an edge to it like he really means what he's saying. He's shaking his leg a little. I don't respond to the ridiculous sentiment.

"I just came by to bring you the documents but fine, sure, I'll come back when it's more convenient for you."

He stands up quickly and his chair scrapes across the floor a little. "Sorry about that," he murmurs as he makes his way to the front door.

"Christ, just give me the documents already," I groan, holding out my hand. When he hands me a manilla folder, I lean back in my chair and begin reading. "Well, sit down. This'll take a bit."

He nods and sits quietly. "The thing is..."

I look up at him and again my eyes zip straight to his mouth. I force myself to look into his eyes. It feels like dragging rocks up a mountain.

"I really just came to drop them off. I didn't mean to…for you to read them all the second I walked in the door."

Shame fills my body, that dreadful heavy embarrassment, as Lucy goes over to him and sniffs at his legs. He turns his gaze to her, to her soft eyes that always seem to know just how someone is feeling. She really drills into your soul when she looks at you.

"Oh," is all I say, and I set down the papers. "Well. Thanks then."

"Yeah. Of course. I mean, thank you."

He stands up, and Lucy again jumps at him, placing her fat paws right on his stomach. He grips her paws and dances with her while she bounces on her back feet to steady herself. "Were you lying when you said she doesn't jump on people?"

"No, she really never has before. She's always been so well-mannered."

"What kind of dog is she?" he asks, wrapping Lucy's paws around him and grinning at her big, square head.

"Um, I don't know, tell you the truth. I found her in a dumpster. She looks like a black lab mix to me."

I lean back a little and bounce my pen against my thigh, a bad habit that annoyed everyone all throughout my school years.

"Right?" I ask, looking at him to verify for some reason.

"She does, yeah. A bit big for a lab, though. I was just wondering. She looks a lot like my old dog did, but she was a mix – never knew what she was, either."

"You had a dog?"

The random self-disclosure surprises me. I've known Chris since he was a college boy and I was about 10 years old, and I've never known him to have a dog.

"Just for a few months." His answer is mysterious and his voice strained, and for a moment I see pain across his face. I've never known Chris to be so serious.

"Ah, I'm sorry."

"Oh, yeah, well, it's okay. I just – I had a puppy with Julie, but she took her with her when she left. Well, anyway, who knows if my dog would have looked like Lucy? She was so little then. But you know, doggie parents have a sense of what our little guys will grow up to look like."

I smile at the sentiment. I know what he means. I've often pictured Lucy older, her face smattered with gray across her nose the way my freckles fall.

"We do, yeah. Hey, I'm sorry about your puppy. You never saw her again? So you and Julie don't share custody?"

I remember the wedding – well, the almost wedding -- clearly. It was the most intense thing I'd ever been a witness to.

I'd been Tyler's plus one that day, and the silence had been agonizing, crushing while Chris stood at the altar waiting.

Julie never showed, and the moment had stretched out in front of all of us until it seemed like it would never end.

Eventually, someone went up to him and whispered something in his ear, and he walked out tearfully.

His dad told us all that he'd refund the people from out of town and that he was sorry, but there wasn't going to be a wedding.

He'd said it was open bar and we should all drink and party, that we should not waste the day, but continue to spend time with friends and family, anyway.

At that point, both the bride's and groom's families left.

After an awkward few moments, one brave soul stood up, gathered her purse and cardigan, and walked to the bar. Others then followed.

I had only been 20 back then, so I opted to leave at that point, calling an Uber and high tailing it out of there, leaving Tyler to catch up with old college friends of his and Chris'.

I know it was hard on him; I can't imagine going through something so publicly humiliating.

He laughs bitterly. "No, I never saw Julie again."

"Ever?!" I shriek accidentally without thinking. "Sorry, oh, my God." I clamp my hands over my mouth in embarrassment.

"Nope." He flips his lower lip out of his mouth casually and shrugs. "I went to Cancun by myself." He grins at me.

"And I got laid like every day of my honeymoon."

My hands slither down from my mouth into my lap. "Chris, that's bat shit crazy."

"I know."

Silence fills the space between us, and I go back to answering emails, giving Chris a moment with Lucy. I know personally how healing she can be. I swivel back around in my chair. "Your dog's name was Noodle?"

He's winding Lucy's ears around his finger, and she seems to be falling asleep in his lap as she lets him do it.

His grin is infectious, his dimple deep and his teeth strong and white. He has one small freckle on one of his lips that I find myself drawn to.

"Yeah."

"That's adorable."

"It is, isn't it?" He looks down at the sleeping Lucy. "Uh oh, I think I put her to sleep. Now how am I going to leave?"

I shrug. "Don't. Just stay here and keep me company."

The words slipped out of my mouth so easily, and I'm a little surprised at myself.

I've never invited a man to keep me company before, let alone a man about whom I fantasized about just the night before.

I pat my cheeks to discourage the blush I feel rising in them.

"I mean, if you don't have anything else to do. You're probably busy."

"No, no, I'm not busy. I can stay and...keep you company." His voice is soft, guarding Lucy's sleep. His smile is just as soft.

# Chapter Six
## Christopher

The warmth of Hannah's office envelops me like a comforting embrace, contrasting with the chilly reception I received moments ago.

I can't shake off the awkwardness of our interaction, my mind replaying the exchange with Hannah over and over again. Her firm words cut through my attempt at casual banter, reminding me that, to her, I'm just another client.

As I feel Lucy's warm breath on my thigh as she snoozes peacefully in my lap, I can't help but feel a sense of envy for the connection they share. The ease with which Hannah interacts with her furry companion highlights the stark contrast to my own failed relationships.

Julie's departure still stings, leaving behind unresolved questions and lingering doubts about my ability to connect with others.

Lost in thought, I catch myself tracing the outline of Lucy's fur with my fingertips, marveling at the softness of her coat. She stirs slightly at my touch, her tail wagging in response, and I can't help but smile at the sight.

In this quiet moment, surrounded by the comforting presence of Hannah and Lucy, I feel a sense of peace wash over me.

The passing couple of hours are sweet. It feels good to spend time with a woman I have no sexual relationship with.

Besides my mom, obviously, I do spend time with her.

Hannah feels familiar, too, like banana bread you only get on holidays when, the moment you bite into it, you remember the tire swing in your back yard.

Hannah tells me about the ins and outs of her job, including the needy Tom who emails her far too much for her discounted rate, in her opinion.

She has an easy way about her when she talks about work and then a somewhat less easy way when she talks about herself.

I like the confident Hannah, the one who knows her worth, whose shoulders fly back when she tells me about the work she puts in to make this business successful.

She seems less confident about herself as a person – or as a woman.

I sit in the chair, eating some string cheese she handed me so that I didn't have to get up and wake Lucy. My legs are falling asleep under the big dog's body, and every once in a while I stretch out my feet, spinning my ankles in circles.

I'm facing Hannah, away from the door, while she types away on her little laptop.

I study her delicate profile, the curve of her ear kissing the slope of her neck. I note the small smattering of freckles against her jaw line and wonder what it would feel like to press my lips to each one, to trace the path they make.

"...so basically, because of that reallocation, he'll be able to retire ten years earlier and spend the rest of his years on a houseboat with his wife," Hannah brags, her smile wide.

She throws herself back against her desk chair, rocking back and forth, and clasps her hands together behind her head.

"That's incredible," I tell her, stroking her ego, watching her smile spread even wider under my words.

"It was pretty simple. He had everything already in front of him. He just needed someone to show him how to do it."

Her chest is puffed, her shoulders back. Her voice is thick with pride.

"When did you know this is what you wanted to do with your life?" I ask her, looking over her shoulder at the documents she feels comfortable showing me, that don't have any identifying information. Lucy's ear is warm in my hand, and I have a feeling that I belong right here.

Shrugging, she says shyly, "I guess I can't really say when I knew, but I've always been good with numbers. I used to balance my mom's checkbook."

"That's a lot for little Hannah," I tell her, suddenly feeling protective over her as a child.

I want to scoop her up, pluck her out of her childhood, and make it so that she never has to worry about adult problems again. I wonder who she would be instead, what she would be doing instead. Her body language shows her walling herself up.

Worrying that I touched on something too much to acknowledge, I reach out and touch her knee.

When she turns back to her laptop in silent response, I lap up the string cheese with just my tongue and tell her, "You're incredible."

I see the color creep up her neck and into her face and she pretends not to hear me.

For a moment, I consider repeating it and forcing her to acknowledge the truth about herself, but instead I just look at her concentration face, at the slight pursing of her lips, almost a pout, and the way her eyebrows disappear under her bangs.

Her hair shines in the sun like a penny on the sidewalk, and I can practically feel the warmth of the top of her head just looking at it. My hand aches to reach out and stroke it.

What is going on with me? You cannot have a crush on little Hannah Jackson.

Even if I did, I'm not sure I could allow myself to open up to Hannah, to let go of the past and embrace the possibility of something new. The fear of rejection claws at my chest, threatening to suffocate the fragile hope blooming within me. I sit on my hands and look around.

"So, what have you got in that kitchen?"

"Pretty much nothing," she shrugs, grateful for the tone switch.

"Why not?"

"I don't know, I don't really cook. And it's really not much of a kitchen."

"Why don't you cook?"

"I just don't. Why do you care?" she snaps at me, her eyes turning into slits as she swivels her head to look at me with bitter annoyance.

Her green eyes, a still and calming bed of clover just a moment ago, flash with anger.

Where did that come from?

"Whoa, I don't care. I was just asking." I put my hands up like I'm fending off an attack, and Lucy shifts a little on my lap.

"Well, don't." Her tone is still laced in venom that I don't understand. I feel blindsided by it.

"I'm just hungry, you little turd," I snap back, lashing at her the way I used to when she was just a youngster, full of angst and insults. "I'm not asking for an inventory of your kitchen."

"Good." Hannah turns back around, her wide mouth set in a look of defiant anger, and I relax my hands back onto Lucy's soft fur, twisting the short hair between my fingers.

"Good."

I'm embarrassed that I reacted like a frat boy bully instead of asking what was wrong. I consider broaching the subject now but fear the moment's passed.

"Well, I guess I should leave you to it. You seem like you have a lot going on here, and I'm intruding."

"Are you sure?" Hannah asks, her voice slightly warmer than before despite her not looking at me.

Although I feel slightly confused by the back and forth, I know she's younger than me by about ten years.

Sometimes I try and remember what I was like ten years ago, the ball of anxiety that being 25 can be.

I imagine how I was back then, starting a business and trying to understand what it means to be a good man all at the same time.

All the hormones and the frustrations, the growing pains.

I see the little girl in Hannah, the one that wants me to sit back down and ask her what's wrong. But I've also learned in those ten years the value of letting things simmer a while and not pushing boundaries.

"Yeah, you know, if we're going to be working together, I'll have to learn to avoid Lucy's siren call."

I flop one of her jet-black ears and try to lower her to the ground without waking her. She's roughly the weight of a $3^{rd}$ grader, and my arms strain at the odd angle mixed with the weight.

"I still haven't figured that out, so good luck." She smiles weakly and looks back at her screen.

"All right." I stand awkwardly, not sure how to end the day. I reach out and pat her shoulder twice with a flat hand, and I swear I see a smirk flicker across her face before disappearing.

"Well, I'll see you later."

Her earlier invitation to stay echoes in my mind, tempting me to cross the threshold into uncharted territory.

My body is screaming at me to pick her up and sit her on her desk, but my mind is screaming at me to walk out the door before I do something I can't take back. I listen to my mind and walk toward the front door.

"Bye, Chris," she says as the bell rings above my head. "Don't forget to make an appointment next time."

I don't say anything in return, the dismissal stinging.

# Chapter Seven
## Hannah

The room swells with Chris' absence. This place has been my haven since I opened it six months ago, but sometimes it's an aching reminder of the loneliness that allows me to live here without anyone noticing or caring.

Well, except Lucy, I think happily, looking down at her crumpled sleeping form. It amazes me how much she can sleep, drool pooling beneath her open mouth, her impressive canines poking out from under her purple bottom lip.

My parents would care, Tyler would care, but I haven't given them the chance. That's my fault, of course. I've been digging my hole of solitude even deeper.

I don't know quite why I reacted the way I did, except that it's embarrassing to admit that I never learned to cook. It's also embarrassing that I don't have any way to learn while living out of my office.

I'm approaching 26, and I'm only getting better with a microwave.

I'm afraid that if I tell Chris that, he'll just ask more questions, and eventually the truth about my upbringing will come out –

that my parents were rarely around, both working two jobs, that no one taught me how to ride a bike, either.

I think he's starting to put it together, though. I shouldn't have told him that I used to help my mom with the checkbook. I saw pity on his face, and I hate that.

Tyler's a doctor. I'm a CPA who owns a business. We're doing just fine no matter how we grew up.

But the truth is that everything I know how to do I've taught myself, and all that I'm missing is a mystery that may or may not be revealed to me eventually.

And now, how would I learn to cook, anyway? I don't have an oven or a stovetop, or even a real kitchen.

No, it's too much to tell someone, especially someone who looks at me the way Chris does when he doesn't think I'm paying attention.

And if I were to catch his gaze, would I return his look in the same way? And why does he look at me in an almost sexual way?

The way he talked to me at the end of the evening, that's the real Chris. An emotionally unavailable asshole, he's someone who shows up uninvited and then calls his CPA names after trying to raid her kitchen. He has no manners or respect for others.

Besides, Tyler's told me all about Chris.

I know he sows his wild oats endlessly and treats women as disposable.

He hasn't had a real relationship since Julie left him, but he's evidently had plenty of sex. What kind of guy has sex with a different woman every night on what was supposed to be his honeymoon?

No, I don't care how he looks at me. I'm not entertaining any of it. And I'm not entertaining him.

The loneliness rather overwhelming, I pick up my phone and call my mom.

In a strange twist of fate, or perhaps in exactly the trajectory it was always meant to go, Tyler and I leaving the nest, albeit several years apart, allowed both her and my dad to go back to school and then build up enough money to live well.

They now live the life I always wanted to have while growing up.

It's a bitter pill to swallow, but one I can't begrudge them. They tried and did their best. But it's why I know I need to have a modicum of success before I even consider marriage and children.

"My baby!" my mom calls out excitedly. "What did I do to deserve a call from you on this sunny day?"

"Well..."

"Oh, I know. Let me guess – darling, heart of my heart, do you need to use my washing machine?"

I glance over in the direction of my bedroom, picturing the pile of clothing I have in the closet. "Who do you think I am? I just wanted to talk to my mom."

"So you don't want to come over?"

"No, I do."

"And you won't have clothes in the back of your car?" she needles, her voice cloying with sarcasm.

"Fine," I admit, "I need to use your washing machine."

"Okay, but you can't use the dryer," she teases, and I sigh heavily as I stand and walk to the back to gather my clothes.

"I'm kidding. I'll be home a little later. You can come on over now. God knows with that LA traffic, you won't be here until after dinner."

She's right, so I go to the kitchen and grab a couple of granola bars for a snack in case the drive ends up feeling more like a road trip.

I take Lucy out to go to do her business and then pour out some kibble for her. I tell her to wait until dinner time so she's not hungry later, but she doesn't listen. Her ears twitch as she scarfs down her food.

Before I drive away, I change my mind and go back inside to bring Lucy along. If I know my mother, she'll beg me to stay, and if I know myself, I'll want to.

***

When I arrive at my mom's house, I feel that familiar pang of resentment for the two story house and the big yard; all things that feel somewhat wasted on them but that I would have really appreciated as a kid.

She's sitting in the porch swing with my dad. In his hand is a newspaper; in hers, a book that looks to be some kind of smut.

It still embarrasses me how openly she reads that stuff, but it makes her happy. Whenever I protest, she always tells me, "Don't be such a prude, Hannah, everyone reads this stuff. No one cares."

I can't tell which one of us is right. Maybe I really am a prude and, once I lose my virginity, I might actually have a change of heart.

"There's my baby!" My mom waves so hard the bench starts to swing left to right instead of forward and back. My dad grips the wooden arm and shoots her an enamored glance before returning to his paper with a subtle smile.

I start to walk toward her, but she yells, "Oh, and there's Hannah!" as Lucy runs up to her.

I roll my eyes at the corny joke, and she says, "Now, don't be coy – go get your laundry, dear thing."

Caught, I turn back and go get the bag. She jumps to her feet, and the chain on her side of the swing trembles with the weight displacement. "You should really just make a standing appointment."

I smile gratefully as she takes the bag from me and heads for the front door.

"I'll add you to a shared Google calendar," I mutter, rolling my eyes.

"Well, I don't know why you're saying it like a joke. That could work."

She stops expectantly at the door and nods at it. "Finally, thank you. Who raised you?" she asks sarcastically when I open it for her.

"I don't know, but I hear she's a real piece of work."

"Watch your mouth now," she laughs as she leads me to the laundry room.

I'm so jealous of it. It has a folding ironing board that collapses into the wall and a shelf above the appliances for laundry detergent and other supplies. Her cleaning supplies hang on the wall and there's a whiteboard where she's written who's been doing the laundry.

It brings a smile to my lips that my dad has done it the last three times.

"Seriously, when is that no-good landlord of yours going to give you a washing machine and dryer?'

"Probably never, Mom," I say honestly as I dump my clothes into the machine without sorting. I know you're supposed to, but I did it once and didn't notice a difference. I'm a numbers girl. No difference, no change for me.

I used to feel little twinges of guilt when my mom mentioned my imaginary apartment landlord, but we've all basically repeated the lie into existence.

My fictitious landlord is a man named John who has long brown hair and a two-year-old daughter named Ruby. He's a chatterbox who often drops in and keeps me from my work. He's nice enough but cheap. I swear I could draw him if I needed to. I might, just for the challenge.

"Come sit with me and your dad."

"Is there room?"

"Sure, you don't mind being squeezed together, do you? Like old times?"

She's referring to when we shared a bed because we surely never had a porch swing. Or a porch.

We used to have two rooms in our apartment, and my brother got his own because he was a growing boy who needed privacy. When he moved out, I got his room.

Being essentially an only child, albeit one with a much older sibling, was hard, and it's a weird thing to explain to people, but the one time I was grateful for it was when he went to college and I got that room – and a modicum of privacy.

It was all I could do to keep myself from moving my stuff in there while he was packing up the family car. But you can believe I helped him pack.

I still remember waving at him from the curb, and the second the car disappeared around the corner, running back inside to begin the process of moving into his room.

I didn't feel the crushing blow of loneliness, of not having him there, not hearing him snore through the paper thin walls, until later that night.

I wept quietly into my pillow until my mom came into my room and slid into bed with me to hug me tight and stroke my hair.

It's a painful memory and one I wish she hadn't reminded me of, however accidentally.

I look at my mom, at all the love in her green eyes, and I shake my head. "No, I don't mind," I lie.

# Chapter Eight
## Christopher

"—I think she's going to need surgery. She called me and said the physical therapy she's doing with you is making it worse. I don't know, is there any chance her form is wrong and she's irritating it?

"Chris?..."Chris!"

I snap out of a haze of sweaty bewilderment as Tyler shouts my name a foot away from me and I turn to look at him.

The freckles on his face stand out in the sun on the café patio, and it brings me back momentarily to the caramel freckles across Hannah's jaw line, the ones that distracted me into becoming lost in the question mark curve of her neck.

"Sorry, what did you say?"

"Ellen, the patient I referred to you last month, called to say her shoulder still hurts. She says it hurts worse after she has physical therapy. She wants you to write her a referral back to me so her insurance will cover it, I guess."

He chuckles. "Red tape is the worst."

"OK, sure, I can do that." I shift in my seat and straighten my shorts out."

"What are you staring at, dude? That woman? That's creepy, bro. I thought you had game."

Tyler takes a swig of coffee out of the ceramic mug. It's green with gold swirls across it that eventually meld into the words 'Make Your Own Destiny.'

It's cheesy in the worst way, and Tyler says he comes here all the time on the weekends.

So here we are on a Sunday, enjoying our coffee in the corny mugs, and I'm already starting to feel jittery.

I once asked him why he doesn't work weekends; don't most doctors work weekends?

He told me that since he's an orthopedic surgeon, he usually schedules all but the most urgent cases during the week.

I shrug nonchalantly and run my hand over my left pec.

"Doesn't that woman across the street look a lot like Julie?"

Tyler's amicable face morphs into one of pity, and I flinch away from the sincerity of it.

I hear the clink of his cup hitting the wrought iron of the table. I feel him shifting, leaning toward me.

I keep my eyes on the woman. She's too far away to clearly make out her features, but from a distance, she looks just like Julie.

"It's been five years, man. And you haven't really had a serious relationship since. We gotta get you off the Julie train."

I shade my eyes with the hand that isn't cupping my coffee.

It's nice of him to say "haven't really." The truth would just be "haven't."

I don't need him to sugarcoat it, but I appreciate the gesture.

"I'm not on the Julie train, Tyler," I tell him, pronouncing 'Julie' like my first curse word.

I couldn't be on the Julie train if I wanted to be. That train left the station with me still holding my luggage.

"I just think that woman across the street looks like her."

Tyler lowers a heavy hand on my shoulder in a gesture more appropriate for someone who's just lost a pet hamster.

"Grief will sometimes make you see someone everywhere you look."

I turn to him with a look that I hope portrays my disgust accurately.

I stand up and throw the rest of the lukewarm drink I've been nursing down my throat rather than taste it. I set it down and tuck a five dollar bill under the empty cup.

"Do me a favor, and the next time you want to say some lame shit like that to me again – don't."

"You can't ignore it forever! You've gotta deal with it eventually!" he calls after me.

I don't wait to respond but make my way down the shopping center. The breeze is in my hair, and the sun on my face is a reminder of how lucky I am to live in a place like this.

Sometimes I look in the mirror and see the fine wrinkles sprouting on my forehead, years of sun and very little sunscreen. There are always two ways to look at things.

I walk through the farmer's market, stopping to admire the particularly large vegetables that farmers have managed to produce. I grab a few onions as big as my hand and multicolored carrots still attached to the stems.

Halfway through, I'm holding the vegetables in the bottom of my shirt like a child collecting acorns. I have to buy a reusable market bag made of cotton mesh just to hold it all.

A younger farmer is standing behind the strangest assortment of mushrooms. They look like the roots of trees and then there's something that looks like a white carrot, and another that appears to be the leafiest, greenest cabbage I've ever seen, with a long stem to go with it.

I've only ever seen it uncooked in pictures. "Is this bok choy?" I ask him, pointing eagerly.

"Sure is," the man says, tucking his hands into an apron he's wearing.

He's got an accent that borders on being Appalachian, and his mustache is slightly uneven. He doesn't seem like he belongs here in the heart of LA, where everyone's hair is perfect and they try to disguise their accents as soon as they arrive.

"How do I cook it?"

"Stir fry, steam, all the same ways. Just be quick about it or it turns to mush real quick."

He smiles. "Here, this one's on me. Practice round. You come back next week and get more if it doesn't go right." A twinkle shines in his eye.

"No, no, let me pay you."

I scramble to find my card in my pocket, but he puts his calloused hand out and lowers my wallet from his eye line. "Nope, not this time."

"Well. Okay. Thank you."

Definitely not from around here.

"Where's are you from? I can't place your accent," I ask lamely as I take the head of bok choy that he deems to gift me.

"Oh," he laughs gaily. "Pennsylvania. My wife got a job out here, so we compromised and now we live out in Mariposa County. I still get to farm my days away and stay away from the hub bub of, well, you know." He gestures widely as if to gesture to the entire city.

"Oh, I know." I smile. "Thank you for this." I lift the bag and nod at him.

"Oh, no worries, you'll be back for more."

"I'm sure I will," I tell him.

He seems happy, happier than most of the people in this city, clawing their way to the top, wishing to be actors or singers or whatever else they think will bring them fame and fortune.

I wonder what his view is like in Mariposa, if they have a few farm animals and if his wife wakes him up with coffee and pancakes.

Swinging the bag and whistling to myself, I pop in my ear buds and turn on a meditative podcast, something to get me through the three-mile run back home. It's a sunny day, and I know once I'm about two miles in I'll be wishing I'd just driven to meet Tyler.

Once I'm through the throng of farmer's market shoppers, I break into a jog to warm up my muscles, but I stop short after only maybe 50 feet when I see an easel in the window of an art store.

The store is small and the windows are stuffed with things I can't quite make out.

Alongside the easel is a stack of ribbon spools, arranged in rainbow order, and what looks to be a vintage typewriter, though I probably wouldn't be able to tell a vintage typewriter from a new one.

A compulsion to buy that easel itches at my fingers, and I realize how I must look standing and staring at it without movement. I'm frozen to the spot, considering the way Hannah might react if I bought it for her.

The picture she drew of me was so good that I can't help but think that she must have even better art, art she's taken her time on.

I can see her now, paint splashed across her face, a dot on her nose, her tongue peeking out. I shake my head. She's not an artist in an indie movie, Chris.

She seemed so upset at me the last time I saw her just a week ago.

I haven't drummed up the courage to make an appointment and I know I need to.

Every time I start to, a sickness balloons in my throat, and I stop. I know at some point I have to. She's surely looked at all my financial reports by this time.

Maybe buying her a gift would help. Maybe buying her a gift would make it worse. My palms start to sweat with the effort of thought.

Finally, I give up, and I jog away.

About a block down, I pivot on my heel and run back to the store.

I'll give it to her when this all blows over. Maybe for her birthday. She won't ever know how long I agonized over it. To her, it'll just be a birthday present. Easy.

Why am I making this such a big deal?

And then, Tyler's going to kick my ass, right before he's out of my head and his image is replaced with the image of Hannah's scrunched nose over her sweet smile and a blush crawling up from her chest when she opens it.

# Chapter Nine
## Hannah

Something about fresh laundry just makes me feel like all's right with the world.

I stuff my bag into the backseat and turn to hug my mom.

I stayed the entire weekend, telling myself it was for her, but it was for me.

I haven't been feeling myself lately, been feeling like I'm standing on a cliff and someone could come up behind me and push me off at any moment.

Her hand glides over the space between my shoulder blades, and she makes an 'mmm' sound as she squeezes me to her. Her hair, once copper like mine but now fading into a coppery brown, tickles my nose, and I pull away.

"I hope your landlord never installs a washer. Or a dryer," she tells me, smiling obliviously, patting Lucy's side before I open the car door for her.

She bounds eagerly into the backseat. She loves the car, loves sitting up before smashing into the back of my seat when I brake. She loves when I open the window for her so she can chew on the rapid air.

I walk around the front of my Toyota Corolla, lightly dragging my fingertips against its greasy exterior.

"Me, too, Mom," I assure her as I open the door, that odd champagne color that seemed so popular in the early 2000s.

"But we won't worry about it – because he never will."

I wave and dip my head to pop inside the car. Standing at 5'9, getting into most cars is a head wound waiting to happen, and this one's no different.

Hitting my head on the roofline of this car enough times has trained me to bend down when getting in and it's become my version of Pavlov's whistle.

I could go back and do some work, but I've been trying to be better at asserting work/home life boundaries lately, and it's Sunday. It's the day of rest.

I drop off Lucy at the office. She runs to her food bowl and gives me a look of confused misery as I head to the door to leave, but I tell her, "No, don't. I saw Mom sneak you all that rotisserie chicken. You're not getting anything else right now."

There's still daylight left, and I want to get to the bookstore, so I can spend some time in the office supply section first before buying a book from the clearance section.

I do just that, ordering a latte, then heading straight for the office supplies section where I stare at calendars and budgeting books and pens. They are my weakness, all the soft pink pens and post it notes.

A woman a few feet down the aisle from me strongly considers a leather bound journal with a ribbon for saving her place. She finally chooses it, tucking it under her arm in a signal of finality, then considers getting a second one in a lighter leather.

A flash of jealousy surges through me; that she can afford two of these ridiculously priced journals. I let the feeling sink me for a moment before swimming my way out of it.

It isn't her fault that she's everything I'm not. She has no idea that I'm watching her and thinking about all the ways she's better than I am.

Her wavy brown locks cascade down her back like the side of a mountain. Her shorter stature allows her to wear a little, yellow sundress that doesn't expose her entire butt to the world.

I sigh and put away the multipack of post it notes in my hand.

It would be a ridiculous purchase anyway, and if I get those, then I can't afford a book later.

I know I'll get more enjoyment out of a book, so I'll prioritize and wait. My little exhale gets the attention of the woman, and she glances at me.

My blood runs cold, and I feel my eyes widen without my permission.

"Are you okay? You look terrified," she says with a nervous laugh, her eyebrows leaning into each other in her confusion.

Terrified isn't the right word. I'm sure I'm looking at Julie for the first time in five years. I blurt out, "Don't you live somewhere else now?"

She cocks her head and turns slightly toward me, although her feet stay facing forward. She doesn't want to be in this conversation. "Do I know you?"

"Well, I was younger, but yes, I'm Hannah." She looks somewhat confused and I then realize that she never really met me.

"Sorry, I'm Tyler Jackson's younger sister." When her face doesn't move, I jut out my chin. "Tyler. As in Chris' college roommate?"

"Oh!"

She knocks her forehead with the heel of her hand in an overdramatic gesture. "Duh! Hannah, hi. How are you?"

The confusion on her face has melted into stiff condescension. She didn't just leave Chris, apparently, but all of us. I'm reminded of the cruelty Chris described, and I see it on her face now.

"I'm fine...what are you doing back here?" I ask warily.

"I got a new job out here, so I moved back."

She smiles and spreads out her hands, her elbow still tucked in holding the leather book, like it's good news that she's back, as if any of us would welcome her back.

I think she expects me to congratulate her, but I couldn't if I wanted to. I feel sick for Chris suddenly, my stomach churning at her words.

"How's Chris?" she asks me.

"He's good." I feel a blush spread across my cheeks. I want desperately to push it down but that only makes matters worse.

"Do you talk to him at all?"

"I'm helping with expanding his fitness center business," I tell her mildly. "So I talk to him a bit, yes."

A pause passes between us, so I add out of a sense of loyalty, "He's very successful. Yes, I talk to him a lot, actually. He's great."

The words spill out of me. I open my mouth to say more, then clamp it closed.

Something flashes in her eyes, and her smile changes into a smirk. "Do I detect a little crush, Amanda?"

"Hannah."

That stupid hand flies to her stupid forehead again. "Right, sorry. Anna." She nods as though she's solidifying it.

I shake the pack of pens in my hand. "Well, I've gotta go, just came to get these." Why am I explaining myself?

"Okay, nice to see you!" she calls, her voice disappearing into the air as I walk as slowly as I can out of the aisle.

Once Julie's head is hidden behind the shelves in the foreground, I pick up my pace and speed walk to the register. I'm practically jogging when I reach the automatic doors, and the clerks hollers at me to pay for the pack of pens I'm still holding.

I throw them onto a table of book recommendations a foot away and hurry out the door before running to my car.

Breathing heavily in my driver's seat, I turn the key and hear the bumpy humming of my old car's engine.

Pulling out of the parking lot, I try to slow my heartbeat by breathing out through my mouth in a slow pace, feeling my lungs empty.

What is wrong with me? Why did she get to me like that? Do I tell Chris? Does he know?

***

I rush home to throw myself in work so that I can stop thinking about Julie. Forget work/home life boundaries.

Lucy greets me like I've been gone for weeks, and I squat down on my heels to envelop her in a hug. She frantically tries to lick my face while I hug her around the neck, forcing her to lick my hair instead.

I open the folder Chris gave me with his financial statements so that I can input the information into his client portal. I scan the documents in one by one when one catches my eye. I snatch it off the glass surface and look at it more closely.

A discrepancy between the projected profits of the last quarter and the actual profits isn't too strange, but the last few quarters have had eerily similar discrepancies.

Hesitating for only a moment, I call Chris. It's been a few days since our awkward moment, and it's still in my mind, but I have a duty to tell him.

He answers in a disjointed voice, his breathing up and down. "Hello?"

"Hey, Chris. Sorry to call, but I noticed something unusual about the financials you gave me."

"Hannah?"

"Yes? Who else would be calling you about financial documents?" I roll my eyes and Lucy walks up to me to soothe me. I pet her head when she rests it heavily on my thigh.

"Sorry, it's just. How did you get my number?"

"You included it in the first email you sent me."

"So you agree that our relationship is too personal to restrict to emails." His voice is smug, and I almost feel bad that I have bad news for him.

"No, Chris, I definitely don't agree, but this is kind of urgent, if you don't mind shutting down the asshole attitude for a minute and being serious."

"Oh. Well, why don't you come over? I'll text you the address."

"You can just come—" I realize he's already hung up, the phone silent in my hand.

# Chapter Ten
## Christopher

When I arrive home, I try to decide whether or not I'll have time to shower before Hannah gets here. Just when I decide to go for it, peeling off my shirt, I hear the buzzing of my apartment's box.

I stand still for a moment with my shirt above my head before yanking it off to hit the button and tell her to come on up.

When she knocks on my door, I let her in, and she stands smiling for a moment before nonchalantly commenting, "Nice hair" and pushing past me to sit at my dining room table.

I look in the mirror on my wall and see that the static has animated my dark curls. I smooth them down quickly and try to snap back, "Nice…" but nothing comes to mind.

She looks beautiful. Her hair's glossy sheen seems especially bright in the warm lighting of my penthouse apartment and she's put on eyeliner that accentuates the almond shape of her eyes.

"Good one," she chuckles, her eyes shining.

I shrug, resigned, and sit next to her in a chair, shaking my legs. I feel an unnamed tension bubbling inside me at having her in my house. She looks natural in it, like she's been here before.

"What did you need to tell me?"

"Why are you sweaty? And shirtless?" She squints at me and tucks her long hair behind her ears as she shuffles her chair closer to the table.

"I just...went on a run. Why, do you like it?" I tease, running my fingers down my chest.

She wrinkles her nose, but her tongue flicks out to lick her bottom lip unconsciously, and I can't help but smirk at her body language betraying her.

"Here." She lays down the papers in front of her like she's reading my tarot cards or about to do a magic trick. "Do you see anything strange?"

"I wouldn't know what to look for. That's why I pay you the big bucks."

Hannah snorts. "Well, who would? Who's in charge of your finances?"

Her question takes me aback. I'm not sure if I should say. Maybe she's misunderstanding whatever it is.

"What did you find, Hannah?" I ask, lowering my voice and scooting in. I squint at the papers trying to understand what it is she thinks she sees.

"Chris, your projected profits versus your actual profits are markedly different."

"So? Like the actual profits are lower?"

"Yes, lower."

"So? It happens. We got cocky with the projections."

Hannah's mouth twists uncomfortably. She drops her elbow heavily on my table and lays her face in her hand, covering her mouth with her cupped palm.

"That's not really what projected profits are. There's no reason to be overly cocky with them. Listen to me. You could be right, okay? It could be a simple mistake, but it has happened to you practically every quarter. Your company is consistently underperforming. Why would someone continually make that mistake and project high profits when historically the profits were not rising to that level?"

"So what are you saying?"

"I think someone who has control of the company's financials and bank accounts is stealing from you," she says simply. "And if you could get me an itemized list of your company's financial transactions, I could confirm it."

Her words shoot ice into my veins. I drag the papers over to me and look them over, staring at the numbers she's highlighted and her math in the margins.

I look back up at her with my mouth open.

"Is this right? $30,000 a quarter less than projected? For—" I shuffle through the papers, then look back at her again, "—years?"

Her nod is silent, allowing me to soak in the information.

$30,000 a quarter. $120,000 a year. For years.

I put the papers facedown and stand. And the only person who has that kind of power is Sarah. Sarah, who I've promised an even bigger position. Sarah, who's been with me since the beginning.

A cold sweat now mixes with the sweat from my run. "Are you hungry?"

"I, uh—"

"Let me make you something. I just went to the farmer's market. I got some bok choy I'm very excited to experiment with. Have you ever had bok choy?"

"Yes, but Chris—" She turns around in her chair, her body following me as I walk over to my kitchen.

"Well, so have I, I guess, little wilted things in American Chinese dishes, but look at these bad boys." I pull out the large head of it, look at her, then back at it, then hold it up next to my head. "You see that? As big as my head."

"Impressive," she says grimly and stands. "Listen," she tells me, walking to me slowly like an officer at a standoff, like I have hostages she needs to save.

"I will help you with this. There's no need to panic, okay? It will be easy to figure out who did it and then you can figure out how you'd like to proceed. If you want to press charges or sue for restitution, we'll do our best to get your money back."

Rinsing off the bok choy, I let her words wash over me as I look out the window down at the ocean glinting in the distance, shining bursts of lights at everything metal and glass that people have built.

"I'm not worried about the money," I finally respond.

It isn't quite true, but it's true enough. I bring the vegetable over to my butcher block countertop and start cutting it into strips, unsure if I'm doing it right. I realize halfway through that in my state, I haven't looked up any recipes or anything.

"Okay, so tell me your concerns. We have to do something about this. It can't be allowed to continue."

Something about her saying we and meaning the two of us sends a string of fire that I can trace from my heart down to my toes and back up to my skull.

"We don't have to do anything right away."

"Don't you want—"

"What I want to do, Hannah, is eat. It's Sunday, and I should be relaxing, and you came tearing in here with bad news, that I don't really feel equipped to handle right now. Is that okay with you? If I just make us something to eat, then for an hour or so we can forget about all this? The money will still be gone after we've eaten, right?"

She backs away from me slightly, then straightens.

Her eyes harden for a moment before softening. I watch all the emotions pass over her, something like pity enter and leave.

"Yeah, okay. I'm sorry. You're right."

In a lighter tone, Hannah continues, "You know, it's funny, I tell myself all the time that I need to get better at work/home life boundaries. Today, I tried, I really did. I tried to not do any work because it's the weekend, but sometimes it feels impossible."

She looks at her interlaced fingers and sighs heavily, then back up at me.

"Well, hey, if anyone gets that, it's me. You're in the beginning stages of a business. That's how that first year goes. Before you have help. Will you put that pan on high for me?" I gesture to a pan near her, hanging on a peg on the wall.

"This one?" she asks quietly, pointing. I nod, and she places the pan on the burner.

She turns the knob to high, looking at me as though for acceptance, and I smile reassuringly as I find a bowl to mix seasonings in.

"Can I tell you something? I want to explain my reaction the other day. I know it was…weird."

I set the wooden bowl down to give her my undivided attention, staring into her mascara-rimmed eyes. "You don't have to explain anything to me."

"I know. I just want to," her eyes downcast.

"If you think it will help me understand you better, go ahead, please."

I can see the agony in her eyes, the unsureness of telling me whatever it is she thinks she needs to say. It's a gentleness that's not usually present in our conversations.

"When I was younger, my parents didn't have much money. They both worked two jobs, and Tyler and I were home alone a lot. Tyler practically raised me. I feel bad about it, that he used up his childhood on me."

Seeing her nibble on her bottom lip eats me up, and I feel terrible that she feels that way. I reach out and stroke her shoulder. I run my hand down her arm and interlace her fingers in mine. Her hand twitches as though she might pull it back, but she doesn't.

"Tyler doesn't feel anything but love for you. He talked about you a lot when we were in college. He was so happy that the two of you were close. He does feel a sense of responsibility for you, but it makes him happy, gives him purpose. Tyler felt rather alone before you came along."

Her smile is unsure, a gentle teasing at the corners of her lips. I shake her hand a little.

She says, "Well, anyway, he was a kid and I was a kid, and I never...learned how to cook. At all. No one ever taught me, and I've tried, but I always mess it up." Her gaze dips to the floor.

Her 'confession' makes me a laugh a little, but when I see her wounded expression snap back up towards me, I swallow my chuckle back.

"I'm sorry. Is that all? I'm sorry you didn't feel cared for as a child, but you should know that not knowing how to cook at 25 is quite normal. You aren't far behind me and I've had about ten more years to practice than you've had. Here, I'll give you some pointers now. Do you want to help me make this?"

The hurt expression slips off her face, and an easier one of relief replaces it. "Really?"

"Of course. I'm 35, Hannah. Most people learn to cook when they want to eat something. For me, it was a stir fry. I was craving it so badly that one day I learned how to make it." I grin.

"Maybe you just haven't had a craving like that yet. Don't sweat it."

I bat away her insecurities with the hands we're holding. Hers is warm and soft with a heartbeat, like a small animal.

Shyly, she tells me, "Well, there's something else."

"Oh, gosh, what? You don't know how to do laundry, either? The shame of it all."

My other hand takes her other hand, and the intensity of my own heartbeat rushes into my ears, a tidal wave of heat and self-consciousness.

She breaks eye contact. "I don't really have a way to learn to cook right now. I'm sort of…living in my office."

Her eyes come back to find mine, searching for something, maybe understanding, maybe judgment.

Hurriedly, she continues, "The plan was to live there for a little while the business got legs, and then time kept passing, and the business kept being hard, and…I'm barely making ends meet, you know? I can't really afford to lease that place and pay rent. And I don't have a real kitchen there, just a microwave and a fridge in the office kitchen, so."

"But…Tyler wouldn't let you do that. He'd have you stay with him," is all I can think to say. It's sad to think of her living in her office. I've seen it. It's small and cramped. She and Lucy in there together must make her feel stir crazy.

"He doesn't know. No one in my family knows."

Her voice is quiet, but then her lips curl up a tiny bit and her voice cracks with a chuckle she's holding back. "They think my landlord's name is John."

"John?" I ask, letting go and handing her the wooden mixing bowl and setting some spices next to her on the counter.

"Put those in and stir them together. Taste it as you go to see if you like what you're doing. That's the biggest rule in learning to cook, making sure you like it."

She reaches out hesitantly and stops, her milky, freckled hand suspended above a bottle of soy sauce. "You won't ruin it," I assure her, "And if you did, I wouldn't care."

Dumping sauces into the bowl haphazardly and stirring with a wooden spoon, she continues, "Yes, John. He has long brown hair. Oh, and a daughter."

"Fake John has a fake daughter?"

"Her name is Ruby. She's two."

Hannah's grin is devilish, and I can't help but laugh at the mischievous twinkle to her eyes. She's bouncing on her heels, like someone who can't wait to say something. It must feel so good to say this out loud. I can't help but chuckle with her. It's a ridiculous thought.

"Is she a redhead, too?"

"She is! Little self-insert moment, I know, embarrassing," she tells me as she brings the spoon to her lips to taste it.

"You might want to put that on your finger to taste it. It's not a soup, so it might be a lot of flavor to slurp up. If you're feeling fancy, you could use your pinkie."

With a childish look of joy, she cradles the big mixing bowl in one arm and uses the hand holding the spoon to dip her pinkie into it, splashing specks of sauce across the counter.

"Sorry," she whispers before sucking on her pinkie, her peachy lips forming a small O.

"I think it's good?" Her opinion comes out like a question, with a tiny shrug to accompany it. It's cute to see her unsure of herself, looking to me for answers.

I join her, moving close to her body, only a bowl between us, and dip my finger into it. "It tastes good to me."

I can feel her body emanating heat, and I see that her chest is moving rapidly, shallowly, a thing of flight. "Don't doubt yourself. Have confidence in your choices."

Her eyes meet mine, inches away, inches close, and she stumbles backward and bumps into the pan that I left on the hot burner.

It clatters to the ground, and Hannah instinctively moves to catch it. I grab her hand to pull her away before she can burn herself and pull her body into mine, swiftly taking the bowl out of her hand as I wrap my other arm around her waist. Tucking her head into my naked chest, she chuckles, "Thank you."

Flutters wave through my stomach. "You're welcome." I snake my arm off her waist. "A couple of rules of the kitchen – don't catch a falling knife and don't catch a hot pan."

Taking a step back, Hannah covers her eyes before ruffling her bangs. Sighing resolutely, she slaps her thighs with both of her palms.

"I'm going to let you do the rest."

Before she can walk away, just as she pivots her hips away from me, I catch her by the hand and pull her back, smiling at her.

"No, no, don't give up. Pick it up and let's keep going, Hannah Jackson." I pick the bowl back up and push it against her chest.

# Chapter Eleven
## Hannah

Chris turns on the oven and hands me a pair of tongs. Using the knife he cut the bok choy with, he pushes the slices off into the bowl and says, "Mix it gently so you don't tear the leaves, okay? You've got this."

My mind races with the moment we shared earlier. What was that? Was he going to kiss me? Why would Chris kiss me? And why did I want him to?

Because I did want him to. I've kissed men before. Not many, but I have kissed them. The thing is that when I go on dates, they always lean in for the kiss, and I pull away, afraid of what comes after the kiss.

What does come after the kiss, I wonder, as I absentmindedly stir the bok choy.

"What are you thinking about over there?" Chris asks me as he cuts a chicken. I'm grateful that he doesn't ask me to help him with that. He seems aware of his audience.

Kissing you. What comes after a kiss.

"I need to use the restroom," I blurt out.

Looking confused, Chris tells me, "Okay, you're allowed. Right down there."

He uses his knife to point to a door visible down the hallway.

Embarrassed by my earlier admission, I nod and set the bowl down then walk calmly to the door, so that it doesn't appear that I'm about to burst.

Once in there, I close the door of the bathroom and lean against it with both hands, holding it shut as though barricading it, as though Chris might break the door down and tell me that he knows I'm thinking about him romantically.

And I am, right? I'm thinking about Chris romantically? I'm having fun and thinking about having fun like this every day for the rest of my life...well, it doesn't have to be Chris.

It could be fun to build a life with a man, and for the first time, I see that. I see how easy it would be to cook dinner together and giggle and...well, anyway, it doesn't have to be Chris.

Just a man. If Tyler can find a good man just by accidentally being his roommate, maybe I could purposefully find love.

My breathing returning to normal, I turn and survey the bathroom for the first time, unfurling my eyes from their anxiously squeezed position.

I realize, not the first time, that Chris has money.

You know someone has money when they miss the theft of over $120,000 a year from their business. He lives very well and his apartment is to die for.

His appliances are high end stainless steel, with a sub-zero frig and a Wolf range. The beautiful carved wood trim in his home is painted a deep forest green.

His floors are made of a dark gray concrete that looks surprisingly elegant against his plush, white furniture. Small pops of color like the yellow runner in the hallway and white curtains with orange flowers show evidence of his keen design eye. Or someone's keen eye, anyway.

The bathroom is no different. Soap, mouthwash, and lotion all sit next to each other on a large vanity sink, labeled in amber pump bottles. The sink is a copper basin – and this is just the guest bath.

I pull aside his tasteful gray shower curtain to reveal a bouquet of eucalyptus and lavender hanging from the showerhead.

I flush the toilet to make it seem like I actually used it, and turn on the faucet.

As I turn around to leave the bathroom, I see that on the wall right next to the bathroom door is the sketch I drew of Chris. He's framed it in a small, copper frame that matches the sink.

I rip the door open and walk with purpose back to the kitchen where I find Chris closing the oven. His hands are covered in small, baby blue oven mitts.

"Are you okay? Did you find everything—"

"Chris, did you frame that picture I drew of you?"

A playful, childish smile, like one you might see on a young boy after pulling a prank, crosses his face.

"I did. It's good. And I bet since you signed it, it's going to be worth a lot one day."

"You think so, huh?"

"I know so. You're special, Hannah, and even if it isn't for art, you are going to be known, and I'm going to pay off a small boat with that one day."

"You don't really think that," I tell him seriously.

"You're right, I don't."

"I thought so."

"I won't really sell it. I love it too much. I might just get it blown up even bigger. Maybe I'll commission a mural, a Hannah Jackson print on my wall. Everyone will be so jealous."

He's leaning against the oven, cocked at an irregular angle, his dark spirals of hair flopped over his forehead. His grin is self-assured, easy going, and teasing.

"What wall do you think it would be good on? I'm thinking right there in front," he points, "so that when you walk in it's the –"

I can't take it anymore. His floppy hair, his chiseled arms twitching with movement, his red lips glistening from licking them. I take one big step toward him, so that I'm right in front of him.

He straightens, and I wonder if he knows what's coming. I place my hands on his cheeks, close my eyes, and stand on my tiptoes to press my mouth against his.

His body immediately responds as his hands fly to my waist, landing on my hips, then spreading across my lower back. He pulls me into him, his hands pressing into my back, pushing our hips against each other's.

My hands slide down his cheeks to the tops of his shoulders, settling on his traps. I relax off my tiptoes, and he bends to meet me where I am before walking toward me, forcing me backward against his kitchen counter.

His kiss is firm and warm. His lips feel tethered to my vagina, and the more pressure he uses, and the more his tongue probes my mouth, the wetter I get.

Chris' hands sink down to my ass, and I don't know if I should let it keep going or not.

I should tell him I'm a virgin, I know I should. I should stop him and ask about Tyler, ask about him being a client, ask about Julie.

Julie. My eyes fly open with the memory of running into her at the bookstore. I completely forgot to tell him, and I don't want him to think I'm keeping it from him.

Would Chris pine after her when I'm right here? If Julie wanted him back, would he go back? She is older, and she seems like everything I'm not.

"What's wrong?" Chris asks, pulling away. His hands still rest against my ass, and I wonder if he knows he left them there. He kisses my cheeks. "Tell me."

# Chapter Twelve

## Christopher

The air between us crackles with newfound tension as Hannah and I stand in my kitchen, our lips still tingling from the heat of our first kiss.

It's a moment suspended in time, teetering on the precipice of uncertainty and possibility.

But then, just as quickly as the spark ignited, it fizzles out into an awkward silence.

Hannah's words hang heavy in the air, the weight of her confession settling like a stone in the pit of my stomach.

My hands are still on Hannah Jackson's ass. That's a sentence I never imagined being true. Hannah breaks away from me, her hands flying to cover her mouth.

"What's wrong?" I ask her again, swallowing, afraid that she already regrets it. I can still taste her mouth on mine.

"I'm a virgin," she murmurs, her cheeks flushing with embarrassment as she averts her gaze.

For a moment, I'm at a loss for words. My mind races, grappling with the weight of her revelation.

Disgustingly, the first thing I think of is Tyler. I wonder how bad Tyler would kick my ass if I not only dated his sister but took her virginity, too.

And it was going so well just a moment ago.

I want to reach out to her, to reassure her that it's okay, but I'm choked by the swell of emotions swirling within me.

Instead, I simply nod.

She pushes my body off hers. I want to grip her hand and tell her not to leave, not to be embarrassed.

I want to tell her that I don't care about any of that, but instead I stand looking at her. She looks small, which is impossible at 5'9", but she does. She's hunched her shoulders forward and her hair falls forward like a curtain.

My heart aches for her, but words elude me. I hold my hands out and bend my fingers at the knuckles like if I try hard enough I can pull them from the air, the perfect sentence already prepared.

Hannah gathers her things to leave, her bag and her papers, and at the door she turns to look at me, her teeth grinding at her bottom lip.

She wants me to say something, and I want to say something, too. A strange sound comes out of me, a word stifled before it ever turns into one.

"Bok choy?" comes out, but it's not what she wanted to hear, and it's not what I wanted to say, and she rolls her eyes before slamming the door.

The weight of her confession hangs heavy in the air, casting a pall over the room as I watch her retreat, a knot of regret coiling in the pit of my stomach.

I'm left standing in the wake of her departure, grappling with the aftershocks of our encounter.

I run my thumb over my lips, thinking of her warm mouth on mine, the serious look she had given me before taking my face in her hands.

Little Hannah Jackson being a virgin was not at all a twist I had considered.

She's so beautiful, so self-assured, that I wouldn't have thought that men were something she had trouble with. And if they aren't, does that mean she's been waiting…did she tell me because she wanted me to take her virginity? Could I even do that?

I don't know that I have what it takes to deal with the emotional aftermath of our encounter.

Since Julie, I've struggled with emotional vulnerability, and only Hannah has been able to reach down far enough to find it.

***

A few days later and my mind has been bustling nonstop from Hannah to my finances, back and forth like a very confusing game of ping pong.

Work used to be my solace when life got hard, but now work feels like a minefield because I've got no idea when it's coming, the realization, the bomb dropping.

Eventually, I have to face the money problem, and I know that.

Or do I? It's only $120,000 a year. No biggie. Joking, I really do know I have to face it.

Worse yet, I've been avoiding Tyler, afraid that we'll hang out and he'll see the kiss on my face somehow.

I keep imagining it so vividly, him showing up to meet me for a run or me showing up to meet him at a coffee shop and he takes one look at me and goes, "Dude, did you kiss my sister?" and before I know it he's on top of me, wailing on me.

I'd have to give it to him, too, I know. Just lay down and let him have at me because who kisses their best friend's sister, anyway?

He'd probably yell "She's ten years younger than you are, you freak!" and then everyone around us would gasp, and it would turn ugly.

That's probably the worst case scenario, but it likely wouldn't get much better than that.

I'm at the grocery store, mindlessly scanning the shelves for something to make for dinner.

I reach out for a tube of anchovy paste to make a Caesar salad when I see her. Julie. Or I think I see her.

I try to dodge quickly to get a better look, but when I turn around, I smash directly into someone's cart and tip it over a little before they can right it back onto the wheels.

The older woman steering the cart cries out, "Excuse me!" as though I tripped on purpose, and I drop the anchovy paste on the linoleum tile.

My heart pounds in my chest, and I rest my forehead in my hand for a moment, steadying my breathing.

The woman continues to squawk at me, saying "Excuse me? Are you going to pick that up?" and other variations of the same question while I attempt to regulate my heart beat and a sweat bursts open on my palms.

"Chris?"

Oh, yeah. It's definitely Julie.

I sigh, lift my face up from my hands, and look at her. Our eyes meet, and she smiles unsurely, lifting her fingers to wave.

# Chapter Thirteen
## Hannah

As I step into CHOICE Fitness, I can't shake the feeling of unease that has been gnawing at me for days.

I hold my breath as I look up at the employees manning the front desk. No Chris. Thank God. The last thing I need right now is for Chris to be here, and the whole plan to be ruined.

I sign the guest waiver and pay my $10 before making my way onto the gym floor. The unfamiliar scent of sweat and rubber greets me as I make my way through the crowded space, my eyes scanning the rows of exercise machines and weight racks in search of Tyler.

I spot him near the back of the gym, his shock of auburn hair standing out in the sea of sweaty bodies. With a sense of relief, I quicken my pace to join him, eager to discuss the troubling suspicions that have been weighing heavily on my mind.

"Hey! Tyler," I greet him with a too-excited voice.

But I'm anxious, and I feel out of place in the gym, used to getting my workout from running with Lucy at dog parks and swimming at the beach.

Los Angeles has a million gyms and yet somehow also feels like a place that doesn't really need them, as there are so many ways to exercise naturally outdoors.

Tyler quirks an eyebrow in my direction as he sits on some torture device, kicking his legs up and down while weights lift high in the air as he does.

"What are you wearing?"

I look down at my outfit, a brown two-piece outfit consisting of a sports bra and booty shorts that the lady at the store assured me were perfect for working out at a gym. "You don't like it?"

"You look like you're starring in a porn movie made in a gym," he tells me. "But sure."

"You watch a lot of those, huh, Sargeant Lonely Heart?" I flick his knee bone, hoping to mess him up, but he doesn't falter at all.

"It's Sargeant Pepper. He has the Lonely Hearts club," he tells me, as he breathes heavily while pumping his legs.

His hair sticks to his forehead, the ends brownish from the sweat.

"I can't believe you corrected me on such a stupid thing," I tell him, sitting on a machine next to him and reading the little sticker tutorial.

"You're one to talk," he grunts, straining with effort.

"Hey, a guy gave me his number at the dog park just the other day!"

"What's his name?" he asks, sitting up to take a sip of his water, which is an entire gallon jug.

I look around to see that several men have gallon jugs of water, which is weird, but I can't exactly make fun of him for it as it appears to be some niche part of gym culture I don't understand.

"Scott."

"Is it serious? When do we get to meet Dog Park Scott that we've heard so much about?"

I roll my eyes. "Can we just move on already? I have something serious to talk to you about." I make my tone grave to force him to drop the subject of my love life.

"Go for it. We'll get to your love life later," he tells me, spreading his legs apart and leaning his arms on his knees.

Not likely. I steel myself for the sentence I need to say next, breathing in deeply through my nose and closing my eyes. I lay my body forward against the workout machine.

"Well, you know how Chris hired me to help him grow his business, possibly outside of the United States?"

"Yeah, duh, I'm the one who sent him to you."

"Well, I think someone is embezzling money from Chris' business."

His eyes widen in surprise, and I can see the gears turning in his head as he processes my words. "Embezzling? Are you sure?" he asks, his lip curled.

I nod, my heart pounding in my chest.

"That's so...Ocean's Eleven."

I sigh. "You know I've never seen any of the Oceans."

Tyler pinches the bridge of his nose before looking up at the ceiling as though begging God for help with me. "Just keep talking. How did you find out?"

"Well, obviously, I have to go over his finances as his CPA. Basically, his projected earnings are way lower than his actual earnings. Year over year, every quarter. And the discrepancies add up to about the same amount every quarter."

"What do you want me to do about it?"

My voice shaking slightly with emotion, I explain, "Chris is too afraid to face it. I told him about it the other night and that I need to take a better look at the transactions of the business, and he just changed the subject. I'm worried that if we don't do something about it, Chris could lose everything."

Tyler's expression darkens with worry, and I can see the tension in his jaw as he absorbs the gravity of the situation. "Damn," he mutters under his breath, running a hand through his hair in frustration. "So, do you have any idea who it is?"

"Not really. I don't know anything about his employees, do you?" I prompt him, eager to gather any information that might help us identify the culprit behind the embezzlement.

Tyler pauses mid-rep, his brow furrowing in thought.

"Well, I mean, this is heavy, Handy. I don't want to, like, implicate someone, but if I had to place bets," he begins his voice thoughtful, "well, Sarah's been with Chris since the beginning. And, I mean, she is technically in charge of finances -- inventory, that kind of thing. But she's always been reliable. And Chris loves her. If anything, he wishes they were closer. He feels like she's a little closed-off."

My interest piques at his words, and I can feel a sense of suspicion beginning to creep in. "Closed off?" I echo, my voice tinged with curiosity. "Why do you think that is?"

Tyler shrugs, his expression thoughtful. "I'm not sure," he admits. "But it's definitely something worth looking into."

I grab the handles of the weight machine, checking the weight to make sure it's nothing unmanageable, and pull with all my might. I mull over the information about Sarah. "Where is she?"

"Sarah?" Tyler clarifies. "She's just in her office back there. That's where she works."

"Alone?"

"Yeah, Chris has been wanting to give her a bigger office, but that's what they're working with right now. It's basically her and a desk."

Alone, with access to the company finances. No one breathing over her neck, double checking her work.

Tyler interrupts my thoughts with a pointed question, his voice laced with curiosity. "Do you normally put in this much work for your clients?" he asks, his gaze fixed on me.

I feel a flush of embarrassment creep into my cheeks at his question, and I quickly avert my gaze, pretending to be very focused on changing the weight on the machine. "I, uh, no, but he's your best friend, so I'm a little closer to it. I want to make sure he's okay."

Tyler nods, seemingly satisfied with my response, but I can't shake the feeling that he sees right through me.

As we continue our workout in silence, I can't help but wonder what other secrets lie hidden beneath the surface of Chris' business and what role Sarah might play in unraveling the truth.

# Chapter Fourteen
## Christopher

Yep, it's definitely Julie smiling at me like she didn't leave me at the altar after cleaning out my house, taking our dog, and disappearing into the night five years ago, while I waited for her at the church in front of all our friends and family. But hey, I'm not bitter or anything.

I force a smile. "Hey, Julie. It's been a while."

"Yeah, it has," she replies, her tone cautious. There's an awkward silence between us before she speaks again. "How have you been?

"Good, good," I answer, trying to sound casual. "Well, for the most part. And you?"

Julie shrugs. "Oh, I've been good, too. Staying busy." She laughs. "Well, you know how it is. A bit too busy, usually."

I nod, unsure of what else to say. My mind races, searching for something to fill the awkward silence.

It's strange. I have so much to say to her and yet really have nothing to say.

What does someone say in a situation like this?

'Hey, why'd you leave me?' seems a bit much for the condiment aisle. So does 'I haven't ever emotionally recovered and my therapist isn't sure when I will.' More of a diary aisle thing.

"So, you here for a bit?"

"Oh! Yeah." She rocks back and forth on her toes, a pained expression on her face. Please don't say what I think you're about to say. "I've got a new job out here."

"So you'll be staying, then."

I flatten my lips, my heart and mind racing as I imagine having to run into Julie at the grocery store every week. I want to ask to see her calendar, so I can schedule my grocery trips for another time.

"Great," I say with feigned cheer.

She laughs wryly. "Yep. Well, hey, you've had the last five years without me. It's time to face your fears, yeah?"

She's joking, but her words still sting.

Her hair is in two long, brown braids that hang over her breasts, and she takes one and nervously twirls it like a rope. It's sort of comical, like it isn't attached to her head at all.

I guess she's right, anyway. Maybe it is time to face my fears.

Already, I can feel my adrenaline subsiding as my body seems to acclimate to Julie being in front of me.

"Well, um, hey, I was just talking to someone the other day, and maybe it's good you're here! Because I was wondering: how's Noodle?"

Her expression darkens for a moment before she replies, "Oh, well, okay. Promise not to be mad?"

I laugh. 'What is this, 3$^{rd}$ grade? Julie, we're well past me being mad at you."

My empty living room, my empty bedroom, her clothes gone, her dishes gone, her art gone. Our dog gone. Her gone.

"Okay, well..." she continues to twist her braid anxiously like it's a toy of some kind.

I stop her hand with mine. "Can you tell me, please? Is she okay? Did she get sick or something?"

"No! No, she didn't get sick. I just... I got rid of her."

I furrow my brow, surprised by her response. "Really? I thought you loved that dog."

Julie looks at the ground with something that looks like a tinge of shame or regret. But it's hard to tell with Julie. She could be feeling anything.

As I learned the hard way, I evidently can't read her emotions well.

"Yeah, well. She wouldn't stop peeing on everything, okay? It was driving me crazy. She peed on the floor and on my purses and in my shoes."

I let out a bitter laugh as anger, resentment, and sadness all fill the caverns of my ribs at once. It's unbearable, this mixture of emotion.

Noodle was my family. Noodle was our family, I thought. I thought she took her because she loved her so much.

"She was a puppy, Julie. That's what puppies do."

She scoffs. "I know what puppies do, Chris, I'm not an idiot, but I was dealing with a lot."

"You caused that. I thought you took her because you loved her and couldn't bear the thought of being without her, and you're telling me you not only weren't willing to actually put in the work to raise and train her, but also wouldn't let me do it? What is wrong with you, Julie? Are you actually made of stone?" I tap her arm as though I'm checking what material she's made of.

She yanks her arm away from me and walks back to her cart. "I'm not made of stone, Chris. I was young, okay? I made some mistakes. I should have called you. But it's been five years. Get over it."

"Are you serious? Get over it? Are you a villain in a Lifetime movie? Noodle loved us, Julie. I loved Noodle. I would have taken her if you didn't want her."

"That dog didn't care who she ended up with, Chris. She just wanted to be fed. Anyone could have done that."

She walks away, one wheel of her cart screeching and wobbling horribly beneath the weight.

# Chapter Fifteen

## Hannah

As I'm settling into my evening routine, the soft knock on my door pulls me out of my thoughts.

It's late, and I'm not expecting anyone, so I'm surprised when I open the door to find Chris standing there, his expression a mix of distress and vulnerability.

"Chris, what's wrong?" I ask, immediately concerned as I step back to let him inside.

He enters with heavy steps, his shoulders slumped with a weight I can't quite decipher.

"Hey, Hannah," he greets softly, avoiding my gaze as he shuffles into the living room.

"I know that we left things kind of weird, but I just—I need someone right now?"

It's a question: Will I be that someone, he's asking.

"That's okay," I tell him.

Truth be told, the moment I saw his furrowed brow, his tearful eyes, I forgot all about the anger I felt the last time I saw him. It was childish, of course.

I can see instantly that he didn't mean to hurt me.

Closing the door behind him, I follow him into the room, my worry growing with each passing second.

"Chris, what happened?" I press gently, taking a seat beside him in a big, leather chair.

He's in one chair and I'm in the other.

It's times like these I wish I had a living room with a big squishy couch so that I could sit next to him, wrap my arms around him, and close this gap between us when he so obviously needs it right now.

He runs a hand through his hair, his movements tense and agitated. "I... I ran into Julie today," he confesses, his voice laced with sorrow.

My heart sinks at the mention of his ex-girlfriend – ex-fiancée- knowing all too well the complicated emotions she stirs within him.

She stirs complicated emotions within me, too, one of them being guilt that I didn't warn him she was in town.

This gutted feeling he's having right now is my fault.

"I'm sorry, Chris," I murmur sympathetically, reaching out to place a comforting hand on his arm.

He glances up at me, his eyes filled with a mixture of pain and frustration.

"Oh," he says, when he looks in my eyes. His soften, and I think again what teddy bear eyes he has, rimmed by long curly lashes.

"No, it's not that. I mean, yes, it was hard to see her. But it's something else."

"Something else? What do you mean?"

She had seemed fine when I saw her last, happy even, excited about her new job and not nervous in the least to be back in the same town with her ex.

"I asked her about Noodle," he continues, his voice barely above a whisper. "And she told me."

Noodle. The sweet, energetic pup Chris had shared with Julie.

My heart clenches at the thought of her, knowing how much she meant to him.

The clench only gets tighter when I imagine them picking her out together, so in love, holding hands as they look in at sweet puppies whining behind glass walls.

I can see them now, Julie saying, 'Aw, Chris, look at that one' and Chris saying 'She's perfect.'

A shared look between them. It makes me sick. After the kiss we shared, I don't want to think of any shared moments between him and anyone but me.

"Told you what?" I ask softly, dreading the answer. I stare at him as his head hangs between his knees.

Chris takes a deep breath, his gaze distant as he recounts Julie's words. "She... she got rid of her," he admits, his voice heavy with desolation.

"Got rid of her?"

His head snaps up and he narrows his eyes as he looks at me. "Yes. Just abandoned her like she meant nothing."

The news hits me like a punch to the gut, my empathy for him completely devastating, and I reach out to squeeze Chris's hand in silent solidarity.

"Oh, I'm so sorry, Chris," I murmur, struggling to find the right words to comfort him.

"Thanks, Hannah," he says softly, his voice thick with emotion. "I just... I needed to be here. Is it okay?"

I nod in understanding. I stand up and cross to him to hug him, letting him rest his warm cheek against my stomach. "Of course, Chris," I reply, offering him a small smile. "I'm here for you, always."

"Thank you," he whispers, leaning into my touch as if seeking refuge from the storm raging within him. I rake my fingers through his curls, swirling them across his scalp.

In that moment, as we face the sorrow together in the quiet comfort of my office, I realize just how much Chris has come to mean to me.

As I hold him, my hands stroking his hair, the back of his neck, his shoulder blades, offering him whatever solace I can, I think about all the other ways I want to offer him solace.

The other day, in his apartment, I had wanted to lose my virginity to him.

More than I had ever considered it with anyone else.

I had been on the edge of asking him to take me. I've been imagining it, and I don't know how long I can pretend I don't want it anymore. Even now, having his body against me is shortening my breath.

In the dimly lit room, the weight of Chris's pain hangs heavy in the air. I search for something, anything, that might offer him a semblance of comfort in this moment of heartache.

"Would you like something to drink?" I offer gently, hoping to distract him momentarily from his grief.

He shakes his head, his gaze fixed on some distant point beyond the walls of the small room. "No, I'm okay," he replies, his voice barely above a whisper.

"Are you sure? I might not know how to cook, but I can mix liquor with mixer," I joke, squeezing him against me.

He shakes his head without comment. I nod, respecting his silent request for solitude as I remain by his side, offering silent support in the face of his pain.

Minutes pass in silence, the only sound the soft hum of the air conditioning and the occasional rustle of fabric as Chris shifts. I resist the urge to speak, knowing that sometimes, the greatest comfort comes from simply being present.

Eventually, Chris breaks the silence, his voice barely audible as he speaks.

"I didn't think it would hit me this hard," he admits, his words tinged with regret.

"I never expected to know what happened to Noodle, but I also didn't expect it to be that she doesn't even have her anymore."

My heart aches at his anguish. Even more than that, I'm filled with anger thinking of Julie inflicting this pain on him without care.

"It's okay to feel this way, Chris," I assure him, my voice gentle yet firm. "Noodle meant a lot to you, and it's only natural to grieve her loss."

He nods, his eyes glistening with unshed tears. "I just wish I could have done more," he murmurs, his voice thick with emotion.

I pet his head. "You didn't do anything wrong." I wait a moment before asking a potentially painful question. "What did she say happened?"

Chris laughs bitterly. "Oh. Noodle was peeing on her floor, so she just...got rid of her."

"Got rid of her where?"

"I don't know. I didn't ask. I guess I should have asked."

"No, no, that's okay. I'm sure it was hard to think."

"Well, that, and she practically ran away from me when we started talking about Noodle."

He pulls away from me, pulling me into him by my waist. I feel my skin light up at his touch as he does.

"Why didn't you tell me Julie was in town, by the way?" he asks, looking me right in my eyes, looking to see a hint of deception, I know.

The question catches me off guard, and I feel a knot form in the pit of my stomach.

"What do you mean?" Wrong answer. "No, I'm sorry. I know what you mean. But how did you know?"

A small chuckle escapes his throat. "Hannah, Julie hasn't been in town in five years, and you reacted like I said I saw Tyler. You saw her, didn't you?"

Busted. "I did. At a bookstore."

"So, why didn't you tell me?"

He pulls me down to sit on his lap. His arms wind around my waist, and he props me up against his shoulder so he can look into my face.

I feel strangely off-guard in his lap, like he could ask me anything and I'd have to tell the truth.

Swallowing, I say hesitantly, "I... I didn't think it was important," finding that I can lie after all, my mind racing to find the right words.

Chris' expression morphs from curiosity into one that's a mix of disbelief and hurt. "Not important?" he echoes, his voice tinged with anger. "Hannah, come on."

I swallow hard, feeling the weight of his words pressing down on me. "I know," I admit quietly, avoiding his gaze. "I knew it was important. I was afraid of how important it might be. I was afraid that..."

"Afraid that what?" he interrupts, his tone softer now, but no less intense.

I take a deep breath, gathering my thoughts before meeting his eyes. Just a few days ago, I told him my biggest secret, something no one in my life knows...and then I told him another.

He was kind, and I walked out like he wasn't. If I tell him this, I have to deal with the consequences. I have to sit and let him respond.

All of my skin feels electric. I'm terrified to speak. My mouth is dry, and my heart is the inside of a metal drum.

"Afraid that if you saw her, maybe you'd meet up, and maybe she'd tell you she wanted to give it another shot, and maybe..."

"Maybe what?"

"Maybe you would want to. Give it another shot, I mean. Maybe you'd choose her over me," I confess, the words tumbling out before I can stop them.

"She's beautiful, and she's older, and her brother isn't your best friend," I say pointedly, and Chris chuckles.

I continue, "And she's from your past. This, whatever this is, it just started. I still don't even know what to call it. I didn't want to risk losing you to her."

Chris's expression softens at my words, and I can see the conflict raging behind his eyes.

"Hannah, you have nothing to worry about," he says gently, reaching out to cup my cheek. "I don't know what to call this yet, either, but whatever it is, I want to keep doing it."

His touch sends a shiver down my spine, and I lean into his hand, relishing the warmth of his touch.

I leave his lap briefly and get up to lock the office door.

I climb back onto Chris and lean down, kissing him deeply, feeling his erection against my thigh. His teeth catch my bottom lip and pull it out slowly before letting go. I moan at the sensation and palm his cheeks with my hands.

His hands knead into the meat of my waist as I press my tongue between his lips. He returns with his tongue against mine, our tongues competing and swirling around each other.

I sit up and wrap my legs around him, straddling him in the chair, my hands still on his face, my mouth pushed against his, my breathing heavy. My heart feels like it might beat out of my chest as his hands explore my body.

I lean away from him, holding myself up with my thighs, and pull my shirt off.

He helps me and throws it to the ground. He sighs longingly at the sight of my breasts in a brown, silk bra, and runs his hands down over my ribs, down across my lower back, igniting a trail of fire where his skin touches mine.

I feel a wet patch grow in my panties as he does, and I arch my back to moan at the ceiling, covering my face in embarrassment.

His hands shoot out to pull mine away from my eyes.

"Hey, don't be embarrassed," he murmurs, his voice low and husky with desire. "I love that every little thing I do turns you on."

His smirk is deep, and he knows he's mocking me. When I hug him to avoid looking at him, he repositions my hips so that his bulge is against the crotch of my jeans.

"Can't you feel that every little thing you do turns me on, too?" he whispers in my ear, and I feel the walls of my vagina lurch and clench at his breath on my skin and his cock against me.

His hands still on my hips, he moves my hips against him, pulling me in a circle against his bulge, grinding me against it, his breathing ragged in my ear. With one hand, he grips my hair at the roots and pulls my head to the side so he can suck on my neck. His hand travels over to the strap of my bra and moves it aside so he can continue to kiss and suck on my shoulder, on my throat, on my ear.

"Do you want to be a virgin, or do you want me?" he asks me.

"I want...I want you," I tell him, and I know it's the truth. I've wanted him since the day he walked into my business and I ran off to fantasize about him and touch myself alone in my bed. He's been special to me from the moment I laid eyes on him.

"You do?"

"Mhm," I say quietly, burying my face in his neck.

"Let's get you out this bra," he says quietly, his hands finding the clasp of my bra and unhooking it. For a moment, I hold my bra against my breasts, knowing that the moment I let go, everything changes.

"I'll be slow and gentle," he assures me, sensing my hesitance. "You don't have to do anything you don't want to. If you change your mind, you let me know. Okay? It won't change anything about how I feel."

"Are you sure?"

He laughs a little and leans up to kiss me. "I'm sure."

I feel safe with his chest against mine, and I let go of my bra, letting it stay between us.

I can feel his smile against my mouth, and he pulls the bra out from between our chests and throws it to the ground.

"Hey, there you go," he whispers. "That was brave."

His wide palms spread out against my back, and I feel small for the first time in my life like that. One hand sneaks around to the front and he palms one of my breasts with it, tweaking my nipple the way I tweak my nipple when I'm alone.

I can't help but shudder at the feeling it ignites between my legs, and I feel my pussy dribble into the crease of my inner thighs.

"God," I whisper against his mouth, unable to make my lips into the shape of a kiss, only able to feel.

"Does that feel good, baby?" he asks me, his eyes on my face, watching my every reaction. His mouth is dropped open as he does, like I'm a fascinating scene in a movie.

"Uh-huh," is all I can manage to squeak out.

"How good do you want to feel? Can you handle feeling better than this? Why don't you let me taste you?"

I gasp at the thought of Chris Stephens between my legs, and I clench my thighs reflexively in response.

"Oh, you want that, don't you? I bet you've thought about it before, haven't you?" he asks me.

He holds me by the lower back and leans me back so he can fit his mouth around my nipple. His tongue flicks against it, lighting it up, enjoying my small squeals of delight as he does so.

He laughs a little at the sounds and ignores me bashfully covering my eyes.

I can't decide what I want more: to be fucked or to be eaten.

Thinking of Chris' tongue in my pussy is enough to send my walls into an attack of convulsions, but thinking of his cock pressing against my little hole excites me even more.

"I want you right now, Chris," I tell him honestly. "I'm so wet, and I just want to feel you inside me."

I feel so lusty that I can't even feel any shame over being so candid. My eyes stare into his as I unbutton his and my jeans. I stand and pull them down slowly for him, then turning around and shaking my ass.

His laugh is tender and he leans forward and bites my ass cheek a little before spanking it.

"Dinner and a show?" he asks me before pulling me into him as though he's going to hug me. He pulls my panties to the side and positions his head where he can slide his tongue between my flaps like he's licking shut an envelope.

His flat tongue swipes against my slit a few times, his knuckles pressed hard against my thigh as he holds the cotton of my underwear.

I spread my legs to allow more room for his head between my thighs and rest my hands in his hair, gasping at the feeling of his tongue, wet and warm and probing. I want to cry from how good it feels, so alien to me and yet like a sensation I've known all along

The tip of his tongue plunges inside me and I almost-scream as it does. His hands grip my ass and pull me in tighter.

I push his head away and yank his pants off. "I need you. I can't wait anymore," I tell him.

"Sorry. I just needed to taste you," he tells me, his eyes on mine as I pull his pants down over his legs and mount him.

I look down, afraid to see one for the first time, and see his thick cock standing at attention, the head of it lightly spilling pre-cum out. The skin of the head is reddish and seems to be bursting at the seams, his veins standing out.

I reach down and wrap my hand around it, feeling his sticky pre-cum on my palm.

"How big are you?" I ask curiously.

"I could tell you anything and you'd believe it, huh?"

He's smiling earnestly, and I giggle as he pulls me against him.

"I guess so, yeah."

"I'm 13 inches long, then. Spread the word."

As he says 'spread', he knocks my legs open with his hands. He pulls my underwear to the side.

"God, you have the most beautiful little pussy I've ever seen, Hannah. Has anyone ever told you that?"

I laugh. "You know they haven't."

"So you've lived all this time not knowing? Oh, I'm so glad I get to change that."

I'm positioned right above him, and all I have to do is sit, feel him enter me. I hold myself above it, cherishing the moment.

There's something special about it, holding onto the second you are still a virgin but know you won't be soon, like falling asleep before your birthday.

I brace one arm against the back of the chair and lower myself slowly. My head flies back as the tip of his penis presses against my entrance, stretching just a bit but sliding easily against my slickness.

Tears instantly surface at my ducts, merging into one watery tear at my waterline, obscuring my vision.

"Are you okay, Hannah?" Chris asks, wiping my tears away with his thumb.

"I am, I am. It feels good. I'm just...overwhelmed. It's okay, keep going."

I gasp as he holds my hips and lowers me another centimeter. The feeling of his shaft entering me and touching every nerve ending I've only ever touched myself overwhelms me even more, and I groan with desire.

I let myself sit down entirely on his hard cock so that the length of him can fill me. It's a sensation I've always wondered about, the fullness, and I can only handle it for a moment before I start wriggling against it, moving up and down on it.

I look down at his face, and he looks sick with desire, his eyes on me, his mouth slightly open as he lets me take control. I hold him tightly and rock up and down, feeling him harden and expand even more than I thought possible.

"Oh, God, Hannah, it's too good," he tells me, and I feel him pulsing against my walls.

And it is too good.

As he says that, I feel his pulsing, and all of a sudden I feel my vagina contracting in a rhythm that can't be tamed, squeezing on and around his cock dangerously fast.

I'm sliding against him faster now, able to feel his length inside me with no pain now, and I hold him tight so that his face is in my neck.

Our hips feel fused together as one, and he pushes against me with my rhythm, the squelching of my pussy audible in the silence of the room. In this dark space, it's just our breathing, our moans, and my juices.

I start to scream an orgasm, feeling it rip through my body, up to my chest and out of my mouth.

He holds me tight and continues to pump inside me, letting me ride the sensation until it's over. "Cum inside me," I tell him. "Please."

He needs no convincing. The words are barely out of my mouth before I feel ropes of his cum being emptied inside me, spraying me as he grunts against my neck, his hands squeezing me with the effort.

# Chapter Sixteen
## Christopher

The morning sun filters through the curtains, casting a soft golden glow across the room.

I can barely remember how we ended up on her bed, a little mattress that she pulled out of a futon in the back room.

I was too lusty, satisfied, and tired all at once to chide her for her set-up. Soon, though, I know I need to help Hannah find a real place. She needs boundaries. This is no life for her.

I look over at her sleeping face, her still mouth and roving eyes under lightly purple eyelids. Yesterday's mascara is smudged under her eyes, and I see a faint hint of the tears she shed last night as I penetrated her.

I pull her warm body closer against mine and snuggle into her. I trace lazy patterns on her skin with my fingertips, finding freckles to connect like stars in a constellation.

"Good morning," she murmurs, her voice soft and melodic as she stirs beside me. She props up on her elbow and kisses my scruffy cheek.

"Morning," I reply, my voice husky with sleep. "I have something for you. I got it for you that day you ran out of my kitchen."

She giggles. "How did the bok choy turn out?"

"Perfectly. You seasoned it perfectly," I assure her, kissing her on her full lips. They're even puffier with sleep.

"Okay, okay, no more small talk. Go get my present! I can't take not knowing what it is."

"Oh, wow, you're a child," I chide her, rolling her around like I'm flattening dough.

"Yes, I am. Now get me my present, please."

"Fine, but won't you miss me? You'll be cold under there without me."

"I'll live," she says seriously, sitting up as I roll out from under the blanket. I kiss her on the forehead and go out to my car to get the present.

An anxiety over the gift starts to fill my chest, even though I know it's silly. After our shared intimacy, I'm worried she'll take it as an insult or a jab, even though it's really meant purely as a present.

I bring it back to her and hand her the box, wrapped in old Christmas wrapping paper, while I strip again and climb back into the makeshift bed with her.

She laughs at the paper before tearing it off. She pulls the tape off the box and laughs at the paper inside the box.

"This is a fortress," she jokes before finally getting to it. Her eyes widen in surprise as she sees the portable camping cooktop and beginner's recipe book nestled inside.

"Wait, Chris," she says, her voice filled with emotion even as a joking smile spreads across her face.

"This is actually so sweet. This is, like, one of the most thoughtful presents I've ever gotten."

"You're worth it," I tell her, ruffling her hair. I reach out and brush a stray lock of hair from her face.

A soft smile spreads across her lips as she leans forward to press a gentle kiss against my cheek. "Thank you," she whispers, her breath warm against my skin.

With a grin, I climb out of bed and offer her a hand, helping her to her feet. "Come on," I say, my excitement palpable. "Let's go shower and make some breakfast together."

"Wait," she says, laughing bashfully. Her hair is so bright in the sunlight that the top of it looks like pure gold. Her freckles stand out like chocolate chips in the bright light.

"Okay, but I have to tell you something you may not have realized."

"What?" I ask, putting my hands on my hips, so that my penis reaches toward her in a goofy pose.

Laughing, she tucks her head into her knees. "Please, this is so embarrassing."

"What? Say it. If you can't tell this guy, who can you tell?" I ask, whirling my penis around in a circle.

"Chris, I don't have a shower here. I have to shower at a community center." She looks up and scrunches her nose in an expression that tells me she knows it's a lot.

I sigh. "Okay, well, we definitely have to talk about this living arrangement later," I tell her, offering her my hand and pulling her out of bed and to her feet.

"But for now, let's go grocery shopping and focus on a beginner breakfast: eggs and pancakes. And after, you can come to my house and shower since you're a dirty girl."

I wrap her up in my arms. Even after the sex, she still smells so good somehow. I must be in trouble if her pheromones do this to me after a night of sweat and cum.

"Okay," she mutters, kissing me on my cheek. "Right after we talk about how someone's embezzling from you and you won't acknowledge it because of your deep-seated fear of betrayal."

"Holy shit, you are cold, Handy Jackson."

"Do not start," she warns me, looking up with her eyes squinted into small slits.

"Awww, but now it's accurate."

"I should just let someone steal from you, then, do you know that?"

I hold her tightly. "You would never do that. Deep down, you're entirely too sensitive for your own good, aren't you?"

I kiss the top of her head, the warm sun in her hair and on my lips.

"Just in your arms," she whispers, tucking her lips into my arm.

I hug her and cradle her head and think of all the things we need to say and confront.

# Chapter Seventeen
## Hannah

The cool air of the grocery store hits my face as we step inside, a stark contrast to the warm sun outside.

Chris grabs a shopping cart and playfully insists I hop in, but I roll my eyes and push past him to grab a basket instead.

"We're here to shop for breakfast, not to goof around," I tell him and myself, even as my heart does a little skip every time he smiles at me. I can't keep the warmth from my voice, remembering the thoughtfulness behind his gift.

As we walk down the housewares aisle, I can't help but feel a flutter of excitement at the thought of cooking together. It seems so domestic, so normal, and yet nothing about our relationship has been normal from the start.

We first choose a skillet and a small griddle, along with a spatula, a mixing bowl, and a measuring cup. Then we head toward the breakfast meats.

"What do you think? Sausage links or patties?" Chris asks, holding up two bags as if they're trophies.

"I'm partial to patties," I decide, pointing.

"Good choice," he grins, tossing the box into the basket and steering us towards the dairy section for milk and eggs.

As we walk, I can't shake off the conversation we need to have about the embezzlement at his gym. It's been eating at me, the numbers not adding up, and now the uncertainty of who he can trust.

But looking at Chris, seeing the easy way he navigates through crowds, always with a protective eye on me, I feel a pang that I can't protect him, too.

The walk back is quiet, each of us lost in our thoughts, Lucy trailing behind us on the leash to smell every single leaf, it seems.

She finds dirt deeply interesting. I make a pained expression for Chris' benefit, but it's clear he doesn't mind, oohing and aahing over her found treasures as though he himself were a big puppy in a human's body.

He keeps his hand wrapped around mine, warm and inviting, as though he's been holding my hand all our lives.

Back at my place, we unpack the groceries and supplies in the small employee breakroom, and he kisses my cheek when he notices that I'm overwhelmed by the process. "Don't worry," he tells me, "I'm right here to help you."

"I just don't know where to start," I tell him honestly, melting into his kiss.

His hands snake around my hips and I moan without thought. He smirks at my body's response, kissing underneath my ear, and tells me, "Start at the beginning."

Chris puts on a song on his phone, and a woman's honey-thick voice wafts out of the speakers as he pulls out the ingredients in a row for me. He plugs in the cooktop and turns it to medium-heat.

He whirls around to me and wraps his strong arms around me, tucking his chin on my shoulder. "Okay, read the first step. You got this."

I flip to the page we're on – pancakes – and think to myself: and we're off.

I tell him, "You know, this feels nice. Just...us. No money or gym talk, just us." I snuggle into the crook of his arm and let him pet my hair.

He whispers into my ear, "Are you stalling?"

"Mmm, and you already know me so well," I joke as he pushes me away from him. He catches me before I crash into the wall, and I dissolve into laughter in his arms.

As I crack eggs and pour milk and mix batter, in the back of my head two thoughts compete with one another: one, that I can't wait to shower with Chris, to shampoo his hair and touch his warm body, and two, that I need to confront Julie.

***

After breakfast is completed and pancakes are eaten, we head to Chris' place to shower and clean up.

Once Chris drops me back off at my office/home once more, I immediately begin to sleuth, even as I know I shouldn't.

I sit in my desk chair and open my laptop, chewing on my thumbnail as I type in my password.

I look behind my shoulder to make absolutely certain that Chris really did drop me off and leave, my guilt manifesting as anxiety.

And then I do the thing I shouldn't: I type Julie's name into a search engine and look to see what social media profiles come up.

Last night when Chris came by and seemed so upset by Julie's arrival and by the knowledge of Noodle's departure, his words kept ringing in my ears: that Julie had abandoned Noodle.

Chris has been the epitome of a positive force, someone who enters your life and instantly makes you feel seen and understood.

I wonder if I could track down Noodle for him. And it's definitely not because I think that I'd be more appealing to him if I could.  More appealing than Julie. I'm definitely over that fear.

With trembling hands, I click on a profile that looks like her picture in a tiny little circle. It unfurls itself to reveal squares upon squares of pictures of Julie at her best: Julie up against a brick wall, Julie looking back and laughing, Julie doing yoga on a mountain top.

That last one in particular really stings – she sure has got the aesthetic of a fit, successful young woman down. A part of me wonders that, if I scroll, will I find pictures from five years ago?

Not what I'm doing right now, though. A few swift taps bring me to her latest post — a casual invitation to a brunch with friends.

The irony is not lost on me. While she sips mimosas with her companions, I stalk her life from afar, alone in my office, the lights turned off, the harsh light of the screen in my eyes.

Against my better judgment, I find myself making a spontaneous decision. I need answers, closure for Chris. He deserves that.

Without giving it a second thought, I grab my keys, Lucy's leash, and head out the door.

The drive to the brunch spot is a blur, my thoughts consumed by the impending confrontation.

What will I say to Julie? How will she react? Is this crazy? Am I crazy? What would Chris do if he knew?

I push aside my doubts, steeling myself for whatever lies ahead.

As I step into the bustling restaurant, the smell of coffee and chatter fills the air, mingling with the palpable tension coursing through my veins. Scanning the crowd, it doesn't take long to spot Julie, her familiar silhouette seated at a table near the window.

She sits straight up, as though someone is watching her and judging her posture. Her hair falls in perfect waves down her back, and she has a book open on the table as she waits for her friends. I can't remember the last time I had time to read a book.

Summoning every ounce of courage, I make my way over to her, my heart pounding in my chest. She looks up as I approach, her expression shifting from surprise to guarded apprehension.

"Anna," she greets me, her voice tinged with uncertainty. "What are you doing here?" I slide into the seat across from her, and she lifts her chin, telling me, "Oh, I'm sorry, I'm meeting friends here."

"I know. And the name is 'Hannah'," I tell her, nodding at a waitress holding up a pitcher of water questioningly at me.

She walks over and places a glass down in front of me. She pours water into the glass, smiling, unaware of the tension between Julie and me, thinking there's friendship, thinking we're here for a giddy brunch like the rest of her patrons. Adjusting her glasses, she smiles at me and says, "Can I get you something to drink?"

"No," I tell her, scrunching my nose at Julie. "I'm leaving soon. Thank you, though."

"Aw, who's this?"

The server's eyes are on Lucy and her hands shoot out to pet her shiny black coat. Her fingers fiddle with Lucy's dog tag and she reads the name.

"Lucy, aww, you're so sweet. Okay, well y'all let me know if you need anything."

As soon as the waitress leaves, I don't waste any time with pleasantries. "We need to talk, Julie," I say, my tone firm and resolute. "About Noodle."

The color drains from Julie's face, her eyes widening in alarm. "What about...about Noodle?" she asks, her stammer betraying her unease.

Her uneasiness softens me a bit. I lean forward and ask, "You told Chris you got rid of her. What exactly does that mean?"

Julie's finger trails the rim of her mimosa glass, and she tells me as she lifts it to her mouth, "I got rid of her. It's exactly what it sounds like. She was pissing all over everything. It was exhausting cleaning up after her every day, sometimes multiple times a day. Pets are supposed to enrich your life. She didn't."

She shrugs, and I can tell that she's deflecting, pretending to care less than she really does. I wonder how guilty she felt when it happened, if at all.

"Okay, so you didn't want her. But where did you get rid of her? Where did she end up? When?"

Julie shifts uncomfortably in her seat, avoiding my gaze. "It was a long time ago," she mutters, her voice barely above a whisper. "I don't really remember."

I interlock my fingers together, placing my elbows on the table. I drop my chin onto my hands and lift my eyebrows at her. "Try. What do you remember?"

"I left her...in a dumpster."

The confession hits me like a punch to the gut, leaving me reeling with shock and disbelief.

I never knew Julie. All I knew of her was a few holiday appearances. The appearance she didn't make had made more of an impression.

Back then, I had given her the benefit of the doubt, considering that marrying someone was a big commitment, considering the fear it must have taken for her to just not show up, the anxiety that must have consumed her.

But now, anger surges through me like a tidal wave for Noodle and for Chris.

"Why didn't you just give her back to Chris?"

She shrugs. "You sound just like him."

Her friends have shown up. One slides into the seat next to me, a big smile across her face, expecting that I'm a new friend she hasn't yet met, her curls springy and her green glasses poised on her nose. Julie looks at her and shakes her head.

"Like who?"

"Like Chris. He asked the same thing. Why didn't I just give Noodle back? As though that was an option."

"Wasn't it?"

"No!" she scoffs. "I had just gone through the worst breakup of my life. It isn't as if I could exactly call Chris up and ask him to come get her. So yeah, I dumped her in a dumpster over by the art district. I figured some hippies would find her and give her a better life or whatever."

She flicks her hand at me, exhausted with the conversation, embarrassed, leaning into the villain narrative.

"But why? Chris loved that dog," I whisper, the anger in me ebbing, sorrow taking its place.

"Wait, you left a dog in a dumpster?" Julie's friend asks, looking over at the other friend in horror.

"Sure did!" I tell her chipperly, standing up. "This dog, I'm pretty sure."

Lucy pants dutifully at my side. "This is Lucy, who I found in a dumpster in the art district several years ago. Lucy, who reacted ecstatically when she first saw Chris. Lucy, who fell asleep on him. Lucy, who I'm pretty sure is Noodle."

Unable to bear the weight of the conversation any longer, I turn on my heel and storm out of the restaurant, my eyes blurred with tears.

As I make my way back to my car, I can't shake the feeling of betrayal, the bitter taste of it lingering on my tongue.

In that moment, I vow to myself that I will do whatever it takes to make things right.

For Noodle, for Chris, for myself. No one deserves to be treated like garbage.

Even a dog. Maybe especially a dog.

# Chapter Eighteen
## Christopher

At the gym, I help a client with some physical therapy for his weak knee ligaments, an issue that involves mostly retraining his body to use those ligaments in order to strengthen them.

The man isn't much younger than I am, in his early thirties, and the weakness has left him unable to pick up his children, walk up stairs, or even put on shoes without debilitating pain.

It just about broke my heart to hear he couldn't pick up his kids. He'd been grateful, though, to hear that he likely wouldn't need any kind of surgery.

He'd been hypermobile his whole life without even realizing or understanding it, and the looseness of his joints had caused his body to compensate by forcing him to put weight on his hips instead.

"How does that feel, Nick?" I ask the guy, a thin lanky brunette with wire frame glasses currently fogging up as he breathes heavily, watching him do grapevine exercises, the silicon bands cutting into his thigh meat as he moves to the right and then to the left.

"I'm not gonna lie to you, Chris, it doesn't feel great," he tells me through a grim smile that almost looks more like a grimace with teeth bared.

"Well, you look great, so no one can tell," I lie to him, standing to the side and watching his form, "You keep doing what you're doing. Just five more reps on each side and then you're done, okay? Do you need any water or anything?"

Nick can barely look at me, his face contorted into one of extreme focus. He shakes his head in response, and I take the hint and shut up, letting him do his exercises.

After a few minutes, he extricates his legs from the band and hands it to me. "Here you go, you medieval torturer."

I chuckle at him as I hang them up on the wall. "I wear it like a badge of honor. Why don't you go up to the front and make another appointment, and I'll see you next week?"

"Fine. How many more sessions do you think I need?"

"Well, I can't tell you for sure. Your insurance covers nine more sessions. I can tell you that based on your reaction to the band, it'll take a few more. Okay, dude?" I slap him on the back, the worldwide known manly gesture for rallying.

"Okay. Yeah. I mean, it still really hurts, I'll be honest."

"I know it does, man."

"And you're sure it's not a surgical issue? That I don't need surgery?" Worry passes his face, obvious in his knit eyebrows and twisted lips.

"I know for a fact that you don't, at least not before we try the non-invasive physical therapy techniques first. You know Dr. Jackson and I agree on this point. You've had every possible test done. Just trust me. We'll get you through this and get you back to picking your kids up in no time, okay?"

I offer him a smile, trying to show him that I mean it, that I wouldn't steer him wrong.

"Okay. Well, thank you for everything."

"Of course, man. Go make an appointment. I want you to do those reps every day for the next week."

"Is there risk of overdoing it? I'm scared. Sometimes it feels like it hurts more afterward." I can feel the fear coming off him.

"It's going to hurt. It's hard work. You're basically feeling the very normal pain of a workout but isolated to one spot. But there is absolutely no risk of overuse right now. Absolutely not. You are in pain because of underuse. Trust me. Do you trust me, Nick?"

"I trust you." Nick sighs, gathering his things, stuffing his pockets with his phone and his keys. He takes a swig of water. "Bye, Chris."

"Bye, Nick!" I call out to him. I write down my notes in the little notebook I keep during physical therapy sessions. I write down the reps he did, my recommendations, and the pain that he's describing feeling afterward.

With my pen in my hand, I feel the vibrating of my phone in my pocket. I pull it out of my shorts and answer without looking. "Hello?"

"Hey, Chris, it's me."

Julie. Even after five years, I would have recognized her voice, but it helps that I saw her at the grocery store just…God, when was that? It feels like a lifetime ago.

My breath catches in my throat as I answer, "Um, who is this?" I don't know why I insist on playing it cool, but I don't want her to know that I know her voice like the back of my hand.

"Funny," she says coldly, and I can practically hear her rolling her eyes. "We need to talk."

"I can't imagine why," I tell her honestly.

"You're full of jokes today, huh?"

"Who says I'm joking?"

"Listen, can we meet?"

I lean against the mirrored wall, hesitance rendering me silent. I can't imagine Julie has anything good to say to me. Nothing I want to hear, anyway.

"I don't think that's such a good idea, Ju-Julie." I almost called her 'Jules', my old pet name for her. A pang shoots through me.

"It's about Hannah. Thought you might want to know that she's been stalking me."

Sighing deeply, I stand up straight. "Sure. Where?"

My curiosity is piqued enough to see her, despite the knot of tension forming in my stomach.

"71 Above in two hours?" The restaurant I used to take her to all the time, a place with $100 plates and gloomy, romantic lighting.

"How about somewhere else? There's this new place that I love, somewhere that opened up while you were gone. Philippe the Original. You'll love it."

"Sounds like a plan," she purrs.

"See you there." I hang up, an ominous sense of unease settling over me like a blanket.

Julie hasn't been up to anything good in years, and I can't imagine she's changed that much. Or maybe she has. Maybe I shouldn't judge her by anything but what she is now. I wouldn't want someone to do that to me. Still, she's never apologized, and now she's calling me up for lunch.

Whatever it is, I'm sure Hannah didn't do anything wrong. It's probably just a miscommunication, something I'll be able to explain easily.

# Chapter Nineteen

## Hannah

I go home after seeing Julie, my nerves unable to settle.

I don't know what exactly I want to do with the information that I am now certain is true: that Lucy is Noodle. If that's true, it means I have a slice of Chris' former life sitting in the backseat with warm brown eyes and a wet nose right now.

The first thing I do is make myself an omelet for lunch on the cook top Chris got me, which is one of my favorite meals now.

I had really underestimated how much better an egg would taste cooked over a burner versus coming out of a microwave.

After eating it feverishly, like someone who had never eaten a meal in her life, I gather up my painting supplies, put Lucy on a leash, and walk to the nearby dog park, my mind wracked with repetitive thoughts about everything.

Lately, my mind is a thick fog of questions and curiosities. I don't know what to do about losing my virginity to my brother's best friend.

I really don't know what to do about how good it was and the fact that I am looking forward to a repeat performance.

I don't know what to do about Chris' business, the whole reason we're together in the first place.

As long as he has a thief in his midst, he's losing money, and that scares me.

I know how much he struggles with betrayal, so the thought of him being betrayed on an ongoing basis by someone else he trusts just breaks my heart.

I don't know what to do about Lucy.

What if I tell Chris and he's angry that I met with Julie? What if he doesn't believe me? What if he doesn't care? What if knowing about Lucy makes him want to avoid me because it's too hard for him knowing that she's actually Noodle?

I sit on the grass at the dog park, finishing the painting I started of Lucy in what seems like a lifetime ago now.

I paint the background of the trees and deepen the greens of the grass.

Painting on the grass is one of the best feelings in the world because if you get paint on your fingers, you just wipe them off right there on the earth. It's like a present from Mother Nature.

Lucy runs back and forth across the park, her mouth frothy and her eyes wild, her ears flapping backward in the wind as another dog happily chases her and they play bow to each other. I tear up thinking about the way Julie just threw her away.

Not very happy with the outcome of this painting, I prop the canvas up against the tree I'm under and pull another out of my bag to start anew.

Maybe if I do a really good job of painting Lucy for Chris, he'll see what good news this really is.

I start by sketching her face, her soft eyes filled with love that look as though she's never once suffered, and the nose that twitches at the slightest smell.

I paint her head tilted at an angle, the way she looks when I answer the phone and she listens to my conversation. I think about painting her in technicolor, to show what she has added to my life and what joy she can still bring to Chris.

"Hey, there, working on another?"

I look up and see the man I met briefly at the dog park before.

Scott stands over me, blocking the sun directly with his body. He casts a long shadow over me that gives me a chill in the otherwise sunny spot.

"I'm sorry?"

"You were painting the last time I saw you here, too. Looks like you've started another."

"Oh." I look down. "Yeah." I shade my eyes with my hand.

"Oh, I'm sorry. Can I sit?"

"Sure." I shrug.

Scott sits down, a tangle of legs and arms. "You left kind of quick last time. Wasn't sure if I upset you for some reason."

"Nah," I say, continuing to work on my artwork. "I was just done already. Bad timing."

"Ah." Scott points over at our dogs together.

They're jumping and biting at each other's necks, their tails wagging wildly. "Looks like they like each other."

"Lucy likes everyone," I respond honestly.

"Ouch. Not even gonna let me feel special for a second?" I look up at him to see if he's serious and he raises his eyebrows at me, a sideways small across his lips.

"Do you normally only need a second?" I ask, and he returns my question with a grin.

Is this flirting? Why don't I feel nervous? Was all that was necessary for to be able to talk to men was to lose my virginity?

"Wooooowww." He drags the word out, throwing his head back to laugh. "You're a cruel one, Hannah."

I smile politely, satisfied with the way I responded, satisfied with my ability to talk to a man and make him laugh, and I go back to my sketch as I hide a grin into my canvas.

Once I realize I've lost the light, I stand up, my bones seeming to creak with the effort.

Scott looks up at me and protest, "Nooo, don't go."

"Ah, but I...," I turn my painting around, "I've lost the light for the day."

"Well, so? That doesn't mean you have to leave. Our girls are still having so much fun."

Standing awkwardly, I look over at Lucy and Scott's golden doodle. They do still seem to be having fun somehow. Their endless energy is remarkable, inspiring even.

"Yeah, but." I check my phone and see the time, that hours have passed already.

"Well, I really do have to go. I have a life."

"You saying I don't have a life?"

"Well, I do see you here a lot," I snicker at him, gently tapping my canvas with the pads of my thumb to make sure the paint is dry before I slide it back into my bag.

"Hm, well, maybe I'll see you here again, then? For a play date? Our dogs are too in love for us to ignore it, don't you think?"

"As long as it's only a doggie play date."

I hold my bag in front of me like a barrier, suddenly worried about how Chris might feel if he saw me talking to Scott like this.

Would he care? Would I want him to?

Scott crashes his hand into his chest and frowns dramatically, "You're breaking my heart."

"I'll be back later in the week," I tell him, slapping my hand against my thigh for Lucy to come back to me.

"Also, not to really rub it in, but you're sitting on my blanket." I point at the ground.

"Oh. Well, if I keep it, you'll have a reason to come back. Like Cinderella."

I roll my eyes, already tired of this flirting game.

"I have a reason to come back because of the dog park, Lover Boy. Give me back my blanket, please."

"Fine." Scott stands and picks up my blanket. He shakes the grass and dirt off, folds it, and hands it over to me. "Until then."

"Bye, Scott," I tell him, clipping the leash to Lucy's collar and walking out.

# Chapter Twenty
## Christopher

I arrive just a few moments before Julie, as I want to see her reaction when she enters the restaurant and sees the space I chose, a cheap little chicken place despite its fancy name.

My leg jiggles as I watch the door. Finally, it opens, a bell tingling over her head, and she scans the room before settling her eyes on me. They narrow sarcastically and she waves from the door.

She crosses, the small heels of her shoes clacking on the floor. She sits down across from me and crosses her legs, a piece of her tan thigh flashing from under the table.

"Hey Chris," she tells me, her voice bubbly as she suppresses a small smile. "Nice place, this. Interesting choice."

"I thought it was what you deserved," I respond, my eyes flitting to follow her movement as she tosses her hair to the back, exposing her neck.

I roll my eyes and clear my throat. I pick up the menu. "So. Fried chicken or grilled chicken?"

"How about we just make this quick? I can tell you don't want to be here," Julie smiles tightly, folding her fingers together.

"Sure, works for me. Go ahead."

I drop the menu back on the tabletop, running my hand over the plastic sleeve.

"Hannah showed up at my brunch today." She waves at a nearby waitress.

"Water please. With a plate of lemons on the side."

"How did she know you were having brunch?" I ask her tactfully, as the waitress sets water down for both of us, smiling as she does so.

I smile back thinly and watch as Julie picks the slimy, oval seeds out of her lemon slices.

Julie drops her shoulders in a gesture of exasperation.

"I don't know exactly. But if I had to guess, I think the poor thing probably looked me up on social media. Bless her heart, I know what it's like to worry about someone's ex, but still, totally inappropriate, you know?"

"Sure." I lean back in my chair, placing my hands behind my head, and keep my eyes on her. I can't help but let a smirk slip onto my face, and she looks at me sharply when she sees it.

"I feel like you aren't taking me seriously, Chris. She was really unhinged today, and it made me feel unsafe."

"Oh, did it? Tell me about that. In what ways did that 25-year-old make you feel unsafe?" I grin at her and flick my straw in her direction across the small table, my wrist sticking to the plastic, checkered tablecloth.

Julie sits up straight and looks down her nose at me, her big brown eyes glowing with anger.

"You're going to say "25-year-old" like that? Aren't you fucking her? I wouldn't think you have a right to be dismissive of her because of her age."

Her fingers tent on the table, and she leans her body forward in an intimidating posture.

I almost laugh. "Is that what this is about, Julie? You're jealous? God, that's sad. You left me. At least be confident in your decisions, huh?"

Julie crosses her arms and leans back in her chair, too.

"Jealous. That's a good one. You're right, Chris, I did leave you. Maybe you should remember that."

I sip my water, swish it around, and tip my head at her. "Do you think so? That I should "remember" that? So Julie, when Hannah showed up, what did she say?"

"She was being totally insane. She showed up asking me about Noodle. It was so weird, and I was with my friends, too. Everyone thought it was completely worrying. If you're not worried, then forget it, I guess."

She shrugs as if she doesn't care and sips her water.

"She was asking about Noodle, huh?"

"Yes."

"So is all of this because you feel guilty? And instead of saying you're sorry, then what? Trying to make her out to be crazy or unstable or something? That's a bit much, Julie."

Julie sits for a moment, gulping water down, her eyes over the rim of the glass.

She sets her drink down too noisily, making a clank that she cringes at, and leans forward toward me. She places her hand over mine.

"I never said she's crazy. I just think she's young. She probably doesn't know what to do with all those feelings. I get it, actually. Still, it's a bit much, you know? She had to find me on social media to know where I was. Unless she was following me for even longer than that. It's scary. Obsessive."

I process her words slowly, skepticism mounting. I try to picture the Hannah she's painting. Obsessive, unhinged, showing up to Julie's brunch after following her all day. It doesn't make any sense. She isn't even that obsessive about me, let alone Julie. I can't imagine it.

"That doesn't really sound like her..." I trail off, sliding my hand out from underneath hers.

Still, I can't say it didn't happen. How else would Julie even know that Hannah and I are close?

"Oh, Chris, you've always been so naïve, so unaware of the effect you have on women. She really likes you. If you thought you'd have a little one-off tryst with Hannah, well,

I think you underestimated how she feels about you. That's all."

I look into her face.

"Julie. All due respect, I don't think she's jealous. She knows I don't talk to you. I think it's possible I piqued her interest talking about Noodle, but that's it."

"So you were talking about me."

"I told her I saw you, yes."

"You need to be careful with what you say to a girl like that. She could hurt you. Or me. I mean, you don't want me to get hurt. Why did you bring me into it?"

"Because, I mean, she isn't a one-time thing. I like her. A lot."

"Chris, what are you thinking? Tyler is going to lose his shit when he finds out you're fucking his baby sister, you know?"

She pinches the bridge of her nose like the weight of the knowledge physically pains her.

I inhale heavily through my nose and tighten my shoulders.

"When he finds out? Do you plan to tell him?"

"Maybe I should."

Suddenly, a deep concern that Julie will tell him just to be nasty slinks its way into my mind, settling like a cat sunbathing in front of a window, a cat with waiting claws.

I look into her eyes and see a person I don't recognize anymore, someone who would hurt me easily, who is maybe considering hurting me now, just for the hell of it.

"I'd rather you didn't."

"Well." She crosses her legs in the other direction and pulls her shoulders back, sitting up straight. She looks down at my outfit. "You ran here, didn't you?"

"Mhm," I answer warily.

"You're so good about that, exercising. I never had your discipline. Maybe I could drive you home and we could talk more about it."

It sounds more like a demand than a suggestion.

# Chapter Twenty One
## Hannah

I let Lucy into the backseat, knowing she'll manage to wrangle her way into the front seat next to me, anyway, clever girl that she is. I get into the front seat and wrestle her front paws away from me as I pull out and head for Chris'.

Even though I'm afraid to see him and tell him my strange news, I know that I need to, that it's only fair, that it would be cruel to wait any longer.

I shouldn't have even let it go this long, but at least I have the painting almost done and I'm hopeful that will soften the blow.

The afternoon traffic does nothing to soothe my nerves, the crammed-together cars seeming to mimic my mind, the thoughts stuck to each other, dribbling through.

How do you tell someone that your dog is the same dog that their ex, the one who abandoned you at the altar, left in a dumpster? How do you tell him that his past is unknowingly intertwined with your present?

I pull up to Chris' house, the weight of the revelation sitting heavy on my chest.

As I kill the engine, I look at Lucy—or should I say Noodle?

She sits on the passenger seat, her tail wagging slowly.

I always suspected she was smarter than the average dog, and I wonder now if she senses the gravity of the situation. I take a deep breath and pat her head before we step out of the car.

I push the little metal button at the front of the building, the one that corresponds with Chris' apartment, and wait for him to answer.

When he doesn't, I look around, suddenly feeling silly for showing up without calling. Did I forget he has a life? Of course he's not home in the middle of the day. He's probably at work.

I look down at Lucy as she sits on her haunches next to me, waiting patiently.

I think, not for the first time, that I won the lottery with her. She's so good at waiting and at knowing when she needs to wait.

"Good girl," I tell her quietly, as I decide that I should likely just go home. "Sorry, Luce," I tell her, pulling her back to the car with me.

As I turn around, my gaze locks onto a scene I wasn't expecting, something that hadn't ended up in any of the iterations I'd daydreamed about.

I see Chris stepping out of a sleek, silver car. I see him before he sees me. I also happen to see Julie before she sees me, in the driver's seat, her smile radiant and her tan glowing.

I freeze, suddenly unsure of what I should do next. I wish desperately for a tree to magically appear in front of me just so that I can hide behind it.

The sight of them together, Julie waving, seemingly carefree, and Chris comfortable enough to get a ride with her, so at ease with each other, feels like a cold splash of reality.

They seem...right together, somehow, a perfect match, the right age and the right world.

My mind races with every possible reason they could be together, but one possibility screams louder than the rest: they were on a date.

Panic claws at my throat as Julie leans out of the car and says something to Chris that makes him nod.

Without fully realizing what I'm doing, I pull on Lucy's leash, hurrying back to my car.

Suddenly, we're practically jogging, Lucy's ears back as she runs with me, always my partner-in-crime, happily my partner-in-crime.

As I usher her into the backseat, I meet Chris's eyes, his expression shifting to utter confusion, then to a dawning concern as he recognizes the turmoil in my gaze.

He looks back at Julie as she pulls out of her space, then back at me again, his head shaking wildly.

"Hannah!" His voice reaches me faintly, the name floating across the wind to me, urging me to stop.

He starts toward me, his hands outstretched, but the distance might as well be miles, there might as well be a world between us.

I can't do it. I can't face it, listen to the excuses, hear him tell me that I was right, that he wants Julie back, that they want to give it another try, that they're going to get it right this time.

Meanwhile, he has my virginity in his pocket, something precious I can't ever get back.

With a shaky breath, I turn the key and the engine hums to life. I drive off, the rearview mirror briefly capturing Chris' figure, looking at me with a mix of hurt, bewilderment, and concern.

The drive home is a blur, tears threatening to spill over as I navigate the streets back the way I came.

When I arrive home it's quiet, a stark contrast to the turmoil inside me. I sink into the couch, Lucy curling up beside me, her head resting on my lap as if she senses my distress.

The softness of her fur under my fingers brings a momentary relief, while the image of Chris and Julie haunts the back of my mind.

I bury my face into Lucy's back and inhale, smelling the warm scent of a dog who's had a good day.

How could I have been so wrong about everything? About his feelings, for Julie and for me and for us?

Had I been wrong about the potential of something real blossoming between us? Had it all been just a joke to him? Was I just a Chris Stephens conquest?

Why had he told me he chose me when he could have just kept quiet?

I would have never pursued him if he hadn't made me feel like it was possible, this thing between us, this heat I feel when I see him.

The thought of confronting Chris now, of explaining why I had fled without a word, seems impossible.

The weight of the unspoken truth about Lucy – about Noodle – lingers heavily on my shoulders.

It's not just about a dog. It's about closure, about the past, and about the complex web I'm now caught in.

I consider calling and telling him what I saw, telling him what I know, and asking why he fucked me if he never intended for it to go any further.

But I decide instead that tonight is a night of mourning for the possibility of what might have been, my heart heavy with words left unsaid and paths not taken.

# Chapter Twenty Two
## Christopher

I sit with Tyler, eating a croissant as I watch Tyler drink coffee.

I look momentarily at the other patrons drinking coffee and eating little sandwiches. They all seem so carefree.

Just a few weeks ago, I felt that carefree feeling.

Julie was somewhere else in the world, far away from me, and Hannah was just Tyler's little sister. Now, it's all complicated.

I wish I'd never called Tyler.

Sometimes, all you want is your best friend. But the way that I've complicated this relationship, I can't look at him without a twinge of guilt.

The confusion and hurt that I saw washed over Hannah's face has been haunting me. It haunted me all night, and it haunted me all morning, and finally I had to phone a friend, unable to handle it anymore.

Still, even with all the secret strings from me to him that he doesn't even know exist, his face and voice are full of the usual cheer and camaraderie that has defined our friendship since our college days at UCLA.

"All right, Chris," he says, his goofy demeanor helping with my mood already.

"I've been watching you nurse that croissant for a half hour now. I can't take it anymore. Tell me about your woman troubles, dude. I know you've got them."

I snap my head up to face him, my fingers twirling crumbs around in circles.

"How do you know I've got woman troubles?"

"Because I'm a man, and I know when a man is having issues with a girl."

I cringe at girl. Even though Hannah is an adult woman, Julie's voice echoes in my head, the way she'd mocked me for being intimate with her.

She'd got me wondering if the age difference was too much. She also got me wondering how Tyler would take it.

I feel guilt eating at me that I hadn't really considered him.

But Tyler's always been astute. We've known each other so long that he feels like an extension of my brain sometimes, like a friend and a journal and a brother all in one.

"Yeah…" I trail off, unsure how to continue without revealing too much.

Tyler laughs, his green eyes sparkling the same way Hannah's do sometimes.

"So spill, dude. What's going on? Wait, no, let me guess. Julie's back in the picture?"

Terror seizes at my heart, a sudden fear that Julie made good on her covert threat, that she called him before he came over and he's play-acting, playing the part of my best friend who doesn't know. I look at him warily, hesitantly.

"Sort of. I did see Julie yesterday."

Tyler's strawberry blonde eyebrows shoot up into his hairline.

"Please, no more Julie. We barely got you back after the last time."

"Well, it's not that…you don't have to worry about her coming back…in that way."

"What do you mean?" he asks, spilling a splash of coffee on the front of his shirt and wiping it haphazardly.

"She's stirring things up."

"So, in other words, being Julie," he points out, lifting the front of his shirt and dabbing it with a wet napkin.

I laugh thinly. He got me there.

"It's…yeah. I've been seeing someone, and I think she's… Well, I think Julie's jealous, and she's been lying, saying things to try and get me to break up with this other girl."

I tread carefully, pulling on a wayward curl, pulling it down so that it's a tight strand and then letting it go so that it coils up again.

"You're seeing someone? Who?" His curiosity kicks in, and he leans forward eagerly.

"Just a girl I'm seeing. Don't worry about it."

"Well, you have to tell me who, come on."

"Just someone from the gym. You don't know her," I lie, tearing off a piece of croissant and stuffing it into my mouth, trying to fill my mouth before I say too much.

"I thought you vowed never to date someone from the gym. Didn't you say it was a conflict of interest? I specifically made fun of you for it because you're not a lawyer."

Tyler's pointing an accusatory finger at me as though he's caught me in a grievous lie.

"Well, she was really hot, so I broke my vow just this once."

"So give me a name." I have a feeling that he's got a feeling, that the two of us are in a game of cat and mouse.

"God, you're relentless. It's Samantha." I give the name of the woman who'd given me her number long ago, just anyone to shut him up.

Tyler leans back, satisfied that he wrangled my "secret" from me.

"Man, Julie always was a drama queen. What are you going to do?"

I sigh, rubbing the back of my neck.

"I don't know, Ty. It's delicate, you know? Samantha saw me with Julie and she…well, she thought we were on a date, I think. But then Julie had told me something that made me a little nervous about Samantha. It's a mess."

"Hm." Tyler's shoulders droop as he takes it in.

"Well. It's Julie, you know? Julie's hardly trustworthy. I would always give someone else the benefit of the doubt before I would believe Julie. Maybe you're overcomplicating it. Just call Samantha up and explain it. Explain that you're a deeply fucked up man and that you'll need continual therapy for years to get over it."

Tyler grins at me, pushing his cheeks up into his eyes.

His words ring true, and guilt washes over me. He's right. It's Julie.

There's no way she's telling the truth. And Hannah would understand. I just have to call her and explain.

"Yeah. You're right. Yeah! It's Julie, dude, what am I getting all tied up in knots for? Thanks, man. Thank you. I just needed someone to talk to, you know? I needed to work it out by talking it out."

"Anytime. You're my best friend. And hey, if you need a break, come over tonight. We can grab a beer, watch the game. Distract yourself a bit."

I agree, grateful for the offer, though I know my mind will be anywhere but on the game.

"Yeah. But I think maybe I should call Samantha first, yeah?"

My thoughts drift back to Hannah. I need to explain things to her, to clear up the misunderstanding before it grows into something insurmountable.

"Yeah, you do that. I'll be right here."

I sneak away to a corner of the coffee shop and pull out my phone. Usually, my mind would be full of all the usual thoughts of rejection.

What if she won't listen? What if seeing me with Julie poisoned this before it started?

But this time, I feel at peace.

I know I can trust Hannah, that she'll listen and understand the way she has every time I've needed an ear or a shoulder.

I pull out my phone and dial Hannah's number, my heart beating a rapid tattoo against my ribs as the phone rings. Once, twice, three times. She picks up, and my heart leaps at her voice.

"Chris?"

"Hannah! Can we talk?"

"Why are you whispering? Are you with her right now?"

The fear from just a moment before leaps back into my throat.

I hadn't realized I was whispering. Something about the quiet corner had me quietly talking directly into the phone, my hand cupped around it.

"I'm just in public. I'm trying to be polite."

"Oh yeah? Then say something in a normal voice."

Sighing, I raise my volume. "We need to talk. I think there's been a misunderstanding. Can we talk?"

Silence at the other end. But only for a moment.

"Of course. I'll be at yours in an hour."

# Chapter Twenty Three
## Hannah

Armed with my painting and Lucy again, I feel a bit lighter this time, though I'm unsure why. It's entirely possible our "misunderstanding" is that I thought we were together.

But I hope not.

Once again, I hit the little metal button. Once again, I hear the buzz ring through. This time, his voice calls out, tinny through the speaker, "Yes?" and I feel a little jolt.

"It's me," I respond, and the familiarity in the statement – me, you know me – makes me smile in spite of myself.

Even in the midst of everything going on, Chris' presence calms me.

"Oh! Come on up!" He sounds so joyful, and I wonder if he feels the same about me, if my voice comforts him.

I slip into the elevator with Lucy, and she sits next to me happily, her tail wagging and her body wriggling.

I always wondered why she seemed so happy around Chris, and now it seems obvious. Of course she was. She instinctively remembered him.

When we reach the door, he opens it before I even knock, his face flushed and his aura chaotic.

"Hi. I'm so sorry."

He wraps me up into a bear hug, his fingers tucked into my waist, his nose against my neck. He's warm and soft, and he kisses me lightly.

His eyes scan over to Lucy and light up. "And hello to you!"

The back of Lucy's body wiggles chaotically with the energy of her excitement, her tail slamming against me as she tippy taps over to him, sniffing him and licking at his pant legs.

Chris crouches down to be on her level and pats her all over.

I feel my heart warming seeing him and Lucy together again. He always seems so at ease with her, like a younger version of himself. I think I can see what he would have been like as a young boy when he's with her.

I hesitate to bring a tsunami wave crashing down on the moment, but I know I have to.

"Hi."

"Listen, I just need you to know—"

"Can we sit down? Before anything else, I really need to tell you something."

Hesitation and concern cross his ocean-blue eyes, so blue they look like colored glass.

"Is everything okay, Han?"

He takes it upon himself to release Lucy from her leash, and she rewards him with a few licks on the back of his large hands.

A memory flashes through my mind of his hands on me, his fingers inside me. I suppress it and sit down on his plush white couch, tucking my legs beneath me.

"Everything's okay. Everything's fine. Come sit, okay?"

Chris's steps are hesitant as he advances toward me.

He sits down, his body so close that I can feel the heat emanating off him.

His thigh touches mine gently, small places of connection that have me leaping out of my skin. I keep wondering if we're going to have a repeat performance or if it was a one-time thing.

"I'm on the edge of my seat here, Hannah. Let me have it."

The words feel stuck in my throat, like they'll change everything. They will. I know they will. But for the better, I think.

"I met with Julie."

"I—why would you do that?"

The question's fair. Last we spoke about her, I was keeping it a secret that she was even in town, and now I'm telling him that I voluntarily went and spoke to her.

I'd have more than a few questions if it were me, but the maturity of his age is showing. I feel like I can physically see him holding back, keeping his cool.

"I just kept thinking about what you told me about her abandoning Noodle. I felt so bad for you, especially seeing you with Lucy. I wondered if I could find her for you."

As if on cue, Lucy comes and rests her head on Chris' leg. He pets her face instinctively, his eyes still on me.

"That was so sweet of you," he says gently, his voice dripping with tenderness, "but I think that ship sailed. It was five years ago, Hannah."

"Well," is all I say as I gather my thoughts.

"Well, what?" he smirks.

Before I can answer, he reaches out his hand and trails just the very tips of his fingers down my neck.

A shiver goes through my body, and he smirks even more, his eyes smoldering.

"What did you find out, my little detective?" His fingers brush my jawline. "Do you know you have five little freckles right...here?" He cranes his head toward me and kisses my jaw.

My body reacts, flushing a bright pink. I want so badly to drop the conversation right here and now, to sit on top of him and kiss him and feel him. But I know this is more important than that.

"She dropped Noodle in a dumpster by the art district."

He recoils from me. "Why would you tell me that?" he asks, furrowing his thick brows in an expression of genuine pain.

"Oh! No, I'm sorry." I stroke his face. "I didn't tell you to be mean. It's just that I found Lucy in a dumpster in the art district."

"Okay? Hannah, I'm not following." He readjusts, and I can tell he's holding back, waiting for me to make sense.

"I found Lucy five years ago." I keep my eyes on his, waiting to see the realization settle.

I see it, but I see his resistance, too.

"What are you telling me, Hannah?" he asks, his voice hesitant.

"It's too much of a coincidence, Chris. I think...well, what do you think? She does seem to love you."

I smile gently at him, trying to let him know that it's okay to believe in what he thinks I'm saying.

His lips part gently, and he looks down at Lucy's head on his thigh. "Do you really think so?" he whispers.

"I think so, yeah," I tell him, petting Lucy with him.

"Are you Noodle?" I ask her. Her tail wags just a little, her eyebrows heavy over her brown eyes. "And...I painted this for you, but it's not quite finished yet."

I pull out the painting I made earlier, of Lucy's face, her tongue lolling out, a deep purple, and the rest of her fur painted in golden technicolor.

"It's beautiful, Hannah, it really is. Wow, I don't even know what to say. You are...so talented."

He kisses my lips gently.

"And so sweet." His tongue runs across my lip. "You are the loveliest part of my life. And I never for a second want you to think that there's anyone else."

I freeze at the wording. "You don't want me to think that...or there isn't anyone else?"

"Hannah." He nibbles on my bottom lip and brings my hand up to kiss the back of it.

"There is no one else. Julie called me and said she was worried about you." A wry laugh escapes his throat. I watch his Adam's apple bob.

"She said you were obsessed with me, that you stalked her. I knew it wasn't true, but she...she threatened to tell Tyler about us, and so I let her drive me home since I had jogged to the restaurant. She tried to convince me that you were too young for me the entire drive back. And that's it. I told her she was right, I told her I'd break it off. But that's only because I wanted to give you the chance to decide if telling Tyler was worth it to you. Hannah, I'm yours completely."

His kiss is soft on my mouth, and I can't help but return the kiss, his words honey in my ears, his kiss honey on my lips.

I breathe in deeply as I reach my hands around his neck and slip my tongue into his mouth. I feel his tongue intertwine with mine as he holds my waist. My skin is electric everywhere he touches.

"I'm yours, too," I whisper back. "You already have me, any part of me that you want."

# Chapter Twenty Four
## Christopher

Hannah's words make my cock stiffen in my shorts. "Any part of you, huh?" I mumble to her, my mouth against hers, my words becoming her breath and her breath becoming mine.

"Any part," she says again as I lower her onto her back on the couch, lying down on top of her.

A smile crosses my face as I remember that the last time I took her, I was on a couch as well.

Although it started on a chair. There's something so sexy and youthful about wanting someone so badly that you need to take her wherever you happen to be.

"What are you smiling at?" she asks, her voice betraying something self-conscious in her.

"Oh, nothing. Just that I'm always on a couch with you."

She laughs a shrieking, girlish laugh as she wraps her legs around me. "I'm going to keep you on this couch forever."

"Please do. I never want to leave this couch as long as you're here."

I peer into her eyes, see the vulnerability there, and lean down to kiss her cheeks, her lips, and then I kiss her neck and move down all the way to her sternum, pulling her shirt down a little to kiss her chest.

"All you have to do is tell me to stay."

She moans as my lips brush against her skin. I kiss every freckle on her chest, wanting to kiss her nipples the same way. I lift her shirt and kiss her tight, pale stomach.

"Stay," I murmur, lifting her to pull her shirt off.

I pull the cups of her bra off her breasts, exposing her small pink nipples to me. I take one nipple in my mouth and lick it in circles, feeling it harden around my tongue.

"Stay and let me take you. Let me take you and take you and take you until you can't think straight. Please."

She cradles my head in her hands, wrapping my dark curls in her fingers, moans escaping slowly like steam from a pot.

"Does that feel good?" I whisper, watching her eyes as I suckle on her nipple. I watch her eyes widen, the green saucers growing with the pleasure, her pupils dilating.

"Mmmhm," she whispers back, unable to form words.

I move my mouth to her other breast and suck on that nipple instead. I use my fingers on one nipple, flicking it and pinching it lightly until she arches her back into it, while I suckle the other, overcome by lust.

I look up and see her eyes glaze over as she's thoroughly lost to pleasure.

"Oh, Chris, that feels so good. Never stop."

"If I never stop, I can't do other things to you," I tell her, working a hand up her skirt. I rub the outside of the crotch of her underwear. She's already soaked through the fabric of it. "Don't you want me to do other things to you?"

"Yes, please. Oh, yes."

"So you want me to stop sucking your nipple?" I ask, my mouth still around it, my tongue still swirling. I use my fingers to play against her slit, pushing the underwear between her flaps.

"No," she breathes. "I want you to do it all."

I chuckle a little, the honesty of it. I wish I had four hands and two tongues, so I could do everything to her all at once. I want to see her twist in the agony of pleasure. I want her to feel so much that she can't think, can only be.

"Oh, I want that, too," I tell her, rubbing her swollen clit through her underwear.

She bucks at my touch. Her hips lift and lower as she forces my finger harder against her clitoris. "Please," she mumbles.

I lift my head off her nipple and look at her face to see that her eyes are rolled back, her head tipped back, her mouth open. She breathes heavily, her chest flushed pink. "Did you say please?" I ask her.

"Yes, please, please, please." Her voice is quiet, tight, begging.

I remove my hands from her skirt and lift up to hold her face in my hands and kiss her on her open mouth.

"That's a good girl," I murmur and slide both my hands back up her skirt to slide her out of her underwear.

She shrieks with excitement, kicking her legs, and I laugh as I pull her them all the way down and off her feet, throwing them to the side.

I push her skirt up and lap at her slit gently, tasting all the juice that soaked through her underwear.

"How about that? Does that feel good?" I ask her, rubbing my lips across her clit.

She doesn't answer, completely wrapped up in it, her legs flapping open.

I suck on her clit gently, the tip of my tongue lapping at it. My lips circle her clit and my fingers massage her labia. I plunge my tongue inside of her, searching her vagina for the part that makes her squirm.

My face is pressed against her, her juices rubbing off onto my cheeks and beard, chafing me.

She pushes her hips into me then wraps her hands in my hair, pressing my face deeper against her. She grinds against my mouth, taking full advantage of me, and I let her, smiling greedily, holding her ass cheeks in my hands so that I can pull her into me. I throw her legs over my shoulders and lick my tongue down her slit all the way down her crack. She squirms, unsure of it, and I pull away as I realize she isn't ready yet for something so adventurous.

"Chris," she whispers.

"Mhm?" I ask, my mouth sopping wet and still going, my jaw stiff.

"Please take me. I need to feel you inside me."

"Say please again," I tell her, looking up at her round face as I trace my tongue in circles on her clit.

"Please," she begs, her eyes wide and her mouth open, her need evident on her face.

I slide her skirt down her legs and throw it to the side. I pull my shorts off and lie back down on her, pressing my erection against her thigh as I kiss her lips, savoring in the gentle moment.

"Please," she whines, humping against my leg, wrapping her legs around me. I can feel her wetness on my thigh, in my pubic hair, and I don't think I can deny her any longer.

I part her legs and lean sitting up so that I can press the head of my cock against her opening, feeling it start to suck me inside her already. I press into her gently, letting her warm tunnel envelop me before pulling back out with a delicious, wet plop.

She lets out a delicate moan, a murmur almost, a whisper and a sigh all at once, and pushes on my back, trying to pull me back into her.

I press my palm against her stomach and hold her back.

"Be still. Take it in. You said I could have you anyway I want."

Her eyes widen as she quiets, her body sinking deeper into the couch.

I once again slide the tip of my cock into her, this time a little deeper, feeling the wet, tight warmth of her hole tightening around my shaft.

She sighs in delight, her hands relaxing against my back, my skin electric where she touches me. As soon as I feel her revel in the pleasure, I pull back out of her in one motion.

Her gasp is the gasp heard round the world. She whines, "Please, Chris, don't."

"Don't? Are you telling me what to do?" I growl, my hands pinning her hips down, keeping her where I want her.

"No," she whispers, and I plunge my cock all the way inside her until my pelvis is against hers. Her back shoots into an arc and she screams, "Oh, God, yes, please, please fuck me."

I want so badly to thrust in and out of her, to feel her tight against me, wrapping around me, to feel her walls stretching around me, her virgin pussy widening for my thick cock, but instead, I move slowly, so slowly that it physically pains me.

I want all of me inside her, but I decide to tease her, tantalize her.

"Like this?" I ask her, looking down at her face, her lips open, her tongue braced against her teeth, her eyes wide and rolling around.

"Harder. Faster. Give it to me."

"When will you learn, little girl?" I chide, moving my hips excruciatingly slow, the length of me lighting up as I enter inch-by-inch.

"I'm sorry, Chris, please give it to me."

"There you go." I plunge all the way inside her and lie down on top of her. My cock is on fire with desire as I thrust hard. Her head smashes against the arm of the chair as I do, and she doesn't fight it, her screams telling me she's loving it.

"Oh, yes, Chris. Right there."

I can feel that it's right there. I can feel her muscles clenching as I hit her G Spot, the little bean deep inside her pussy pressing against the tip of my penis.

I continue to rub against it, keeping the entire length of my shaft inside her, the base of my cock against her pelvis, moving my hips while inside her until our bodies feel like one.

She lets out a moan that tells me she's close, so I move my fingers up to one of her nipples and play with it at the same time. Her breathing shallows more and more, her chest lifting, her breasts flushed, as I continue, until I feel her clenching quicken, her muscles spasming so strong that I feel myself being squeezed.

"Hannah, I'm going to cum," I warn her.

As I do, an orgasm waves through her, the clenching moving to an obvious orgasmic rhythm.

Her breathing relaxes, her heart pounding with the effort.

I kiss her face all over before I collapse on top of her.

"Chris, that was so good," she whispers after a while, her arms wrapping around my sweaty back, our sweat sticking our bodies together.

"You really have nothing to compare it to," I point out.

"Well, I was being nice. Take the compliment."

We laugh a little before fading away into a nap.

# Chapter Twenty Five

## Hannah

I wake up before Chris does, sliding out from underneath his sweaty body so that he can keep sleeping while I cook him something to wake up to.

I feel so domestic, padding to the kitchen in Chris' house wearing nothing but one of his shirts.

I've never had a serious boyfriend, and I've certainly never cooked for anyone. But, then, I've never had to slide out from underneath someone's body to cook for him, either.

A little thrill zaps through me as I go through his cabinets, looking for his oil and pans and vegetables.

I settle on some carrots and potatoes, something easy to roast that I think will impress him. I do it the way he taught me, tossing them in oil and spices, tasting as I go. I try to do it all as quietly as possible so as not to wake him.

I look in on him, his arms spread out above him, his broad back shining in the daylight, his hair tousled from our fest.

Just seeing him brings a smile to my face. In this moment, I feel like I would do anything for him.

I toss a carrot to Lucy, and when she eats it, I offer her a couple more while I microwave her some eggs to put in a bowl next to a bowl of water. She crunches loudly, spitting splintered pieces of carrot all over the floor.

I slip a pan into the oven and go back to the couch to lie across Chris' splayed body, wrapping my arms around him and under him, feeling his happy trail running down his stomach.

He stirs quietly, a little moan escaping him, before he turns over and yanks me toward him and on top of him. "Got you. Now you're never getting up."

I settle my face into his neck, inhaling deeply and smelling his scent, the fresh pine and the sweat mix that screams Chris to me.

"I won't fight it."

He pets my hair then runs his hand down my body until he gets to my ass, which he spanks. "You're naked still?"

"Mmmhm. I didn't feel like putting my clothes back on. Is that okay?"

"It's more than okay, pretty baby."

He wraps himself around me and holds me tightly.

I feel safe and like the smallest person in the world, something I've never felt before, given my tall frame.

"But, you know, if you don't let me up, you won't get your dinner."

"My dinner? Are you cooking?"

"I am. Are you brave enough to try it?" I tease as he rocks me.

"Am I brave enough. Ha!" He props me back up on my feet and sits up himself, rubbing his eyes.

"I can't wait to taste the culinary stylings of Hannah Jackson. If it's anything like your art, I know it'll be amazing."

"Please, don't raise your expectations so high. It's easier to deliver if they're low," I beg, putting my hands together in a prayer.

He stands up and takes my hand like it's the most natural thing in the world for me. "Let's see," he says.

Then, as though suddenly remembering, he stops when he sees Lucy.

"Oh, I..I don't know how I almost forgot. Hannah, I can't believe everything you've brought to me."

His hands hover over her, wanting to pet her but letting her eat.

"I can't believe this is my life."

"I can't either. Can you believe it, Chris? Lucy is Noodle. It's so crazy. I guess we'll have to co-parent now, huh?" I ask jokingly but sort of meaning it.

This has been on my mind, the idea that once Chris realized that Lucy was Noodle he might want to be a permanent part of her life.

"Well, that'll be easy since I'm your client and all." He winks at me.

"Stop, you make it sound so inappropriate."

"It is inappropriate." His voice is joking, but I see his face fall as the weight of his words hit him. He wraps his arms around me from behind me.

He mutters, "What are we going to do about Tyler? I can't keep lying to him."

I jump back from his touch.

"Well, tell him then. I don't want to be a secret."

He chuckles, running a hand through his hair.

"That's easy for you to say, Han. He's your brother. He'll never stop talking to you. He could decide he doesn't want to be friends with a guy who would screw his sister."

"Screw?" I ask him, taken aback by his verbiage.

"No, come on, you know I don't mean it like that. I just mean that's how it'll look." He readjusts his weight awkwardly, looking around. "You know?"

"No, Chris, I don't know." I cross my arms. "What is this, the 1800s? You don't need my brother's permission. That's disgusting."

"This is all coming out wrong. I'm just concerned that he'll be angry, okay? There's a code. You wouldn't get it."

His tone is so intense, but I'm still upset by the concept that my brother gets any say in who I date.

"A code, huh? So the brotherhood is real. How quaint."

I roll my eyes and pet Lucy as she greedily laps at the water, her eyes looking sideways at me anxiously. She's always been good at sensing tension in a room.

"If there's no code amongst men, what are we?" he asks me seriously as he pulls two plates out of the cabinets, preparing for my dinner.

"Oh, yeah, the code is what differentiates you all from animals. Fine. Don't tell him. We'll wait."

"Well, I don't want to wait if it's going to make you angry."

"I don't want you to hold back from being straight with him just because you might be worried about making me angry."

"And that's not better?"

"No. That's not better."

"Hmm."

He pretends to consider my admittedly insane mental gymnastics.

"Han, how about this? Today, let's go take our dog out for a walk and hold hands and feel how it feels to be a couple. And let's just pretend nothing else is happening."

He reaches for me and holds my jaw in his hands. He kisses me deeply.

"Pretend I didn't just insult your independence, pretend my ex isn't crazy, pretend your brother isn't my best friend, pretend I'm not your client. Let's pretend it all, okay? I just want to feel your little hand in my big hand and watch our dog walk in front of us. Can we do that, Hannah Banana?"

I smile at the nickname. It's a new one from him, and it feels familiar, like he's called me that all the time we've known each other.

"Fine."

"Fine? I pour my heart out to you, beg you, and all I get is fine?" His blue eyes are shining, teasing.

I shrug. "Take it or leave it."

# Chapter Twenty Six
## Christopher

Hannah lets me hold Lucy's leash, and I feel giddy as I hold her hand in tandem, walking through the bustling streets of LA.

I suppress a grin that threatens to fly off my face if I let it go, looking down lovingly at Lucy's snuffling nose, wiggling at a patch of weeds growing from a sidewalk crack, the wet sheen of her nose shining in the light.

Her body follows suit, wiggling with all the excitement of a human who just won the lottery, her tongue drooping down to the concrete as she sniffs.

I think I know how she feels.

"You've done a really good job with her, Hannah. She doesn't pull at all," I tell her proudly, squeezing her hand with mine as we walk.

"Aw, thank you. It was easy. She's naturally a good girl already."

Hannah leans into me, her skin comforting and warm against mine. I look over at her as she looks ahead, her eyelashes golden in the sun and her red hair shining.

"Oh, look, right up there!" I point at the farmers' market excitedly and walk faster, pulling Hannah along with me.

"I have never seen a man so excited about vegetables," she tells me, giggling, as she speeds up. Lucy breaks into a jog, her ears flying behind her.

"It's not just vegetables."

"Oh, fruit, too?" she teases, smiling widely.

"Yeah, and legumes. Just come on."

We slow down as we near the entrance.

I gawk at the community of it all, the booths set up under a wide tarp, people weaving around each other to get to where they're going in the narrow aisle, all the quiet conversations happening at once.

I look around and realize Hannah has broken away from me. She's at a booth of jams, bent over at the waist and reading the labels.

"Your mother is quick," I tell Lucy, who sits beside me calmly, her mouth opened in what appears to be a gentle smile across her furry face.

I gesture with a nod toward Hannah, and Lucy seems to understand, standing up to walk with me over to meet her.

"Found something already?"

Hannah whirls around to me, a grin to match her sparkling green eyes.

"Okay, I get it. This is fun. Look at all these jams. Now I may not be a bok choy expert, but jams I know. I've made plenty of peanut butter and jelly sandwiches in my lifetime."

"Which one are you thinking?" I ask, chuckling at the reminder of her limited cooking skills. I find it so touching that she instantly thought of her childhood PB&J when surrounded by all these options.

I'm suddenly flooded by the image of Hannah and me in the kitchen, making lunches for our children.

I squeeze past her, picturing her cutting them just right into triangles, as I rest my hand on her lower waist and see her flush at my touch.

Tears threaten to prick at my eyes at the realization that I might not have to go through life alone.

Hannah's already enriched my life so much.

While I just want to hold onto her tightly and keep her wrapped in my arms forever, I know that she's younger than I am and I have to let her pursue her dreams of a successful business and hope that she decides to remain by my side.

"Peach habanero? Does that sound good to you, too?" she asks, her finger on her chin as she surveys the options.

"Peach habanero is one of our best sellers," the woman at the booth says.

Her hair is in a fluffy gray bob and her eyes are a gentle brown under a harsh green eyeshadow applied quickly.

She smiles gently at Hannah. "Perfect for an adventurous PB&J."

Hannah straightens. "Well, I was also looking at the blackberry mint."

"Ooh, well now, that's one of my personal favorites. I guess it's up to whether you wanna trust me or the masses."

Her thin-lipped smile reveals perfect, fake teeth, and I wonder briefly if I'll lose my teeth when I'm older, too.

"Do you make these?" Hannah asks, tucking her hands into her back pockets, her eyes trained on the woman's.

Hannah has this way of making eye contact that feels like you're in a tunnel with her.

"Sure do, lovely. Most of them are my grandmother's recipes, been in the family for a long time. But a few of them are my own creations."

She winks at Hannah, who smiles broadly, her eyes flitting to the labels again.

"Which one are you thinking?"

Hannah turns to look at me as I approach her and snake a hand around her waist to tuck my hand into her front pocket. "Which one do you think?" she asks.

"Hmmm," I mumble, pretending to think about it. I look up at the old woman and say, "We'll take them all."

Her eyes widen a small amount, then relax as she decides she's misheard. "Sorry, what did you say?"

"I said we'll take them all. One of each. Do you have a box or something we can carry them in?"

"Sure, sure do, yes." She pulls out a box from underneath her booth and wastes no time packing up one of each of the 26 flavors.

"What are you doing?" Hannah asks through a toothy smile, whispering so the woman doesn't hear.

I shrug. "I want to try them all. Don't you?"

"Well. Yeah."

"Then that's about all there is to it."

I kiss Hannah's cheek and hand the woman $400 which includes a $100 tip. "Thank you," I tell the woman and pass Hannah Lucy's leash so that I can take the box.

"No, thank you. Thank you, thank you."

We nod in response and keep walking, Hannah's arm snaked in the crook of my elbow.

"Why did you do that?" she asks me, keeping a watchful eye on Lucy's leash to make sure that it doesn't wrap around anyone's unsuspecting ankle.

"To impress me?"

Taken aback, I look over at her sharply, and then a laugh bubbles out of me.

"I guess so, yeah. Did it work?"

Smirking, her eyes still on Lucy, she murmurs, "I guess so, yeah."

I kiss the top of her head haphazardly between her bouncy steps, my lips sliding across her hair. I watch with satisfaction as a blush creeps into her cheeks.

"Oh, let's grab some veggies from this guy. His produce is amazing."

Hannah's laugh sprinkles out of her. "God, you're a nerd. Okay, let's go."

I walk up to the farmer who sold me the bok choy. His mustache is freshly trimmed and even this time, but he can't hide his crooked teeth when he smiles.

"Well, hey there. I remember you. Who's this?"

"This is my girlfriend," I announce, looking over at Hannah's widening eyes.

"Does she know that?" he asks with a smile.

"She does now," I respond, knocking her hip with mine as I clutch onto the heavy box for dear life, very aware of the mess that dropping it would make.

"What have you got for me today?"

"Well, congratulations. How would you feel about some radishes and zucchini? They're growing like weeds, just enormous and full of flavor." His eyes twinkle as he looks between Hannah and me.

"Sure, lay 'em on me." I barely finish getting the words out before Hannah doubles over and squats down low to the ground.

At first, I think that she's looking closely at something in his booth, but the farmer says in his heavy accent, "Miss, are you okay?"

I look down at her and realize that her pallor has gone even paler than before, and she's closed her eyes.

"Hannah? What's wrong?"

"You've got your hands full. Let me help."

The farmer crosses over to our side and helps lift Hannah up by her elbow.

We walk out of the cramped space together and to a shady spot under a tree. Hannah leans on the man in a way that tells me she really isn't feeling well.

"What's wrong, baby?" I whisper to her as I set down the box of jams.

I envelop her in my arms and rub her back before she pushes me off her and doubles over to throw up on the ground in the grass by the tree.

I gather her long, copper hair in my hands and hold it away from her face for her as she continues to vomit, her wretches loud and punctuated by agonized gasps for air.

The farmer fans Hannah's face as I hold her hair, and eventually when she stops, she stays still a moment, her hands on her knees. She looks up at me, her cheeks red with effort, and tells me, "I think I need to go home."

"Of course, let me call a cab. Or let me call your brother."

"No, no, she can't wait. Let me drive you. I'll get someone else to watch my booth."

"No," Hannah gasps. "I don't want to bother anyone. If I could just have a little water, please. I'm sorry. I just...I don't know. It's the strangest thing, but I smelled something weird, and it just made me feel so nauseated. I'm okay now. Let's just walk, it's fine."

"Hannah...I don't think that's a good idea. It sounds like you're sick. Let's just let him drive us. It's okay to lean on people," I protest, afraid that something's really wrong.

"It's really not an inconvenience. I'm happy to help."

"No! I just want to keep walking. Please," Hannah begs, her color returning.

"I don't know, Hannah." I look around, as though someone will show up with a sign that tells me what to do.

Anxiety crawls up my chest, and I feel overcome by worry for her, the puddle of vomit at our feet a stark reminder of how bad she felt just mere moments before.

"Well, now, if the lady says she's fine, I'm sure she is," the farmer responds, running his finger through his mustache. He pinches it at the end and smiles at me.

"I'll see you guys soon enough. Go ahead and take those vegetables with you."

"Thank you," I tell him, unsure, and as Hannah starts to walk away, Lucy anxiously bumping her knees with her nose, the farmer catches my elbow and tells me in a conspiratorial tone, "That's exactly how we found out my wife was pregnant. Might wanna convince the little lady to take a test."

"What do you mean?"

"Strong sense of smell. It's how it starts for a lot of women." He taps his nose and then his head knowingly and smiles. "Congratulations, Papa."

"Are you coming?" Hannah calls from down the block.

"Sorry!" I pick up the box from the ground and hurry after her, glancing back at the man. He smiles and taps his nose again.

# Chapter Twenty Seven
## Hannah

"Why don't you go lie down, Hannah? I'll make you some soup or something," Chris tells me quietly, his hand on my back after he sets down the box of jams.

The veins in his arm ripples as he does, and I bite my lip involuntarily.

"Chris, I'm fine." I roll my eyes. "Today was supposed to be fun. Let's just have fun."

I flop down onto his couch and cross my legs, taking up half the seating with my long legs.

Lucy rests her big head on my knee, and I push her off gently, whispering, "You're making me look bad."

"Hannah, that was really scary," he tells me sincerely, his eyes trained on mine, unmoving.

He stands in the kitchen, his hand on an apron, considering. It's sweet he's worried, but I don't want him to think too hard about it. I want today to remain a fun day if it can still be salvaged.

"Just come sit with me," I sigh, "Seriously, I feel better now. I probably got too hot or something. It was cramped."

Chris makes his way to me, a spatula in his hand, though he hadn't started cooking yet.

He has a queer look on his face, the look of someone realizing something in real time. He hugs me standing up, burying my face into his stomach and running his hand down my hair.

"Hannah," he mutters, clearing his throat as if moved to tears.

"What?!" I push him off me and lean back into the couch. "Why are you being so weird?"

He gives me a look filled with sincerity and brushes my hair off my face, cradling my cheeks. "Could you be pregnant?"

At first I laugh, a guffaw that coughs out of me.

But the genuine expression on his face catches me off guard.

My vision tunnels and my skin goes cold as I consider his question.

How long has it been since my period? Have I even had one at all since being with Chris? I don't think I have.

Anxiety sneaks up on me as I notice the tears springing to his eyes, threatening to spill over. If I am, will he regret this?

"Chris, I don't think so. I have an IUD and have had it since I was 18. When I went away to school I kind of thought it would be the responsible thing to do. I've never ended up needing it for birth control until recently, though. I guess I thought I had mentioned it."

"Well, how long are they good for?"

"I don't know...I think they said three to six years, but since I haven't ever needed it until now, I didn't even think about it."

I realized that if I got it at 18 and was now 25 that there might indeed be a problem.

Chris instantly goes into solution mode, sitting beside me, the spatula still held out in his hand like a magic wand he might wave over the situation.

"Hey, hey, it's okay. Let's just get it checked, to be sure, okay? I bet it's nothing, but we should check. For peace of mind. Right?"

His hand moves to move my hair behind my ear, but the motion brings to his awareness that he has the spatula in his hand. He scrunches his face at it and tosses it onto his coffee table, a magnificent oak thing with texture from the tree still in the wood.

A small smile eeks out of me at the moment, but I say nothing.

"Hannah, it will be okay no matter what. I am here for you." He presses his forehead to mine and stares into my eyes before kissing my cheeks gently, one and then the other.

"Just like you were there for me and brought Noodle back to me."

"Lucy," I correct him in a quiet, joking tone.

"We'll talk about it," he whispers back in the same tone. "For now, you lie down while I make you some soup and make you an appointment with an OBGYN."

I sigh as he moves off the couch, tucking me under a fluffy orange blanket. "How romantic," I joke.

"Well, it's not my thing, but I do what I can," he says from the kitchen as he pulls out zucchini and begins to slice it.

"Hey, Chris?"

"Yes, baby?"

His eyes are on the knife, not looking at me as I watch him in profile, his curls bouncing with his movements, his mouth twisted into his cheek as he focuses.

He's called me 'baby' a few times now, and every time it ignites a little thrill through my body.

I've never been called 'baby' by anyone except Tommy Marshalls in $2^{nd}$ grade. And my mom.

To hear a man say it, a man who's cooking for me, a man who I'm pretty sure loves me, is like being invited to a tea party that everyone else in class went to without me.

It's scary to admit, too, but being secretly loved is something I like even more.

Will it be the same once Tyler knows? Could it actually stay this good forever?

"What? Tell me," Chris says more urgently, snapping me out of my secret spiral. His knife is poised above the squash, and concern is etched in his face.

"Do you have any chicken noodle soup? I just want some chicken noodle soup. I don't want anything fancy."

I close my eyes as another bout of nausea washes over me at the smell of the garlic on the pan.

"Oh!" Chris sets down his knife and stands in the middle of the kitchen for a moment, his blue eyes pinging back and forth as he thinks.

"No, I don't think I do. But, I can go get you some. Of course you want soup. That makes sense."

"I have a very distinguished palate," I tell him, and he laughs at me, already walking to grab his keys.

He smashes a kiss atop my forehead. "I'll be back soon. Don't you worry at all." He smooths down my hair. "You just rest. See if you can't fall asleep."

The moment he leaves, I sit up and scramble for my phone. I wait until I hear his heavy footsteps disappear to call my mom.

"Hey, Lovebug," she answers on the first ring, ever dependable.

I try to think of myself as a mom. What kind of mom would I be? Would I always be available to answer on the first ring, too?

I want to have at least enough money to provide for my kids. I sleep on a futon in my office. Panic swells in my throat. "Baby, what's wrong?"

"Mom," I choke out. "I have to tell you something, but I'm scared."

"Hannah, what's wrong?" she repeats, her voice firm. "Tell me right now."

I can see her now, standing up from wherever she is, slapping my dad's forearm.

"I don't know how it happened, but Chris and I...Tyler's best friend...we, and I might be pregnant, I probably am!"

I'm wailing now, and I know I'm making no sense, but I can't stop, spit pooling on my shirt as I sob openly.

"Baby girl, this doesn't seem like something we should talk about over the phone. Right?"

"I don't know," I respond earnestly, wiping spit off my lips with the back of my hand.

"Maybe you should come over. It'll be okay."

"I can't, I can't."

"Well, then, I'll come to you."

"No! I just had to get it out. Please don't tell Tyler. Not yet."

"Hannah..."

"Mom."

"Is that it? You're just going to drop that bomb and go? I can't say anything and that's that?"

"I'll come over tomorrow, how about that?"

"Oh, Hannah. I don't know what to do for you. And that's the worst feeling a mom can have. Okay, baby, you be safe. I love you."

I hang up, a weight lifted off my chest, though I know I just gave the weight to my mother instead.

And isn't that what moms are for?

To help shoulder the weight when it gets too heavy?

Is that the kind of mom I would be? And once I am a mother, do I cease being a daughter? What do I owe to my mom?

I call her back, and she answers faster than the first ring, it seems, picking it up at the thought of me calling her.

"Hannah? Did you change your mind?"

I sigh, not sure if I'll regret my next words.

"Yes. I'll send you the address. And can you please bring some dog food for Lucy?"

# Chapter Twenty Eight
## Christopher

I stand in the soup aisle, poring over the multitude of options. I want to get Hannah exactly what she wants.

It's so endearing that she even wants soup at all, that she'd rather have that than a home cooked meal.

I suppose she thinks her nausea might be quelled with something simple like chicken noodle soup.

It tells me so much about her childhood, and I can see Little Hannah now, sick and slurping noodles. Finally, I decide she might want more than the one kind of soup, so I decide to just grab one of each kind to be on the safe side.

Last minute, I grab every kind of pregnancy test they have, too. My cart looks like that of a madman.

Before I go back home, I decide to stop by the gym to check up on things. I hadn't expected the outing with Hannah to take up my entire day, and this reality check from her has me thinking, again, about the missing money from the gym.

When I started the gym, it was to have a legacy for the future.

And while I didn't know exactly where the future would lead, I knew I wanted to leave my mark on the world. For who, I didn't really know.

It seemed to be less important as time went on and I failed to find someone significant to share my life with.

But now, the possibility of two someones, three if I count Lucy, has me thinking I need to fix this business problem so we can both rest easy.

The soup cans roll around my floorboard, spilling out of their bags, the result of my hurried packing at the check stand. In the final analysis, only one got dinged when it dropped to the ground in the parking lot.

Once at the gym, I get to the office just as Sarah takes her break.

She nods primly at me as she picks up her purse, a small silver number with fringe hanging from the bottom. "Sarah, you getting out of here early?"

"Just taking my break," she replies, squeezing past me to leave. "I'll be back in thirty."

"Okay, I might have a question or two for you when you get back."

"What about?"

"You're off the clock. You go take your break," I respond, smiling broadly at her, the cans in my car on my mind, the insides heating up even as the LA sun sets.

Once Sarah leaves, I begin my secret mission.

I sit down at the desk and look through the financial statements for the gym.

Not the ones that Hannah showed me – that I had provided to her -- but the ones that she originally wanted me to provide.

These documents show the individual transactions that I'd been too afraid to face.

Without Hanna's accountant eyes, I feel lost at sea, my eyes on numbers swimming in front of me, the sea of transactions dark and stormy.

Scanning through the records, lists of number after number, something catches my eye.

I see a transaction that doesn't quite match up to what I know of our inventory. It's not a huge discrepancy, but it's there, undeniably there.

I furrow my brow, tapping my pen against the desk as I try to make sense of it.

It could be a mistake. It could so easily be a mistake.

My heart sinks as I notice another irregularity. And another.

And only one person has control over this. And she's just left the building.

Anger simmers beneath the surface as I continue to sift through the spreadsheets.

I start to realize what Hannah meant about it being dangerous to put one person in charge of all of this, without any checks and balances.

Despite my fear of betrayal, I've set myself up perfectly to be betrayed.

How could Sarah do this to me? I've always treated her fairly and paid her well. I've been fair to her. I've trusted her.

And she's been here for years, working her way up. How long has she operated under the radar, a trustworthy face with backstabbing behaviors?

I take a deep breath, steeling myself for what comes next.

I text Hannah where I am and that I have her soup. Then, I turn over my phone, sit, and wait.

Once Sarah gets back, my feet are asleep, and I shake them under the table as she opens the door.

"Oh," she says, letting out a little gasp of surprise. "Hey, Chris. I didn't expect you to still be here."

I force a smile, trying to keep my emotions in check. "I said I wanted to talk."

"I guess you did," she mumbles from the doorway, her hand poised on the doorknob as though she might run at any point.

"So. Can I talk to you?"

Her smile falters slightly, but she nods and closes the door behind her.

"What's up?" she asks, taking a seat across from me.

I take a deep breath, trying to gather my thoughts. "Sarah, you know I hired a CPA to expand the gym, right?"

"Sure, of course. I think that's a good call. You've got a lot of business here. It just makes sense."

Her words and tone are both cool, her body language relaxed even as she lies to my face. The only perceptible change in her is her compulsory hair twirling. Her silken jet-black hair spins round and round her index finger, sliding over and under it.

I inhale and consider my options. With Sarah in front of me, I don't feel as angry as I did earlier, only sad.

"Sarah." I sit up straighter. "Are you happy here?"

Her eyebrows fold toward each other. "Yes…why?"

"You're sure I didn't do something to you? Offend you in some way? You can tell me."

She smiles, her fuchsia lipstick opening to reveal her straight white teeth.

"I'm sure. Chris." She chuckles lightly, "I would leave if I wasn't happy. Why? Are you okay?"

She crosses one leg over the other and leans back against her chair. She notices herself twirling her hair and stops, flipping it behind her back. She folds her hands into her lap, holding one down with the other.

I look at my fingers, inspecting my nails, and then meet her eyes, a sharp grey that lingers for just a moment before she breaks eye contact.

"The CPA noticed some discrepancies."

Her brow furrows in confusion. "Discrepancies? What do you mean?"

I turn the monitor to her and point at a line. "I mean transactions that don't add up, expenses that don't match our actual business activity or are grossly inflated."

"Oh."

"And I have reason to believe that you're responsible."

Sarah's eyes widen in shock, and her mouth falls open. "What? No."

I drum my fingers on the desk. "Sarah."

I find her eyes again and sigh. "The facts don't lie. And...there's only you. You've been stealing from the business. From me."

Her expression shifts from shock to panic, and she opens her mouth to protest, but I cut her off as the anger switches to indignation.

"I'm giving you two options, Sarah" I say, my voice firm.

"You can either resign and leave quietly, making restitution, in which case I won't notify the authorities or press charges. If you choose not to do so, I'll call them right now and have you arrested for embezzlement."

Sarah's face drains of color, and she swallows hard.

"I... I can't pay it back, Chris. It's over $300,000."

Anger and shock surge through me, and I grit my teeth to keep from raising my voice.

"$300,000? My God, Sarah." She nods silently, tears welling up in her eyes. "Why?"

"I don't...I don't know. I'm sorry. I could write you a check for $20,000 if that helps."

"Then write it and get out."

She stands up and fishes in her purse for a checkbook.

I watch her write me a check in the swirly handwriting I've come to know so well She then begins packing the personal items on her desk, random things – a pen with feathers on the end, a framed photo of her and her boyfriend.

"I'm sorry, Chris."

"You're sorry you got caught," I tell her coldly as I print out the remaining pages proving her crime.

"Oh!" I call out before she closes the door. "Leave your keys. Who knows what else you would take if you had the chance? We don't have much nailed to the floor these days."

She opens her mouth to respond, a cool reply on her tongue, but I watch her gain control, offsetting the fear in her eyes with a smile as she pulls her key off the ring and slaps it on the table.

Once she's gone, I slump back in my chair, feeling exhausted and defeated.

I can't believe I let this happen. That I was this stupid.

I trusted her, and she took advantage of that trust. But as angry as I am, I also feel a sense of relief.

The truth is out now, I know who the culprit was and I can start to rectify things.

I'll have to hire someone new and, with Hannah's help, install some sort of system of checks and balances. I'm sure she'll have some ideas of the best way to go about designing a new system of accounting for the business.

Never again will I allow one person that kind of control over my business. I won't let one person's betrayal destroy everything I've worked so hard to build.

I've rebuilt my life before, after a stinging stab to the back, and I can do it again.

How could I have been so blind? She seemed so loyal. But now, I can see I missed so many red flags.

The extra cash she always seemed to have on hand, the lavish purchases she made despite her modest salary. It all makes sense now.

I shake my head, trying to push the thoughts aside as I stand up. This can all be dealt with tomorrow.

For now, I have someone sick at home who needs soup, and no matter what betrayals life hands me, I will never be the one who does the betraying.

# Chapter Twenty Nine
## Hannah

Chris gets back a little over an hour later, his eyes shining with tears and his arms crushed to his chest, balancing bags with cans of soup and pregnancy tests.

His eyes are wild with an almost guilty look in them. "Hi, I'm sorry I took so long, I'll make it for you now."

He drops the bags on the counter, his hands shooting out desperately to catch a couple of cans as they roll towards the edge.

"Chris, what's wrong? Is this about…those?" I point to the mountain of pregnancy tests.

"Oh! No. It's about Sarah."

"Sarah? Who's that? Another ex-fiancée?"

I smile at my own joke and stand up to make my way toward him, stepping over Lucy, who's fallen deeply asleep on the ground.

"No, actually." He pulls at the tab on the top of a soup can and slaps it down. "Sarah's the one who's been stealing from the gym. Stealing from me, I guess."

"Chris, wow, you actually confronted her about it? Hey, I feel okay right now. How about you just sit down and talk to me?"

I reach for his hands before he can pull a soup bowl out of the cabinet.

I interlace our fingers and pull him over to the dining room table. I pull out a chair for him and gesture. "Let me get you a glass of water."

He chuckles, shaking his head. "I'm supposed to be taking care of you," he says quietly.

"You are! You're distracting me. That's priceless," I tell him, pulling down a glass for him and filling it up with the water from his fridge.

When I was a kid, I thought that the pinnacle of achievement, proof that your family was rich, was having water come out of the front of the fridge.

"Maybe I should make you soup." I giggle a little and kiss the top of his head as I set his water down in front of him.

Chris gulps his water down, and I sit next to him, seeing his desperation as he drinks, his Adam's apple bobbing with each swallow.

"It was crazy, Hannah. I never really thought…I mean, didn't suspect her at all, although clearly I should have. Even though there really wasn't anyone else to suspect; no one else made sense or had access to the finances, the records, or the money."

I think about what Tyler told me about Sarah working all alone in the back office, completely in charge of the finances with no supervision.

Chris is right when he realizes it couldn't have been anyone else but Sarah, but I imagine it was a shock all the same and the betrayal isn't something he can just shrug off.

Chris runs his index finger over the rim of the glass.

"It's like…when Julie left me, when she didn't show up?"

He looks up at me, his eyes clear now, "I kept thinking something must have happened, you know? A car accident maybe, or something even worse, something truly mystical."

"Mystical?" I ask, confused.

"Oh, sure. Maybe there was an earthquake that only affected her and also all the cell towers. Something like that. I didn't expect the truth to be as simple as it was. I couldn't imagine that she just…didn't show up."

"Ah. Your brain was protecting you."

"It was. And that's how this feels. It's so obvious in hindsight, but I guess I just assumed it was a mystery, the missing money."

"It's okay for you to trust the people in your life and expect that they will protect you; not betray you."

We sit for a moment, eyes on each other.

He stands up and hugs me from behind, kissing my cheeks wildly.

"The thing is, part of me thinks that I chose bad people after Julie left. That I chose bad people and put them in bad situations so that people would show their true colors and I'd be comforted knowing for sure that people are bad. Or maybe I was afraid to plan for the worst case scenario, so instead I pretended there wouldn't be any more bad scenarios. And then, with Sarah, I got disappointed. And, in some strange way, that was comforting."

I've never heard Chris talk about himself with so much stark self-awareness. His eyes are fuzzy and off in the distance while he talks. I tell him gently, "Sure, I get that. Whatever you're used to—that's comfort. Even if it's bad for you."

"Thank you for understanding. And I know I have to call the police and file this or that, but right now, I'm worried about you. I want you to take one of those tests so we can relax, and I'll make you soup for what I'm sure is a stomach bug. Sound good?"

His kindness forms a lump in my throat. I rest my cheek on his cool hand as it squeezes my shoulder. "Chris, my mom is on her way over."

He slides his hand out from under my cheek. "Okay? Why? What does she know?"

"everything, basically."

"Why, Hannah?" His response hits me like a punch to the gut.

"Are you mad?"

"Well, it seems like something we should have talked about first, right? I mean, we haven't even told Tyler. I thought we'd be waiting a while to tell your family."

I swallow back thick tears that threaten to form as my throat constricts. "I needed my mom, Chris."

"Oh, God, of course you did. I'm sorry, Hannah."

"It's okay," I tell him, wiping my tears. "You're allowed to have an opinion or be nervous or whatever."

"That's not what I mean."

He leans down on one knee, and despite the sadness coursing through me in this moment, a flash of heat runs up and down my body as my heart asks my brain if he's proposing.

My brain responds that he isn't.

"I mean that I'm sorry for all of this. You're so young, and you've only had sex a few times at this point. You shouldn't have to worry about being a mom. You've got a new business to run. I feel like I should have been better about boundaries. I hate that you are in this situation when you have so much else going on and so many of your own ambitions to fulfill."

"I'm an adult, Chris. I make my own choices."

"I know. I know that. But I do have some years on you and I should have been more thoughtful about where you are in life right now."

He smiles thinly as I look up at him from my chair.

"It was my responsibility to give you clarity on where those choices could lead. But, in my defense, you were extremely hard to resist. Well, impossible, really, as it happens."

"Believe it or not, Chris, I already knew that sex could lead to pregnancy."

I stand up and make my way to the pregnancy tests. I pick out three. "Best two out of three?"

He laughs, and the buzzer to his apartment knocks the smile off his face and the wind out of me. He goes to the front door and hits the button. "Hello?"

"Chris?" My mom's voice has a robotic quality to it through the grainy technology. "It's Piper."

"Come on up."

Unable to face my mother until I know, I head for the bathroom.

# Chapter Thirty
## Christopher

Hannah's mother, Piper, stands at the door, her red hair full of static, stray hairs surrounding her head like a halo.

Her hair is a slightly duller color than Hannah's, and her eyes are rimmed in thick eyeliner that settles into the creases of her skin.

In her arms is a massive bag of dog food, as though Hannah was planning on staying here forever.

Maybe she is. That wouldn't be so bad.

"Christopher." Her voice is serious and prim.

I've known her a long time, since Tyler and I were just young men, and she has never greeted me with anything other than a kiss on the cheek and a shoulder shake. To be served this frosty glass of disdain hurts.

"Hi, Mrs. Jackson. Come in, please."

I open the door wider and wave her in, putting a smile on my face even though I don't feel it. I feel a sick wave of anxiety instead, settling into my stomach.

Piper shoves the dog food into my chest and pulls her cardigan off to hang it on my coat rack before crossing her arms. "So. Where is she?"

"Who?" I ask jokingly, but the withering look she gives me straightens me out quickly and zaps me of whatever humor I had hoped to bring to the interaction.

"Sorry. She's in the bathroom taking a test now."

Piper looks up to the sky, her green eyes silently begging for help, recognition, something.

"This is a nice place you have here, Christopher," Piper tells me, walking in circles.

She stops when she sees the small pile of pregnancy tests. "We haven't seen you at the house in a while. Where have you been?"

I shrug anxiously. "Just. Busy. Life."

"You have been busy, haven't you?"

Hannah's mother is shorter than she is and much shorter than I am.

She peers up at me. Despite her stature, she's intimidating. I sense an anger within her that's just waiting to be released.

Sighing, I sit on the couch. "I get it," I tell her, pulling imaginary hairs off my shirt. "Busy. Ha ha."

"Do you find this funny, Chris? Hannah might be pregnant, and she's only just started her life."

"I find this intimidation act funny. Come on, Miss Piper. You have known me since I was a little runt."

She sighs and sits down beside me. Her fingers drum on her thighs. "I have. And you've been like family, but I can't condone this."

"Condone?" I ask, the word slipping from my mouth like a dirty word. It feels wrapped in fire in my mouth.

"What does that even mean? What can't you condone? Me and your daughter being together?"

"You really did it this time, Chris. You have been in our lives for years. Why would you do this to Tyler?"

She spits out the words 'do this' like I hit the family dog with my car.

"What's wrong with us being together? And...to Tyler? What have I done to Tyler?" I ask her, more harshly than I mean to.

Her head tilts at my tone, the look of a woman who is daring me to keep going. I resent the question.

What about Hannah? What about what I've done to Hannah? I took her virginity and maybe got her pregnant. Her entire life is on hold until we have answers, and her mother's question is about Tyler?

I watch her green eyes, so much like Hannah's, light up with excitement at my response.

"What did you do to him? How do you think Tyler would feel about this, Chris? You betrayed him."

How will Tyler feel? Who cares how Tyler feels right now?

I laugh bitterly, throwing my head back. "Betrayed him? You're joking, Piper."

"Mrs. Jackson," she corrects me through gritted teeth.

"Fine. Mrs. Jackson, there is no way you think this is a betrayal. I simply won't believe it. You know me. I would never betray Tyler. He's been the only constant in my life."

I sit, comfortable in my own haughtiness, positive about my role and my morality, until Miss Piper asks, "Well, then I assume he knows about the two of you? Or, on second thought, have you lied to him about it?"

She must see something in my face because she crosses her arms triumphantly.

I run my tongue over my top teeth. Samantha. The invented woman to take the place of Hannah in my stories. Fine, so I've lied. But this still isn't about him. Or me.

"I don't care how Tyler feels right now, to be frank. I am worried about your daughter, who has done everything for everyone else and is probably very scared right about now. I am not worried about Tyler. I love Tyler, but this is not about him."

"Of course this is about Hannah, but Tyler is your best friend. And he's very protective of Hannah. You owe him your loyalty. You know he wouldn't have approved of this."

She isn't backing down, but rather than convince me, it only ignites a deeper sense of protectiveness over Hannah's experience.

I feel further and further from Tyler the more Mrs. Jackson brings him up.

"I did not betray Tyler. This isn't the 1800s. Tyler doesn't have any say over what Hannah does. I don't have to ask his permission or his approval. Hannah is perfectly capable of making her own adult decisions."

I realize I'm using Hannah's earlier diatribe, but hearing my own words thrown back at me really sheds a light on how ridiculous the sentiment actually is.

"Hannah is her own person, a wonderfully capable person, who I will honor by respecting whatever decision she makes or, if she lets me, that we make together about our future and the future of this baby. Who, I might remind you, we're not even sure yet exists."

Mrs. Jackson opens her mouth to respond, although from the look in her eyes I can tell the response won't be 'You're 100% correct, Chris, and you did nothing wrong.'

Before she can lay into me, the bathroom door opens and Hannah stands in the doorway, her face pale, her lips like two rose petals in a snowy bank.

"Hannah? Are you okay, baby?" Mrs. Jackson asks, standing up quickly and moving toward Hannah.

"Mom," she whispers.

"What? What? Tell us."

I let Mrs. Jackson gather Hannah's head into her hands and pet her hair. She might have been ripping into me just moments ago, but she is being the mother to her daughter, and it's clear when the two of them are together.

I desperately want to reach out and hug Hannah, but I leave the moment to them. "It's okay, Hannah," I tell her from the couch.

Her face leans onto her mother's shoulder, but her eyes focus on mine. "Best two out of three."

She holds up the three pregnancy tests, all three with either two lines or the word 'pregnant' in all caps, like the baby is screaming itself into existence.

# Chapter Thirty One

## Hannah

I'm in a situation I never thought I'd find myself in.

I'm sitting in the backseat of Chris' car while my mom rides in the passenger seat.

The silence is awkward and seems to sit on my chest. As awkward as it is, though, I knew that I was pregnant the second Chris mentioned the possibility.

Chris wants to take me to get a blood test or an ultrasound, depending on how far along I am.

I have a feeling I conceived the first time we had sex, which would put me right at seven weeks. I spend the silence in the car googling whether or not I can get an ultrasound at seven weeks. Some say yes, some say no. I give up and put my cell down, opting to close my eyes and lean back against the seat.

"How ya doing back there, baby girl?" my mom asks from the front seat.

She shoots her arm back behind her to grapple at my knee, a familiar mom move that makes me smile. I wonder if that's an instinct that all mothers have, to reach for their children when they are hurting or upset.

"I'm fine, Mom," I tell her, my eyes still closed.

"Are you sure? You can tell me how you really feel, you know."

"I really don't feel like anything. Didn't you both tell me to wait to see a doctor before I panicked?"

"Before you panicked, Hannah, not before you allowed yourself any feelings," my mom clarifies. I can hear the eye roll in her voice.

"Maybe panic is the only feeling she would have right now, Mrs. Jackson," Chris replies, the steering wheel sliding under his hand as he turns into the OBGYN office building.

"Is that true, Hannah? Are you that anxious?"

"Mom, please. No more questions," I beg as Chris pulls into a parking space, stopping gently.

My mom twists around in her seat and reminds me, "You called me, Hannah. I'm trying to be supportive in the best way I know how."

Despite the financial choices she made that led to my current job, my mom and I have a good relationship, and we almost never bicker, and I certainly don't want to bicker right now, so I just say, "Thank you, Mom," as Chris opens my car door and holds out his strong hand.

He pulls me out of the car, snakes an arm around my waist, and hugs me tightly.

With his mouth on my ear, so close that I shiver at feeling his breath on my skin, he whispers, "She's just worried about you. She'll even out." I nod against his shoulder and lean into him.

The waiting room is full of expectant women, and their faces show the entire spectrum of human emotion.

Some look out-of-their-mind terrified, and some look elated, others slightly nervous.

I don't know what I am yet. I won't know until I can get Chris alone and figure out how he feels about it all. I could do this alone, but I don't want to.

I look over at my mother, her hair fading with age and her eyes set deeper, and think about how even if Chris decides he didn't want to do this with me, I will never be alone as long as my mother is on this earth.

She came instantly at my request, even without my father. "Hey, Mom?"

"Yes?" She gathers my hands and pulls them into her lap, smiling sweetly.

"What did you tell Dad?"

"Oh, my God! Your father!"

She drops my hands like a hot potato and stands up quickly, pulling her phone out of her purse with a heightened anxiety I can feel from here.

I raise my eyebrows up into my hairline and watch her with amusement as she finds his contact information.

"I'll be right back! I'm going to step out and call him. I plum forgot about him, I was so worried about you!"

She leaves quickly, the little bell above the door ringing as she does.

I have a flashback to the first time I saw Chris again for the first time in several years.

The bell had rung above his head, too, hanging like mistletoe. He'd given me a start, caused me to catch my breath in my throat.

Now, in this moment of uncertainly, he sidles up closer to me, pulling his chair over a few inches so that he can talk in a low volume.

When he does, I feel my breath in my throat again, the rising attraction to him even under these circumstances, his piney smell. I'm grateful that smell still brings me comfort.

"You have a good mom," he mutters to me.

I nod, and he continues, "Questionable if your dad has a good wife or not."

When I laugh, he bumps my shoulder with his and kisses the top of my head. Butterflies take flight in my stomach.

"Hannah Jackson?" a nurse calls from the doorway, and when Chris and I stand, she smiles warmly at us and says, "Just Miss Jackson for now, sorry."

Chris and I look at each other awkwardly, and I say, "I'd like him with me, though."

"You can have him with you in just a moment, okay?" The nurse's smile is kind, crinkling into her eyes, so I nod and shrug at Chris.

Once we're on the other side of the door, she asks me, "Do you feel safe at home?"

"Yes?"

My face must betray my absolute confusion because she rests a hand gently on my shoulder and says, "It's a routine question. Girls and women in all types of situations come in here. We want to make sure you're okay with the people you arrived here with. Is that Dad out there?"

Hearing 'Dad' like that sends another jolt through my body. Dad? Is that what Chris is now? Someone's dad?

"Um, yea, that's…Dad."

"You're in Room 12. Go ahead and change into the gown that's on the bed, and we'll send Dad in in a few minutes."

Her voice has a warm gentility to it, like a distant aunt who's stepping up during a tough time.

Stepping into the room is my first time in complete silence in days.

The chilly air touches my skin everywhere as I pull off my clothes. I fold them neatly and place them on the small, upholstered chair that seems to be in every doctor's office.

I plunge my arms into the holes of the gown and tie it behind my back. I sink into aloneness as it hits for the first time what's happening and where I am.

If I'm pregnant, what will my life look like? Will Chris be in it? Will I be a good mother? Can I still grow a business while I grow a life inside of me?

I try to quell the thoughts that try to scream in my mind, the anxiety and uncertainty of the unknown.

Since I was a little girl, I've known everything about myself. I understood myself and my limitations as well as I understood my strengths. The only knowledge I lacked was what sort of lover I would be.

I knew that I was good at math, that I was needed by my parents, that Tyler was proud of me.

I knew what kind of life I wanted to lead and the path I needed to follow to get to it.

When I decided to become a CPA, I noted that the other potential licensees were generally at least several years older than I was.

People always seemed surprised to see a young woman just out of school working to become a CPA. But I never doubted my own abilities for a second.

My future has always been written in stone. Until now.

A small knock at my door is followed by the door opening almost immediately. The nurse steps in and smiles at me. "I brought you someone."

Chris peeks out from behind her and smiles with relief, his dimples pressing into his cheeks.

When I look at him, a thought passes through me instantly: There's your future.

# Chapter Thirty Two
## Christopher

Relief is written all over Hannah's face when she sees me.

"Hi." Her eyes soften, and even her shoulders seem to relax, as though she's been carrying a heavy weight.

"Hi, Baby."

I walk over to her and hug her, trying to reassure her with my presence.

She feels so small in my arms, almost miniature despite being almost as tall as I am. I feel like I could wrap myself around her twice more, with room to go. It's hard to imagine she has a baby inside her. I think of the times I'd kissed her stomach, none the wiser.

"So, you two, if you're ready, let's go ahead and see what's what here. If you would, Miss Jackson, lie back, please."

Hannah shoots me a worried look before sinking back onto the exam table, her hair cascading onto the pillow and over the side. I smile reassuringly at her and pat the back of her hand.

I watch anxiously as the ultrasound tech comes around the table to check Hannah's vitals, her blood pressure, and her oxygen level, and then when she's done, she lugs over what looks like the TV's the classrooms had in the 90s, a squeaking monstrosity of tech.

Hannah puts her feet in the stirrups so the tech can perform the transvaginal ultrasound, which I understand is generally done in the earlier stages of pregnancy in order to see as much detail as possible.

I can't help myself. I have to say something. "Hannah."

"Mmm?" Her eyes are on the screen, waiting.

"I just have to say – I'm sorry."

"Sorry?" She turns her head to me, her green eyes wide. "Sorry for what?"

"Sorry that you're in this position. I know you're trying to start a business, and the timing here isn't ideal."

I hold my hands together, cracking my knuckles as I look into her eyes.

She's beautiful in this moment, something about being on tiptoes between one moment and another, knowing that life might soon change in a very large way.

"Chris, do you not want this?"

Her voice is hoarse, her question whispered. It's been weighing on her.

"You keep telling me that you're sorry. If you don't want this, please tell me."

"I do. But I'm in a very different stage of life than you are. And if…if this isn't what you want—" I don't know if I'm using the right words.

I don't know if I'm scaring her more or if I'm reassuring her, but I don't want to her to feel like a burden and I also don't want her to feel like she has to make choices based on me.

She reaches her hand out to me and grabs mine with her long, thin fingers. She has fingers like a pianist, I often think, and I love that she uses them for art and math.

I wonder if she ever looked down at her fingers as a little girl and thought, 'I have good fingers for adding things together.'

She blurts out, "It is! It is what I want. I'm a little scared, but if this is real, if I am really pregnant, I'm just scared you'll think this is ruining your life."

Her admission of fear, her anxiety around me and my 'ruined' life brings tears to my eyes.

She's so gentle, someone who felt her very innocence and virginity had marked her, had somehow made her less than she truly was, and who felt unsure of everything but her mathematical abilities.

I only wish I could adequately express my feelings. It doesn't feel like enough to communicate them. I want her to absorb them, to feel them, to trust them. To know that nothing could be further from the truth than to think this will ruin my life.

"God, no. No, no, no. If you're happy, Hannah, I'm ecstatic."

I rest my cheek on her chest in an awkward hug while she lies down and I sit, and I tell her, "Don't ever for a second doubt that I'm happy, please. You will make a wonderful mother."

"Even if I can only make peanut butter sandwiches?"

"Even if you can only make peanut butter sandwiches," I reassure her, and she laughs.

I look up at her and tears stain her cheeks, resting in the pools of her clavicles.

"Actually, especially if you can only make peanut butter sandwiches. What kid wants roasted vegetables? You can be the favored parent. I'll make the vegetables he or she can play around with on the dinner plate and hide under the table for Noodle."

Hannah sighs deeply, letting her cheek rest on the top of my head. She runs her fingers over my head and through my curls. "For Lucy," she whispers.

"We'll talk about it." I lift my head up to kiss her, then move back into my seat.

"I'm so glad to hear that, Chris, really. I was so scared that you'd resent me forever."

"Never, Hannah. You have done nothing but make my life better in so many ways."

"So we're doing this?" she asks me, her hands touching her stomach as the tech performs the internal ultrasound.

"We're doing this," I tell her firmly, nodding.

"Well, that's good," the ultrasound tech interrupts, a broad smile on her face.

"Because I'm pregnant?" Hannah asks, turning her head to squint at the ultrasound on the screen.

"I think I already knew even before I took the tests." She looks over at me, squeezing my fingers, "I could feel it."

"Well, you were right, Mama, you are pregnant. But it's also good because…"

The technician points at a black dot on the screen, a tiny little mark that I would have missed a thousand times.

Then she points at another, "You're having twins."

# Chapter Thirty Three

## Hannah

My heart drops out of my throat and into my stomach. I shake my head as my mouth dries while I take in the ultrasound technician's words.

"I'm sorry," I laugh, "I think I misheard you. What did you say?"

"No, you didn't mishear me. I know, a lot of people have this reaction, but there they are." She points at the dark spot on the screen again like it means anything to me.

"There's one, and there's two. Two little babies. Twins."

"Twins," I say and look over at Chris, whose eyes have gone as wide as plates, his eyebrows furrowed deeply. He catches me looking and smiles generally, as though I'm a child who needs placating.

"Twins? How could this happen?"

"Well, do twins run in your family?"

"No! No, they don't. I'm not a twin. Are you a twin, Chris?"

"No, I'm not a twin. You know I'm not a twin."

"I don't know that. I don't know what's going on at all." I sit up all the way, dragging jelly across the blanket, and lower my gown over my stomach.

Right on time as always, my mom comes waltzing in through the door, her eyes on the phone in her hand, "Sorry, sorry I'm late. I was talking to your dad, and he started asking me about this and that, and I swear he needs me for everything, he'd fall apart without me, so I...what's wrong? You two look like you've seen a ghost. There's a baby, isn't there? Oh God, is the baby okay? What's wrong? Goddamnit, somebody answer me!" she's chattering too quickly for me to even process it and I'm grateful for the momentary distraction of following her train of thought.

"Babies," Chris responds, standing up to allow my mother to take his seat.

It's a sweet gesture that she barely seems to even realize happened.

She drops her phone into her purse and sets her purse on her lap. "Babies? What do you mean?" Confusion crosses her face, her eyes and nose scrunching.

"Twins," I tell her from my place on the bed. "Do we have twins in the family?"

"Twins? Oh, my God, Hannah, that's amazing!" She perks up. "Oh, that'll be so fun!"

She stands up, her purse falling from her lap to the floor, and hugs me, squashing my face against her breast. She sways me from side to side affectionately. "Oh, that'll be so so fun. Are you happy? Is the panic gone?"

I look over at Chris, who seems to be bathed in amusement, watching my face contort as my mother squeezes me.

"I don't know! Do we have twins in the family or not?"

"Oh, yeah, I guess so. My mom was a twin." She shrugs.

"Gran was a twin? And you're shrugging? Don't shrug!" My voice goes up an octave. It's shrill even in my own ears.

"Well, what? Did you want me to tell you before your accidental pregnancy? Would that have changed anything?"

I'm about to fire back at her when the ultrasound technician, who has seemingly mastered the art of fading into the background while families go through every possible emotion, cuts in. "Oh, Miss Jackson?"

"Yes?" My mom and I say in unison, turning to face her.

"Oh, sorry, I meant my patient Miss Jackson." She smiles slightly, pointing at me with a gloved finger. "Miss Jackson, did you have an IUD?" She tips her head at me.

I shrug, even as the worry creeps in. I look at the screen, trying to see what she sees. "Yeah, but I figured it fell out or something."

"No, darling, you would know if it fell out. Your IUD is still in place. We need to get it out or this will become a high-risk pregnancy very quickly. Okay? Do you understand? We need to go ahead and schedule that as soon as possible."

Fear grips me as I detect the serious tone in her voice. She must see the look on my face because she rests a warm hand on my arm and scoots her rolling chair closer to me.

"Hey. It will be okay. We just need to take it seriously. Okay?"

"We will," my mom says from my other side, and even without looking at her, I can see the motherly stance she's in. I remember it well from all from my doctors' visits as a girl, though they weren't many with our limited income.

Still, I can see her with one arm crossed over the other, gripping her elbow and her lips pursed, her glasses pushed up on top of her head. She looked that way when I got the flu and when I was told I needed braces and when Tyler broke his arm playing chicken on the monkey bars. Always that same crouched forward, scrunched lips face like she was trying to read the fine print of an invisible document.

On the drive back to Chris' house, my mom twists in her seat and asks, "Hey, how come I've never been to your place?"

I'm so taken aback that my first instinct is to lie, badly, as though I'm in high school and just got caught coming back inside my bedroom window.

She hasn't been to my place because there is no my place. If she were to find out that I'm sleeping in my office, it would likely really upset her.

She'd want me to move back home or she'd want to send me money, and I just want to make it, or not make it, on my own terms.

"You have," I say automatically, and Chris chuckles.

My mom looks over at him momentarily, but he keeps his eyes on the road and tightens his grip on the steering wheel.

"No...I most certainly have not. I've seen your office but not your home. How is that funny?"

"Yeah, that's really funny," I say in a monotone voice, my mind still whirring with the events of today. When my mom raises her eyebrows at me, I tell her, "I mean, I just work a lot, Mom. I don't know." I shrug at her. "Sorry. I'm tired."

"Well, why don't we go over there now? I can stay the night and then we can go shopping for baby things in the morning."

Her face lights up and she slaps Chris' arm eagerly. It's nice to see her being happy with him again for a moment. I wonder how momentary it is or if the twins really did turn her opinion around this dramatically.

I meet eyes with Chris in the rearview mirror, and I can see his eyes sparkling. He's been wanting me to tell my family about my living at the office.

No better time than now. She's still high off the idea of twins. Chris is here. It's perfect. Tell her. She'll understand.

"Well. About that, Mom."

"What? You don't want your old mom cramping your style? You two have a lot to plan, I know, but I could call in to work. You might find you need some help. There's a lot to do, Hanny."

"Yeah, Hanny," Chris says jovially, smiling at me in the mirror, to which I roll my eyes.

"No, Mom, it's not that at all. It's just that I don't really have a space for you anywhere at my place."

"You don't have a couch? I don't mind sleeping on the couch."

Her insistence is heartbreaking. And a little annoying.

"Mom, I don't have a place. I've been staying at my office."

"Oh." She turns back around in her seat and is silent for a moment. "Well, Chris, could I sleep on your couch?" She looks over at him expectantly.

He smiles kindly, flashing her his dimples. "Of course, Mrs. Jackson. You're always welcome at my place."

We continue to drive in silence. "So that's it? You're not mad that I've been lying?"

"Hannah, you've been lying about a lot more than where you stay," my mom says quietly, her eyes fixed on something out the window.

I flinch at her response. She continues, "I don't have the energy to be mad about every little thing. I just want you to be safe and happy."

I pet my stomach and imagine where my twins are now, small as they are, if they're near the front or the back or somewhere in the middle. I want to try to feel them, but according to the nurse, I should be careful until my next appointment. I'm just as likely to poke my own IUD as I am to poke the babies right now.

Chris catches my eyes in the rearview mirror and mouths 'good job.'

# Chapter Thirty Four
## Christopher

I set Mrs. Jackson up on the couch with a blanket while Hannah lies down on my bed.

Hannah had asked me to sleep in the guest room so that she didn't have to be embarrassed about her mom thinking we were together.

I had told her "A little too late for that" and touched her stomach, but she pulled away from me and said she was serious.

I bring Mrs. Jackson a couple of extra pillows and show her where the tea is if she decides she wants some later. "Sleep well, Mrs. Jackson," I tell her.

She accepts the pillows and blanket and smiles at me almost forlornly. "Chris, why don't you sit down here with me?" She pats the seat next to her.

I do as I'm told, my heart pounding anxiously in my chest. "Are you still angry?" I ask her as I adjust my ankle over my knee. I glance over at her.

She's taken off all her makeup in preparation for bed and she looks a lot more like the Piper I knew growing up. It's impossible to ignore that we're all getting older, as much as we may want to ignore it. And I want to ignore it pretty badly.

"No, Christopher, I'm not mad at you."

She sighs and pulls a blanket over her bottom half, snuggling into the corner of the couch. "I'm worried about you. About everyone, really." She lowers her voice and whispers, "She's so young."

"She's an adult and has been for some time." I raise my eyebrows at her. "Long enough for her IUD to...expire."

That earns a chuckle out of her, which I'm grateful for. "Well, you're pretty young yourself, you know. You all look like ants from up here."

I throw my head back and laugh. "I know the feeling from my own planet of experience."

"Aw, I know you've had it tough, too, with Julie and all. Tyler tells me you were pretty wild after her, girls and more girls."

"Something like that," I joke, smiling at her.

She smiles back. "So do you think you're ready to settle down?"

"Wait, I have to settle down to raise twins?" I ask, widening my eyes like I just realized. "Well, hang on, let me make some calls."

"I suppose you don't have to stop dating other women to raise twins. Are you and Hannah casual?"

"Not at all. And we never will be."

"Chris, you've always been such a fun addition to this family. I wouldn't mind seeing you more. But I'm easy, it's not really me you have to convince."

"Oh yeah?" I turn toward her and pull my legs up onto the couch, so that we're facing each other. "Who do I have to convince?"

"I imagine Tyler won't be easy."

I shrug. "I can take Tyler." I stand up and throw a pillow her direction. "Get some sleep. It'll all be fine."

"Oh Lord, a grandma."

She rests her head in her hands and peeks out between her fingers before lowering her hands into her lap. "You know, I never thought I'd be one of those women who can't accept their age and insist on being a Mimi or a Gigi, but now? Faced with Grandma? I wouldn't mind being a Mimi."

I pat her knee. "Whatever you call yourself, you'll be great at it."

"And you'll be an amazing dad, Chris. I know you didn't have one yourself, but you can learn from the example of your mother, too."

"I had a dad," I correct her as I walk backwards toward my bedroom and say, "He was just in prison." I point finger guns at her to let her know that I can laugh about it and then I, finally, enter my own room.

Everything I do feels like it's being done with the shadow of two children behind me.

I brush my teeth and imagine a toothbrush holder with four brushes. I gargle mouthwash and imagine all of us piled into a bathroom swishing together. I can see myself now tickling them while they try to hold it, their cheeks ballooned out.

I put on my pajama pants and a t-shirt and think of all the children's pajama sets I've walked by stores over the course of my life. It has to be in the thousands. It never matters and then one day, it matters.

I feel myself drift off, my mind on the babies and the future as the image becomes clearer and more concrete.

The children shift in nature, their heads enlarging and their bodies turning into baby rattles. Their baby rattles morph into rattlesnakes, and I scream in terror for just a second before picking up the snakes and singing them a lullaby. I watch the snakes' fangs retract into their heads and their tongues flit in and out as their mouths upturn into smiles.

I wake up to the sound of my bedroom door creaking open, though I'm unsure if I'm truly awake or still in a dream. The open door throws a slat of light across my face, and I look over to see what's throwing the light.

Hannah stands in the doorway, her silhouette darkened by the light coming in behind her from the hallway.

I smile slightly as I sense her approaching. Her footsteps are quiet and slight, though the wood squeaks underneath them slightly.

She crawls on top of me and I can feel her straddling me, heating my upper thighs and cock as she lowers herself onto me. She pins down my wrists and grinds against my already hardening cock. Her pelvis rubs against mine as she lowers herself, lying her body down across mine, relaxing her weight onto me. She kisses my throat softly, her lips warm pillows against my skin.

"Aren't you worried your mom might hear?" I whisper when I feel her ear brush against my mouth. I catch her lobe between my lips and suckle gently.

"Shhh," she tells me, covering my mouth with her hand. I have a childish instinct to lick her palm, but instead I bring my hand up and grip the back of her neck with my hand.

"That's not how this works," I growl to her, pulling her face into mine and crushing my lips against hers. I suck on her bottom lip and then run her lip through my teeth, tugging on it until I feel her moan release into my mouth. "You don't tell me what to do."

She squeaks a moan, and with my eyes still covered, I hold her hips with both hands and flip her over so that she's on her back. I hear her stifle a gasp from underneath me as she hits the mattress.

Slowly, I trail my fingers up her arms until I find her hands and clasp her wrists to the bed. She tenses beneath me, catching her breath in her chest, and I relax her wrists to interlace my fingers in hers. I lower my face to hers and kiss her lips with a gentle pressure. "Tell me you understand," I whisper against her lips.

"I understand," she moans back.

"I can keep you here as long as I want."

I drag my nose across her cheek and down her jaw until I reach her clavicle. My right hand trails down the outline of her body, tracing the curve of her breast and the dip of her waist until my fingers grip the flesh of her hip.

Hannah wraps her legs around me, and I realize that she's not wearing underwear beneath her nightgown as I feel her slick hole press against the skin of my stomach.

Just the feeling of her button against me makes me hungry for her, and I lower myself to her pelvis while on lying on top of her.

She wraps her fingers in my hair and whispers, "I don't know if I can be quiet if you do that."

"Do you want to be heard?" I ask from between her legs. I ask it as I nuzzle my lips under her clit, feeling the warmth she's giving off.

"No!" she whispers forcefully, clamping her thighs around my ears and laughing. "I'll do it, Chris, I swear I'll pull your head right off."

"Okay, okay, I can help, don't do anything rash," I tease, and she releases me, giggling.

"I didn't want to have to do that, but you pushed me," she warns.

"Sit up, Hannah," I command her, and I feel her obey, sliding to a seated position. I slide up to meet her, only going by the feeling of her body in the still dark room. I lean over the side of the bed and pull an eye mask out of my side drawer.

"Here, put this over your eyes. I want you to just feel what I'm about to do to you."

As soon as she's put it on, I clamp my hand over her mouth and taste her juices with one flat-tongued lick. Hannah covers the hand that's over her mouth with her one hand and arches her back, her other hand digging into my left shoulder blade. She gasps into my hand, and I press it harder against her mouth as I plunge my tongue inside her, eagerly lapping at whatever juices she'll give me.

Her squeals are unrelenting and girlish, her back arching further and further into a perfect semicircle. I use one hand to support her as she does, spreading it across her spine and feeling her twist and squirm underneath me.

I pull my tongue out of her tunnel slowly and let it drag across her opening as I trail it upward to her clit again. I circle my lips around it and suck lightly, applying light pressure with my tongue as I do.

"Chris," she moans into my hand, her tone almost begging.

I can't help but laugh hearing the way she says my name. "Yes?"

"It feels so good," she mumbles, her words muffled.

"Does it? That's good. Lie back. Just relax and feel," I tell her, smiling into her soaking pussy.

When I feel her lie back down, I go back to suckling on her clit but this time I let one of my hands wander up her nightgown and over her breast so that I can pinch one of her nipples at the same time.

Her moans are quick and labored, and I can tell that she's on the brink of orgasming, the quickest she's ever climaxed with me.

She twists to move away as the pressure builds, pushing my hand away from her mouth to tell me, "I'm about to cum. I don't want to stop. I still want you inside me."

I lift my head to say nonchalantly, "So cum twice," before returning my mouth to her pearl where it belongs.

I keep my fingers dancing across her nipple, pulling and twisting it when I feel her sinking into it too much, then moving it lightly when she pulls back against the sensation.

My tongue works overtime, lapping at her clit while I suckle on it. It hardens and grows in my mouth, her button swelling as she grows closer and closer to climax.

I'm careful not to tell her to cum for me, though I desperately want her to. I don't want to spook her out of her flighty orgasm.

Like a deer drinking from a brook, I approach it slowly and steadily, my fingers and tongue all moving at the exact same rhythm as her hips raise higher, along with the curve of her spine.

She gyrates against my mouth and as her orgasm swells, she squeezes me with her thighs, her legs lifting up to rest over my shoulders and on top of my back.

She grabs my hand and presses it back against her mouth so that she can empty her screams into my palm, lightly biting my hand as she does. I let go of her breast and snake my arm around behind her back to grip her shoulder so that I can pull her closer to me.

Her hand finds the back of my head and she pushes me closer against her, grinding herself against my mouth. I suck greedily as she drips into my mouth, milking her orgasm against my face.

Finally, I feel her relax under me, collapsing onto the mattress and sliding back down into a horizontal position.

I gently kiss the soft skin of her intimate folds, slick with her juices, as she relaxes. Her fingers intertwine in my curls, and she strokes my hair as I kiss the insides of her thighs.

I spread her lips open and kiss the pink sides of her inner labia, inhaling the heady scent of her orgasm. She sighs gently at my kisses, and her legs open slightly.

"Chris, that felt so good," she whispers to me, her hand still caressing my hair gently.

I crawl up her body and lie next to her.

I still crave her and want to feel her from the inside, but she seems so relaxed that I don't want to ruin the moment for her. I wrap my arms around her body and pull her onto my chest. When I feel her settled against me, I lift her eye mask and look into her beautiful green eyes.

"I love you, Hannah," I tell her sincerely and kiss her forehead.

She closes her eyes for just a second as if taking in the moment and putting it away as a memory.

"I love you, too, Chris," she whispers back, averting her eyes and snuggling deeper against me.

"What's wrong? Why'd you look away?"

"Oh, nothing's wrong. That was perfect. I just wonder if... this will change everything. What if it changes us?"

"It will change us," I tell her, sitting up.

I can see fear flash across her face as she sits up with me. I press my palms against her cheeks and try to catch her gaze even as she looks down at her fingers.

"Hey, look at me." She flashes me those beautiful green eyes again, and I offer her a genuine smile.

"It will. There is no reality where this doesn't change us. But all change isn't bad, right?"

"Right..." she trails off, looking around. "But this is big."

"You know what else was big? It was big when you decided to become a CPA, and it was big when you decided to start a business."

I jiggle her cheeks a little, and a small laugh sputters out of her.

"It was big to move out and be on your own, big to live in your office. It was big when you lost your virginity. Just now, telling me you love me, that was big. Life is just a series of big, and little, moments."

She nods at me and exhales a shaky sigh.

She kisses me lightly on the cheek, and I pull her into a hug, telling her, "Come here, poor thing."

She breathes deeply against my neck, and I smile as her head squishes into my cheek.

"There is nothing too big for how I feel about you. Everything big has brought me right here to this moment. I chose this life with you in a thousand little ways. You realize that, right?"

When she doesn't answer, I shake my shoulder. "Huh? Do you realize that? That you made all your big choices and it still got you right here in bed with me?"

Hannah squeezes me closer and whispers, "I guess so."

"Hey, don't sound so grateful." She laughs, and I continue, "I'm not so bad, right?"

"No, you're not bad at all," she murmurs into my neck in a way that sounds like a song, and I can't help but smile at the gentle tone she uses.

I pull back and kiss her deeply, feeling the way her lips press back automatically and fit perfectly into the space that mine leave.

"I am going to make life so good for us that you never wonder what else could have been. I promise. Everything will be okay. I love you. I love Lucy. I love your parents and Tyler. What else is there?"

"You called her Lucy," she says, smiling at her lap.

"Don't get used to it."

# Chapter Thirty Five

## Hannah

I wake up a few hours later on top of Chris' chest, though he doesn't seem to mind.

He snuffles slightly, no snoring but noises coming from him that sound like a restful puppy.

I move away from him to go back to the guest room, and he pulls me in again, his arm around my waist. He lets out a little grumble of dissatisfaction and whines as I scoot out from under his arm.

I smile at the boyish way his face crumbles into a dissatisfied frown, his brow furrowed.

I kiss the bridge of his nose and smooth it out with my index finger as though I can erase his feeling of discontentment. Chris sighs gently and rolls over onto his stomach.

I open the door slowly and tiptoe out and down the hall, trying to keep my steps light so that I don't squeak the floor underneath me in a way that will wake up either Chris or my mother.

I make it almost to my bedroom before I hear my mother say, "Hannah?"

I stand for a moment with my shoulders clenched before turning around with a smile on my face. "Hey, Mom, why aren't you sleeping?"

She smiles at me and pulls her knees into her chest, grabbing the bottom of the blanket that covers her. "Come sit."

I walk over to her reluctantly and take a seat, covering my knees with the blanket and fanning it around me. "What are you doing up?"

"Just thinking. Thinking about you as a little girl and how you're going to have your own little ones soon."

She reaches over and tugs at a few strands of my hair like a doorknob before twirling it around her finger and letting it drop against my shoulder.

She smiles ruefully, and I can see that her eyes are rimmed in old mascara. She's either been crying or it's been rubbed off by sleep.

"I hope they get your beautiful copper hair."

When I was younger, it always struck me as so odd that she called it my beautiful copper hair as though she wasn't a redhead herself, but now, faced with the idea of having children myself, I think I understand how something might be beautiful on a little girl but not on myself.

I smile back at her and sigh before relaxing against her knees. "Your beautiful copper hair."

"Your grandma's beautiful copper hair," she corrects even further, running her finger over my scalp and massaging it the way she used to when I was a kid. "Hey, do you want me to braid your hair?"

"Sure, Mom," I tell her and close my eyes, feeling the gentle tugging of my hair as she braids close to my scalp.

It's like a deep tissue massage for my head, one that she used to do when I was a kid when she'd work avocado oil into my hair. I used to complain then, having no idea that I would one day work avocado oil into my own hair and wish that someone else was there to do it.

"You have such beautiful hair. My hair has faded," she says.

I look back and see that she's self-consciously running a hand through her hair.

"Your hair is beautiful, Mom. It's changing. Change is okay."

She kisses my forehead. "When did you get so wise?"

"Guess it comes with the mom territory," I tell her.

"Don't wiggle," she chides me, bumping my arm with her elbow before tying off the end of one of my braids.

"Sorry." I sit ramrod straight as she finishes off the braid. "Did you know that you'd be a good mother?"

"Hmmm," she says to herself, the hair band she grabbed out of her purse dangling from her clenched teeth. She wraps it around my second braid and bumps my arm to let me know that she's finished.

"No. No one knows. Everyone worries. It's natural. Look at me, Hannah."

I turn around and look into her mascara-smudged green eyes.

"You have been my perfect Hanny Bee since you were a very young girl. Do you remember that you used to balance our checkbook?"

I nod, the anxiety-ridden memory overshadowing the brief moment of joy I felt remembering the nickname she had for me as a kid: Hanny Bee.

"But you need to know that no one expects or wants you to be perfect. All you need to be is yourself. That's what your children will want most from you."

I nod quietly, taking in the information. "Sure."

"I mean it. And that's what Chris wants from you, too. Trust me. He really cares about you, Hannah. I know this isn't how you planned this. That doesn't make it any less special. Capiche?"

She says the last part while holding a pretend toothpick in her mouth.

I roll my eyes at the motion but kiss her fragile cheek as I stand.

I remember when her cheeks were fuller and round, but as she's aged they've gotten thinner and softer. Big changes that aren't bad. When my own children kiss my mom's cheeks, they'll only know how soft she is.

"You're right. Thanks, Mom. I'm going to go back to bed now. Try to get some sleep, okay?"

As I walk back down the hall toward the guest room, she calls out after me, "Hannah, the deed is done. You're already pregnant. You can stop pretending you and Chris sleep in separate rooms. Go back to his bed. You two need each other right now."

I hear her laugh trailing after me as I pivot on my heel, sending my nightgown flailing around me, and walk back towards the room I came out of, my cheeks flushed with embarrassment.

# Chapter Thirty Six
## Christopher

I wake up to the smell of coffee and pancakes and an empty bed and walk out into the kitchen to see Hannah and Piper cooking breakfast. Hannah leans over her mom's shoulder, pointing and saying something, while her mother pours the batter into an oiled pan.

Lucy sits off to the side, calm and well-behaved but with a well trained eye on the stovetop, her nose wiggling fanatically.

I watch from the hallway for a moment, proud of all that Hannah's learned and how natural she seems at teaching.

I hear her say, "Okay and see, now there's bubbles, so you can go ahead and flip it."

"Flip it?!" Piper balks, and Hannah laughs, moving a hair that's covered in wet flour behind her mother's ear.

"Oh, hey, sleepyhead," Hannah calls out to me, her grin wide and gummy.

I have this overwhelming urge swell through me to grip her face in my hands and cover her face in kisses, but she's stirring a bowl of batter, so I simply say, "Hi, there. You've got a feast going, I see."

"Not exactly a feast, but there's coffee! And we're working on unburnt pancakes. We'll have some any minute now, I know it."

She looks over at her mom hunched over the stovetop, a spatula in her hand ready for the pancake as though it might hop out of the pan.

"I wanted to get McDonald's for everyone," Piper offers sheepishly.

"No, this is better! I believe in you. What can I do to help?" I scratch at my arm, looking around at the countertops speckled with batter and the egg shell remains.

"How about I clean up as you cook?"

"You know what? I actually would love for you to just…do your thing. Take a shower, go on a run. This might take us a while," Hannah says, almost apologetically.

I nod as I approach the kitchen. "Sure, I can do that." I pick up an abandoned bowl with remnants of batter past and rinse it out in the sink.

"Get! Out of here!" Hannah swats me with a batter-crusted spatula.

"Hey! That touches our food!"

"Well, there would be no arms to smack if you'd go on your run!"

She holds the spatula menacingly above her shoulder like a baseball bat, and I hold up my hands in surrender.

I get changed into my running shorts and a tank and clip Lucy onto a leash to bring her with me. As I walk out the door, I call out, "Please don't burn my kitchen down."

"You don't have renter's insurance?" Hannah calls back.

"I do, but remember that there's priceless art in the bathroom," I tell her, closing the door behind me.

My normal routine has been disrupted though. I have a ritual I'm used to, that tens of women have seen over the years.

Typically, I shower, knowing that I'll be sweaty after my run. I make an egg white omelet, naked, and air dry while listening to my meditation podcasts. Then I get dressed and go for a run.

I shower again when I get back and I only drink coffee if Tyler happens to call.

This morning has thrown each aspect of my routine out the window, but Hannah seems so delighted to be here with me that decide to just roll with the flow.

Still, the run isn't quite as satisfying as it usually is, and I feel it turn into a jog and then slow down even further to a walk.

Lucy seems confused, but happy regardless, as she slows and takes her time smelling various spots that I can't see being unique in any sense, but which she finds fascinating in her own little doggy way.

Seeing Hannah and her mother reminds me of my father and the relationship we never got to have.

The memory of his arrest still haunts me. I looked out the window from the second floor of our home and I saw them encircle his wrists with handcuffs.

I saw him look up and see me, at which point I fell to the floor of my room hoping he hadn't seen me standing there, but knowing I wasn't quick enough.

I found out later that he had laundered money. A lot of money. He had filed fraudulent tax returns, and my family was fractured beyond repair from that point forward.

We visited him once a month in the prison, and my father would tell me to keep my eyes on him while my mother would shield my eyes with two hands when inappropriate things would happen around us.

Those memories were the main reason I initially went to see Hannah and get her advice.

I want to do everything right with my business. I don't want a single thing to go wrong. Hannah found more than I bargained for with my business and finances, and it terrifies me.

What if it had been discovered during a tax audit and the government thought I embezzled from the business to evade taxes? My God, I could conceivably go to prison myself!

I'm still afraid to make a move. I'm afraid if I tell someone about what Sarah's done that I'll end up in the same situation and be blamed for everything.

I kick a rock absentmindedly and pick up the phone to call Tyler, my mind made up that I don't have anything if I don't have my relationships.

Tyler picks up after only a few rings and answers happily. I often think that if Tyler were a dog, I would be able to hear his tail wagging.

"Hey, Bud, you're calling me first? I feel honored."

I kick the rock further down the sidewalk, and Lucy jumps at it as though it were a live playmate, her tail wagging behind her as her bark explodes towards it.

"I sure am. What are you doing today?"

"Oh, you know, I have work. Don't you have to work today?"

I shrug even though he can't see me and try to encourage Lucy to walk ahead of me wherever she wants to go. She struggles to lead, looking back with her wet, moony eyes even as I shake my hand at her.

"I don't know what I have going on anymore."

"What do you mean? You okay?" Tyler's concern emanates through the phone.

"Yeah, I'll be okay. I got another client on Friday, but I'm laying low until then. The thing is, Hannah figured out someone was stealing from me, and it turned out to be Sarah, and honestly, dude? It's kind of messed with me in a big way. I trusted her, you know?"

"For sure, man, that's rough."

"It's got me thinking like, what if I get in trouble, too?" Like what happened to my dad. The thought goes unsaid, as always.

"Have you told Hannah about your concerns? She's a good CPA, Chris, she can help you."

I hang my head back and look at the endlessly blue sky above me.

Of course I haven't told Hannah. There were a few moments that I almost did, and then it wasn't the time and eventually it felt strange to even try.

"Not yet. I guess I should."

"I'm sure you wouldn't get in trouble for it since you had nothing to do with it. Okay, Chris? Don't worry about it. But I'm sorry that happened to you. Well, hey, do you wanna grab a drink when I get off later? We can talk about what your plan is next."

A twinge of guilt tugs at my heart. I know I need to tell him about Hannah. His unwavering support has gotten me through so much of life, and I haven't returned any of the kindness he's offered me. Not that he's aware of that yet.

"You sure you can't come meet me for lunch?"

"Uh, you know my days are tight. And they could turn on a dime. I usually just stuff a sandwich down my throat."

"I know," I say firmly, waiting on Lucy to smell a particularly interesting flower. It really is beautiful, purple and stretching out its petals to the sky.

I lean down and pluck it for Hannah, feeling like a child, but Lucy takes it and eats it in front of me.

I laugh a little and throw the stem on the ground for her. "Well, hey, I wouldn't want to mess your whole day up. How about if you find yourself with a free hour you let me know?"

There's a pause on the other end as Tyler considers my request.

I know he's not actually considering whether or not he's going to let me know if he gets a free hour, but whether or not he's going to take off now just to make sure I'm okay.

I quickly say, "Seriously, don't worry about it."

"You sure?" he asks hesitantly.

"Positive. I'm a big boy," I promise him. "I'll talk to you soon. Like you said, when you get off tonight."

"Okay, great, dude. I really do want to see you soon. Hey, how did things go with that girl?"

I freeze, unable to remember my lie or come up with anything to fill the space. "What girl?"

"That good, huh?" he chuckles. "I really thought you cared about this one. You seemed so upset. Ah, well, learned my lesson again."

"Yeah, I don't know." I scratch my head and pull Lucy away from the weeds cropping up along the strip of grass that she's determined to eat.

She sniffs indignantly and reluctantly follows me.

"Who knows what happened?"

I consider saying something right then: I was lying. It was about Hannah. Oh, also, I got your sister pregnant. But I don't. I let it go.

"Well, hey, you'll find someone again soon enough. I gotta go, they're calling me into scrub. I'll call you later tonight. And hopefully this afternoon!"

He sounds peppy before he hangs up but I know he won't have time to call me.

I shove my phone back into my pocket and sigh. The sound perks up Lucy, who looks backward at me while trotting. I pet her head and tell her, "Come on, girl, let's go see what the other girls are doing."

# Chapter Thirty Seven

## Hannah

The afternoon is normal, although a bit lazier than most of my afternoons. I leave Lucy at Chris' and my mom and Chris and I go shopping for baby supplies.

I'm afraid to say what I'm thinking, which is that I'm not so sure it's a good idea to go shopping for supplies for a high risk pregnancy, at least not this soon. So I don't. I hold the thought in and let it go. Besides, it's hard to stay realistic when there are tiny baby shoes on a shelf in front of me.

I unlace a pair of teeny sneakers and pull the tongue out, imagining fixing them over small feet and tying them tight, trying to keep the wiggly legs still.

From behind me, my mom says, "Oh, you don't want those."

"What? Why not? You don't think they're cute?" I wave them around like they're little airplanes, each shoe on two of my fingers.

"They're very cute," she assures me, patting my shoulder, "but babies don't need shoes, I promise you. You'll never really put them down, and when you do, you put them down on their backs. Plus, they grow so fast, they outgrow things almost before you can break them in."

My shoulders sink and I push out my lower lip as I put the shoes away.

"But what if I just think they're cute? I can't just buy the shoes because they're cute and I want to see the babies in them?" I protest as we continue to circle the small boutique.

"Sure, Hannah, but babies are expensive. Be careful spending too much right away. It's easy to spend an entire savings account on cute things you don't need."

Despite knowing that she means well, hearing my mom tell me to be careful with my money guts me a little. I remember all the late nights spent taking care of myself because my mom and dad were out working their second jobs.

I remember all the things we had to go without and the things that we didn't go without when we should have. I hold my stomach for a moment, overwhelmed by a strange fear that my baby will feel my memories.

As the fear crystallizes into a childish resentment, I call out across the store, "Hey Chris! Get this!"

Chris' head pops up from the baby blanket he's looking at and he turns to look at me. It's a small boutique, just about 650 square feet, so I'm not hard to hear.

My mom covers her face with her hand, tossing a sheepish look to the owner whose brow is furrowed. Chris tilts his head at me, and I pick up the shoes to show them to him.

"I wanted to get these, but Mom says babies are expensive! Have you ever heard that before?"

"Hannah, stop," my mom hisses, and I drop the shoes noisily on the shelf before walking across the store back to where Chris is seemingly still looking for the perfect blanket. I collapse into him and let him stroke my back with one hand as he strokes blankets with the other.

"I don't understand why you are acting so childish. I was just saying that, you know, newborns don't walk, Hannah," my mom continues, at my ear, clearly upset.

"I'm sorry, Mom. I just want to make my own choices regarding my babies. Okay?"

Chris rubs my back and turns to my mom. "Everyone's okay, right? Let's go ahead and get lunch. I think maybe everyone's hungry?"

Not wanting my emotions to be boiled down to hunger but knowing it's a true possibility, I nod. "Sorry, Mom," I mumble.

"It's fine," she bristles. "I am hungry, actually."

She pulls her purse higher up on her shoulder and walks out to the car in front of us without waiting to see if we follow.

"I'm going to get that blanket," Chris tells me, kissing my cheek. "Go ahead. You two can figure out where to eat."

The rest of the afternoon is uneventful. We eat soup and sandwiches. We spend time buying little things we know for sure that we'll need like diapers and cribs.

My mom shows me a wet wipe warmer, and I remind her that I can just hold a wipe between my hands.

Eventually, she leaves to go home to my dad, squeezing me tightly at the car.

Chris is in his apartment, looking through the window and waving. He's just a shadow, but we still manage to see him and wave back.

"Sorry that I kind of flipped, Mom," I murmur into her shoulder, and she shushes me.

"Hey, I know better than to argue with a pregnant woman. I have no idea what I was thinking. Don't even give it a second thought, do you hear me?"

"Oh, so I get a free pass for the next nine months?"

"Quite possibly. If you play your cards right."

She tucks my hair behind my ear and asks, "Are you going to be all right?" her smile dropping slightly into a more serious expression. She flips my hair back behind my shoulders.

"Yeah, of course. Chris will take care of me."

She smiles sweetly and says, "Aw, I know he will. You know what? I was mad when he first told me about the two of you but seeing you together, I can clearly see that he cares about you and will take care of you." She looks up at him in the window and waves again. "You take care of him, too, okay?"

"Okay, Mom."

"Call me when you need something. And Hannah?" She walks around to the driver's seat of the car and opens the door to lean on it.

"Yes, Mom?"

"You two need to talk to Tyler – soon."

She blows me a kiss before sinking into her seat. I watch her buckle her seatbelt and wave to her from the sidewalk, her words heavy on my heart.

What I think I need right now is for Chris to tell me he wants me to live here. I wonder if that will happen?

I look up at the window to see that his figure has gone.

# Chapter Thirty Eight
## Christopher

I watch from the window as Mrs. Jackson drives away and I walk away from the window to get the present that I stashed away for Hannah earlier.

I wait eagerly on the couch for her to walk back up the stairs.

She opens the door and sits next to me with a deep sigh. "Chris."

"Yes."

"I'm exhausted, and it's only 4:30."

"It's been an emotional couple of days. The body does strange things with that. Do you want to go on a run with me?"

Hannah laughs, swiveling on the couch and lying down so that she can rest her feet in my lap.

"Oh, you're not joking. Wow, that's scary." She rests her hands on her stomach and looks down at it as though horrified for the future of our children.

"Well, I guess I could take them through the week and you could take them on the weekends…"

"Ha ha." I pull her shoes off and let them fall to the ground. I peel her socks off and dig my knuckles into her arches. "I have a present for you."

"Oh yeah?" Hannah situates her hands behind her head, her elbows bent, and looks at me from her side of the couch. "What is it?"

"Do you want me to tell you or do you want to open it?" I hand her the box from beside me.

My heart does a couple of flips when I see her eyes light up with joy.

The green of her eyes genuinely sparkles as she sits up all the way and takes the box from my hands.

I lean over and kiss her all over the face, and she nuzzles into my neck.

"Stop, stop, let me open my present, seriously. Or I'm going to burst."

"Okay, okay, sorry." I make a show of sitting on my hands and leaning back against the back of the couch.

She pulls the ribbon off the box and opens the lid. Her shoulders droop as she makes eye contact with me.

"You are an angel," she tells me as she pulls out two pairs of tiny shoes that she saw in the store.

"Nah," I say nonchalantly as I look away. "Well, maybe..."

Hannah suppresses a smile, sucking her peach-colored lips into her mouth. "This is really sweet. I can't believe you went back and got me these."

"I could tell it bothered you," I tell her, leaning over to kiss her on the lips.

I feel her smile against my mouth. "And you have a right to be bothered, you know? These are your babies, and if you want to buy them a silly pair of shoes they can only wear for one week, you do that. I want you to have so much fun in motherhood. You are safe to buy whatever silly thing makes this fun for you. I'm here to catch us."

"Thanks, Chris. I appreciate that." She pulls her knees into her chest and balances the box on her thighs.

"I know the reason it bothered you is more than just some sort of claim to motherhood. I know that it was hard for you growing up and it's probably really difficult to have anyone, but especially one of your parents, tell you how to handle your finances."

Her eyes snap up toward me.

"Yeah, actually. You're pretty perceptive, Chris, for…you know…a gym bro." She looks around before whispering 'gym bro.'

I laugh out loud, a barking laugh that catches us both off guard.

"Wow, so your true feelings come out. Well, do you know why I understand family relationships like that and how they catch up to you so well?"

She shakes her head, nervously fitting her fingers into the baby shoes.

"When I was a little boy, my dad was arrested for committing tax fraud. It was not a small thing. It was a really big deal, what he did, and he went away for a really long time. I didn't see my dad out of prison until I was a teenager and by then our relationship was obviously really different. My mother had married someone else and, you know, it was just not the way life had been before. And so that's sort of ruled my life, along with the betrayal by Julie.

"So. You told me that someone was stealing from my business and rather than face the problem head on, I was afraid that I would get in trouble, so I buried my head in the sand. I just want you to know that I know that how we're raised colors how we do this whole adult and parenthood thing, and that's okay. I'll be here for your stuff if you'll be here for mine."

"Of course I'll be here for your stuff, Chris. Oh, my God. I had no idea that happened to you."

She reaches for my hand, dropping her legs into a criss-cross position and leaning over the baby shoes to pull it into her lap. She caresses the back of my hand with her thumb.

"Thank you for sharing. And don't worry, you won't be in trouble. I can easily prove that Sarah did this and we'll get it all taken care of. Don't worry. Tomorrow, we'll look into starting that process and in expanding the gym business. I don't want you to be afraid of any of that. I've got you."

I nod at her and hold back the tears rising into my throat.

"I know. Will you look under the paper in the box?"

She looks at me quizzically, her lips pouted adorably and her eyebrows knitted together, before lifting up the tissue paper that lined the box with the baby shoes.

Inside are the keys to my building and my apartment.

She looks up at me, her hand in the air clutching the tissue paper. "Wait. What is…?"

"So you don't have to buzz in anymore. Maybe work could be work and here could be home? What do you think?"

I wipe my sweaty palms off on my shorts, but they're sweat wicking so it doesn't work well. I watch her face to try and figure out what her response will be, but her face looks completely blank.

"Are you doing this because I'm pregnant? You really don't have to. I'm fine just, you know, keeping things the way they are."

"Hannah, remember what we talked about last night? Things are going to change. They just are. You don't have to move in with me if you don't want to, but I don't want to hear any more about keeping things the way they are. It's impossible."

She nods. "Big changes can be good," she whispers, the key in her palm.

"That's right. In fact, I'd go a step further and say they're always good even if sometimes the good isn't always obvious. Do you want to live with me? That's what I care about. I don't care about what you think should happen or what you think I'm thinking. I'm asking if you to live with me. Do you want to?"

Hannah's smile spreads slowly across her face, each tooth revealing itself like a dancer behind a curtain. She jumps over the shoes and the box and wraps her arms around my neck to hug me tightly.

"Yes, I want to, are you kidding? Chris, thank you, thank you." She mumbles into my throat, "I love you."

I smile against her head, then put my hands on her shoulders and push her back a little so that I can look into her eyes. "Now, listen, there's still one more thing we have to do."

She deflates and sighs. "I know. We have to tell Tyler."

I smile at her and jiggle her shoulders. "Yep. But we got this. And besides, babies have a way of uniting people, right? No way he can be unhappy knowing he's going to be an uncle."

She laughs. "Uncle Tyler. Oh, that's weird."

"It really is. Uncle Tyler and Lucy Noodle. Not much weirder than this life we've made." I kiss her. "Do you want to go outside and use your key to come back in?"

"Yes!" She bounces up and down a little before standing and leaves, giggling almost hysterically, her cheeks rosy. She closes the door behind her and I can hear her footsteps disappearing down the hall toward the elevator.

I look over at Lucy, who's laying on the ground near the couch.

I raise my eyebrows at her and she raises her head before standing and walking my way

"You wanna come live with me again?" I ask her, kissing the soft fur of the top of her head.

# Chapter Thirty Nine
## Hannah

Chris takes me back to my office to fill suitcases full of my clothes and things, of which I admittedly don't have much.

He seems surprised that all of my things can barely fill up his trunk and backseats. "This is really it?" he asks as he closes the trunk on it.

"Yep, I mean, I got rid of a lot of stuff when I moved in here. I knew I wouldn't have much space."

"Well, I guess we won't have any arguments about decor," he jokes, leaning against the car with his arms crossed. His bulging biceps gleam with the sweat on them.

I shiver a little and grapple at his arm. "Well, I don't know, now that I've got room I can finally indulge the desire I've been harboring for a singing bass collection."

Chris rolls his blue eyes at me and then fixes them on my eyes. When he looks in my eyes with that kind of intensity, I lose my train of thought as my mind swirls with images of him holding me close to him and pumping inside me, his grunts in my ear. "Okay, one argument."

"Wait, you don't like that idea? I saw a special edition one with a cowboy hat, though."

"Get in the car, Hannah."

"It had a little disco ball."

"I'm done with this." He lifts me up into his arms at his side like an oversized bag and walks me over to the passenger side. He squats and sets me onto the seat. "Let's go."

He closes the door on me while I laugh from behind the window.

We spend much of the evening setting up what we bought while we were out, though the cribs prove to be worthy adversaries. We end up sweaty on the ground with pieces of it surrounding us. It's a good thing we have several months to get them put together.

I lay back on my back and splay out, spreading my legs and arms like a starfish. I sigh deeply at the sensation of the cooling wood floor on my skin. "I don't think I can move even an inch."

Chris puts his tools down and crawls over me on his hands and knees. He lays down a little so that he's on his elbows and his forehead is against mine.

"You can't move?" He smirks at me, his sideways smile indenting his cheek in a little.

"Nope, not even an inch," I tell him, closing my eyes and dropping my head back on the floor.

"So if I do this," he kisses my lips, and I don't kiss back, smiling slightly, "Oh, wow, you really are frozen. Hm. Well, what about this?"

From on top of me, he sinks his hand into my waist, running his fingers over my hip.

I giggle a little as his fingers tickle me, but I don't respond to his touch, thinking hard about keeping my hands and legs still. I hold my breath to keep myself from wrapping my legs and arms around him and pulling him down on top of me. "I can't move, honest."

"Oh, no, I'm sorry to hear that." His hand slides up my shirt and his fingertips gently prod at the wiring of my bra. He slips his fingertips underneath it, but he doesn't go any farther, only gently touching my skin. He tugs at the collar of my shirt and kisses my chest. "Do you think true love's kiss could bring you back?"

"Maybe, you might as well try," I tell him breathlessly as I feel blood rushing to my skin and warming me all over.

Chris lowers his lips to mine and slips his tongue inside my mouth. When his hand finds the warm spot between my legs, I can't hold it in anymore. I sigh against his kiss and wrap my arms around his neck, fitting his head against the crooks of my elbows. His other hand weaves into my hair and tugs at it. I moan in response. Satisfied, he pulls back, kisses my lips gently, and pressed up onto his hands to get up.

"No, no, no, you're not getting away that easily," I tell him, pulling him back down.

He laughs and wraps his arms behind my back so he can roll over onto his back and pull me on top of him.

As soon as I'm on top of him, his phone rings, and I pick it up for him. He reaches for it, and I tug it back. "Oh, you want to answer a call right now?"

"Well, I was thinking about it." He leans up on his elbows so that he's half sitting up as I straddle him. "Should I not?"

"If you want to, go ahead." He reaches for his phone, and I pull it back away from him.

"Wow, you were not supposed to really want to."

The phone rings over and over in my hand, and Chris looks at it pointedly. "So wait, I'm not supposed to want to answer my phone?"

"Not when I'm straddling you! Aren't you supposed to be distracted?" I grind a little against his pelvis, and he laughs before collapsing back onto the floor.

Without looking, I answer his phone. "Hello?"

My brother's voice comes through the speaker. "Hannah? Is that you?"

"Uh...yes." I slide down onto the floor off of Chris's body as though he can see me.

"What are you doing answering Chris' phone?"

# Chapter Forty
## Christopher

"Who is it?" I whisper, seeing the look on Hannah's face as she slides off my lap and onto the floor.

She sticks up her index finger to shush me, shaking her head wildly.

"He's in the bathroom. I saw it was you so I answered! We're working on his finances, you know, boring stuff. What are you doing? Do you want to talk to him?"

Her words spill out of her like word vomit, and I realize that it's Tyler calling me like he promised he would.

I check the face of my watch and see that it's already been hours since Hannah and I starting setting up.

It's nearly 8 PM. I hold my hand out to gesture for Hannah to return my phone and she sheepishly sets it in my palm before walking out of the room. "Hey, dude, what's up?"

"I was just calling to see if you still wanted to hang out. What are you and Hannah doing together so late? She works almost as much as I do, and I'm a surgeon."

He chuckles, not stopping to hear my answer. "Anyway, I just finished up, I'm getting my stuff together now."

I stand up from my position on my back and stand in the middle of the empty room, littered with pieces of the crib around me. I consider how Hannah would feel. I can feel her anxiety emanating from the other room.

We said we had to tell him. We should rip off the band-aid. It'll only be harder the longer we wait. "Okay, yeah, I'd like that."

"Where do you want to go?"

"Ummm," I look around the room. "Do you want to come to my place actually?

"Sure, I just need a drink."

"I get it. Just come on over and we'll hang out for a bit."

"Okay, yeah, I'll get us a six pack."

We hang up, and I find Hannah in the other room, hugging Lucy and looking at me anxiously from the floor, her chin wobbling.

"So, Tyler's coming here?"

"He is, yeah," I tell her, crossing the room to pet Lucy alongside her, my hand chasing hers like a bird that wants to mate.

"It'll be okay," I tell her, pulling her head against my leg and patting it.

"I know, I'm just trying to think about how we should tell him." She presses her nose into Lucy's fur and inhales.

"Are you smelling the dog?"

"It's calming! She smells good. Don't judge me, alright? I can't take it." Hannah rolls her head over to press her cheek against Lucy.

Lucy stands and takes it, but her brown eyes look up at me with a tinge of concern.

"Look at her eyes, Hannah Banana, she looks so nervous about this."

"Shhh, get out of here, Judgy."

I sit on the ground next to her. "Listen, we don't really have to tell him anything. I think he's probably going to put it together when he comes over and sees that you're here at night and we have a room with a crib in it. Don't you think?"

She shrugs. "Well, maybe he'll think that I'm helping you negotiate your finances because you got someone else pregnant."

I laugh a little, pulling Lucy closer to me. "Well, let's not tell him that, okay? We don't need to dig the hole any deeper than it already is."

She nods quietly, stands up, and walks back into the nursery to continue setting up the cribs.

We work on the first crib together for the next hour, eventually making enough headway that it really starts to look like something.

I try not to think about the fact that we have another unopened box with another crib in it sitting in the corner until Hannah groans, "Chris! We have a whole other crib to set up!"

Laughing out loud, I say, "Well, maybe we'll get lucky and one of the twins will eat the other."

"Chris, that isn't funny," she reprimands me, but I watch her turn around to hide her smile from me.

"I'm just saying, maybe we shouldn't set this one up until we know for sure one isn't hungry. We could return it later."

"Stop!" She swats me in the arm, her smile wide, showing me her wide white smile that I always find so adorable.

Her smile drops a bit when there's a knock at the front door, and she steels herself for Tyler to enter, pulling back her shoulders and sucking in a breath.

"You ready?"

"Ready."

"Let's do this." I hold out my hand for her to take. She slips her palm against mine and her fingers between mine. We pull back our shoulders, breathe out slowly, and I lead her to the front door.

When I pull it open, Tyler holds up a six pack excitedly, a smile across his freckled face.

"You ready?" he asks me with all the frat boy energy he had back in college. His face drops after a moment of processing when he realizes Hannah's here, and his eyes flick downward to our interlocked hands. "What's…oh, no. Hell no."

Tyler drops the six pack back down to his side, his shoulder bouncing with the force.

He pushes the door open to let himself in further and drops the six pack on the floor where one of the cans bursts open, spraying the sticky drink all across the floor. His fingers clutch the front of my shirt as his face slowly turns redder and redder.

"Wait, Tyler, let's talk about this," I tell him calmly, looking directly into his green eyes, the exact color of Hannah's eyes, passed down from their mother.

I can't see much affection for me in them right now, though; they have a glassy tinge to them, and his pupils are flat black like the bottom of a hole.

His response is to pull me even closer until we're only inches apart. Hannah is still holding my hand, her sweat sticking our palms together. "Hannah, let go of him," Tyler growls.

Hannah shakes her head but doesn't say anything.

"Chris, be a man and step outside the house with me. Don't make my little sister watch you get your face smashed in."

"Come on, dude, you're not gonna beat me up. First of all, I'm your best friend and you love me."

I smile and try to move a bit, but he's holding me so closely that I can barely move and he is definitely NOT smiling.

"Second, you're an adult and a surgeon. You need your hands."

I take a chance on joking with him and reach down to clasp our hands together. I swear I can see a small smile flash across his face before he shakes his head at me and pushes me away from him.

As I stumble backward and Hannah catches me, Tyler turns and walks back down the hall toward the elevator. He hits the button and I call out to him, "Come on, man, don't leave. It's not what you're thinking. We love you, dude, and we want to talk."

Just as he enters the elevator, Hannah yelps in a shrill, panicked voice, "Tyler, I'm pregnant!"

I try to interpret Tyler's emotions from his expression, but his face is devoid of discernible emotion.

# Chapter Forty One
## Hannah

I watch the scene like a horror movie as the doors close on Tyler then reopen instantly.

He steps out of the elevator and walks down the hall back into Chris' apartment. He closes the door behind him and stares at the both of us for a moment, leaning against it.

Finally, he breaks the silence with one word: "What?"

I stifle a giggle, and Tyler shoots me a look that could kill.

I know it isn't actually funny in a "ha-ha" kind of way, but I want to laugh in that nervous way you find yourself in when you start laughing at a funeral or during an exam, the laughter coming without your permission.

"I'm pregnant," I repeat, relieved to have the words out there.

They're easier to say the second time. I want to say it a third time and again and again just to feel the slow leaking of anxiety.

"I'm pregnant," I say again, and Chris strokes my arm from behind me, sensing the manic energy emanating from me.

Tyler notices the motion, his eyes zipping to Chris' hand on my arm. He spreads his hands out like someone stopping a fight.

"I'm sorry, what the fuck am I seeing?" He cranes his neck slightly to look in my eyes.

"Hannah, what is going on?"

When I avoid his eyes, he puts his hands on his knees like the catcher in a baseball game, lowering himself to look at me.

"We never expected this to happen. But it has and we want you to be happy for us, too."

He stands up and puts his hands on top of his head and turns away from the two of us so that he faces the door.

I wonder if he's considering making a run for it. I wonder if he's thinking about leaving and coming back, that maybe he'll come back to a different universe or wake up from a nightmare.

He turns back to us and says simply, "This is crazy. I can't even wrap my head around this."

"I know, I know. We would have told you eventually. We just...have gotten closer. When we were working together, we realized we were starting to have feelings for one another."

I chew on my bottom lip, watching the myriad of emotions cycle on his face.

"This doesn't make sense," he says, his mouth stuck open.

"I don't know what else to say."

"Say this is a joke! Please." Tyler picks up one of the unbroken cans of beer and opens it, spraying droplets about a half of a foot before sitting down on Chris' couch. He drinks while staring off into the distance.

"Wait." He turns to look at Chris. "Was Samantha real? Or was that about Hannah?"

"That was about Hannah," Chris admits, walking over and sitting next to Tyler.

"Dude, I gave you advice about my sister! That's messed up."

Quietly, Chris says, "You're my best friend, Tyler. I needed advice, but I wasn't ready to tell you that it was Hannah I cared about."

"Then you weren't ready for my advice! God, so all this time that I've been wondering where you've been, you've been with my sister?"

"I didn't know you were wondering where I've been. You could have asked me to hang out. You could have asked me what was going on."

"And we could have talked about Samantha? This is…you're sick, man. You're a decade older than she is. You used to come to my house on breaks from college, and she was in third grade. You knew her when she was like eight years old."

Chris lays his head down on the back of the couch. "It's not like I was attracted to her then, Tyler, Jesus. The two don't correlate."

"So you don't think that's weird at all?"

Tyler turns to look over at me, his mouth still open. "And you don't think that's weird, either?"

"Tyler, the fact that we were acquainted through you when I was in third grade is not relevant to this conversation or this situation." I realize I am feeling very protective of the feelings Chris and I now share.

"That was a long time ago. I'm not eight anymore, and he's not 22 anymore. He's not some kind of pedophile. He's attracted to an adult woman, not a child. Not to mention that we happen to love each other."

Tyler sits up and leans forward, resting his elbows on his knees. "Hannah, this man," he points at Chris, "is a certified player. He has been through a woman a week for years now."

"That was only after Julie," Chris mumbles, not putting up much of a fight, his voice quiet.

Tyler shoots daggers at him with his eyes.

"Julie dumped you five years ago. That hasn't been a valid excuse for about four years." He looks back at me. "You are making a mistake with him, Hanny."

"And just what part of this is the mistake? The baby or Chris?" I ask with venom in my voice.

"All of it, Hannah! What the fuck? You just got this business started. Why would you do this?"

"Do what?"

"Make a baby with him!"

He points at Chris and shakes his arm. His face is all twisted up, sweat beading up around his hairline. His freckles are popping out amidst his red face. Combined with his pointing, he looks like he's shaming the town dunce.

"You're being mean, Tyler. I need you to stop this now. I need you to think about the fact that you care a great deal about us both." I tell him, crossing my arms.

"I'd rather you think I was mean now than hold in my thoughts and feelings and watch you do something you'll regret. You'll thank me later, Hannah, I mean it."

He slurps his drink noisily, and I feel annoyance and disgust coursing through me watching him enjoy a beverage on the couch of the man he's demeaning.

"If Chris such an awful person, someone so bad that you can't trust him with your own sister, then why is he your best friend?" I ask, blood rushing to my cheeks as my voice rises.

Tyler opens his mouth, and I hold up my palm.

"Now, I want the next words out of your mouth to be an answer to that question and not another insult. I want you to seriously tell me about why you're running around town with someone who is supposedly your best friend, but is evidently someone you don't respect or trust around women."

Tyler sits back and doesn't say anything. "Come on, then, answer me."

"Just because someone is your best friend doesn't necessarily mean you think he's father material. Chris didn't grow up with a father. How do you expect him to be one?"

"That's cold," Chris says quietly at the ground, his eyes not moving up to look at either of us.

"Get out, Tyler," I say much more softly than I thought myself capable of.

"What?"

"You're my big brother, and I've always deferred to you, but if you think that gives you the right to display some sort of ownership over me, then I don't want you here. You aren't being a good brother at the moment, and you certainly aren't being a good friend. Look at what you've done to Chris!"

I point at Chris, who is clearing fighting back tears.

"Just go home, Tyler. You had your chance to share our happiness, and since you don't seem to want to do that, then we don't need – or want – you here."

Tucking his tongue into his cheek, Tyler looks back and forth between the two of us, his eyes wide but his jaw set.

He's got a stubborn look in his eye. "Fine."

He stands to leave and pulls the door open so hard he sends it flying into the opposite wall as he exits.

From the hallway he calls out, "I'm going to let Mom know what a mistake you are making here, Hannah!"

"She already knows!" I call back, closing the door and locking it behind him. I turn around and sigh.

"Well..."

"That went well!" Chris says jokingly, wiping tears from his eyes.

I walk over to him and get down on my knees so that I can look in his eyes. I wipe the tears away with my thumbs and kiss him deeply.

"He'll come around. You know he will."

"And if he doesn't?"

I shrug, even as the question kills me.

"I know who you are. More importantly, you know who you are." I tap his chest, and he grabs hold of my finger. He kisses softly, like the gentle brush of a butterfly wing.

"What if he's right?"

"About which part?"

I raise an eyebrow, wondering if he means that Tyler might be right that he's a player. I'm not sure I'd know how to react to that, so I reserve judgment.

"That I'm not father material. He's right that I've never really had a healthy father figure. My mom remarried a guy when I was a little older, but by then I was pretty fully..." he trails off before adding, "cooked."

"Cooked?" I laugh.

"I don't know, I'm just thinking out loud," he sighs, burrowing his face into his hands again.

I peel his fingers away from his face.

"I don't think there's only one way to be a good dad, Chris," I whisper. "You didn't have someone else showing you the ropes, so you'll have to be your own version of a good dad. We'll figure it out as we go along, just like everyone else does. You'll be the father you would have wanted to have. You taught me that when you taught me how to make a pancake."

Chris laughs. "Wow, the bar is low."

"No," I assure him, standing up and holding out my hand, "It's very, very high."

# Chapter Forty Two
## Christopher

We start the next day off with a lazy breakfast. Hannah sips on a smoothie and nibbles at a homemade sweet potato hash brown patty while surveying my work as I put together the second crib.

I glance over at her as she leans against the wall and watches my biceps as I screw in the wooden rods that surround the crib. I flex my arm for her, and the blood rises in her chest as she realizes I've caught her.

She looks up at me, and I wink at her. "You like what you see?"

She rolls her eyes. "Well, I was enjoying the art before it talked to me."

"Okay, noted, the art doesn't talk." I mimic sealing my lips with a key and throwing it.

"That's better," she tells me, pushing herself off the wall.

"Hey, baby, when you're ready you meet me at the office, okay?" She walks over to me and pecks my lips.

"Okay, I might get in a run after I finish building this."

"Good, I'm glad. I'll see you soon then. Thank you for putting this together for me."

I look up at her from the floor. "Of course, Hannah Banana. It was easy. I'll put anything together for your little…plantains."

I flash her a genuine smile, pleased with my joke, before returning to working on the crib. I'm so close, and I want to be the first person to see it set up.

I want to stand in the middle of the empty room and turn off the lights and see how it would feel to rescue a crying baby at night.

"What's that serious face?" Hannah asks me, smoothing my hair down and wiping curls out of my eyes and off my forehead.

"Oh, nothing." I smile at her and pull her face down close to mine with my hands cupping her jaw. I kiss the crests of her cheeks.

"Go on, I'll see you at your office later."

"My office," she sighs happily, "I get to leave my place and go to my office. How fancy."

I toss my head back and laugh. "I don't know if we can trust you as the arbiter of fancy considering you thought baking carrots was fancy."

"Wow, my boyfriend's mean!" Hannah says in a jokingly whiny voice, looking down at Lucy, who wags her tail excitedly, looking up at her with adoration.

Hannah blows me a kiss and leaves out the front door with Lucy at her side and a hash brown patty between her teeth. She is the picture of a young, busy mom.

I hear her outside the door as she pulls out her key ring to lock the front door.

Butterflies flutter in my chest at the realization that she's going to use her new keys not because she needs to since I am home, but because she wants to have the feeling of ownership, of living here, of it being her home.

I listen with tender affection as she inserts the key and turns the lock.

As her footsteps fade down the hall, I get up quickly and hurry to the door to unlock it and open it.

With large strides, I rush toward her and pick her up around the waist to kiss her, feeling her melt backwards, her mouth softening against mine.

I set her back down, and she asks, "What was that for?"

"Nothing special." I shrug.

I know today's the day that Hannah wants me to think about what I want out of an expansion for the gym.

Truth be told, I'm not sure. I always thought I wanted to expand to another country, but with the addition of two little ones, it seems not like a dashed dream but just impractical at the moment.

In fact, lately, I've been thinking more and more about the man at the farmer's market, with his off-kilter mustache and kind eyes.

At one point, he'd talked about his life off in rural California, and while that's not exactly what I want, I could imagine something like a waterfront gym, a little town where I could learn to sail and fish and come home smelling salty.

Maybe that's too big a dream for all of us right now. There's still a lot to do here.

But it's a nice thought.

It would be even nicer if I could get Tyler on board, I think to myself as I put together the stroller and the car seat that we bought with Mrs. Jackson.

If I could get Tyler to look at me with a genuine smile and tell me that he likes the idea of me moving to a countryside town with his sister, that's all I would need to pull the trigger on the idea.

Not for the first time, I look over at my phone on the ground and consider calling him again, even though Hannah told me he's the one who should apologize to me. I'm just not sure that's entirely true. The situation is not exactly black and white.

I start my run with the words thumping in my ear: "Strength and growth come from continuous effort."

The rest of the speaker's words melt into the background as I consider that echoing sentiment. It rattles around in my mind while I run.

I find that this happens a lot when I run, that I start off trying to focus on the meditations but end up actually meditating instead, completely unable to keep my mind on the words as my eyes move back and forth between my feet as they slap the pavement.

Before I know it, I've reached the gym, my feet taking me there before I even registered my destination. I stand on the sidewalk in front, hands on my hips, and look up at the sign that says CHOICE in neon lettering.

I named my business CHOICE because the amount of work you put into exercise is your own personal choice. Whether or not someone decides to come to my gym is their choice. How much they exercise and train and how they choose to look – it's all their individual choice.

I kick a rock and consider all the choices that now lay in front of me, the path laid out that I've built brick by brick with my own freewill.

My phone rings, and I answer hesitantly. "Hello? Sarah?"

# Chapter Forty Three
## Hannah

Even though Chris is still in the house, I pull out my key ring and relish locking the door as I leave. A little tingle rushes through my body at the act. It feels almost intimate and I'm grateful that Chris seemed to understand my need to do that.

Lucy and I hop into the car together, and I roll down the car window for her as I drive toward the office.

Lucy's tongue whips in the wind as if it isn't a part of her, her chin balancing against the glass. I reach over with my right hand and pet her back while she relaxes, feeling the hot sun on her black fur.

It's not the first time I realize that I'm having a moment that I have had every day for quite some time but which will likely soon be a thing of the past.

Once there are two car seats in the back and Chris next to me, Lucy won't get to ride in the car with me as often. Even if she does, it likely won't be just me and Lucy on our own very often after the babies arrive.

The realization hits me hard, and tears fill my eyes as I continue to drag my hand down her back, feeling the knobs of her spine under her thick blanket of short hairs.

When we arrive at the office, Lucy rushes to the front door of the office, panting excitedly. She jumps up at it, her front feet scraping at the glass and her ears bouncing with her every move.

"Lucy, little thing, did you miss this place?"

Again, tears spring to my eyes as an awareness sinks in that I've deprived her of the home she's now known for a while.

Just because I know Chris' space is bigger doesn't mean she understands that it's better for us to be there.

These babies are making you emotional, I laugh to myself, rubbing her ears between my fingers. I pull them back into an ear ponytail, which used to make me laugh but now only makes me feel tender feelings for her.

"You are so beautiful, Lucy, you know that?" I squat down so that I'm eye level with her and touch my nose to her wet nose, looking into her black eyes, seeing the sun glint specks of orange in them. I feel emotional over her short black eyelashes and her gentle expression.

I open the door and let her bounce around, sniffing the walls and floors and furniture. I sit down at my computer and open up the financial information that I already have on Chris' gym.

I highlight the transactions that look shady and know that I'll eventually get the more detailed spreadsheet from Chris.

Finally, I open up a map of California and look up what cities have the most gyms in the state.

I also check which cities in the country have the most gyms and which locations have the most active members.

I hold my fingertip between my teeth, nibbling on my nail, before leaning forward and replacing it with the back of my pen.

I'm inclined to say that what makes Chris so successful is Chris, but I know that there's more that goes into it than that.

It's hard to be impartial, though. Chris is successful because he's kind, thoughtful, ambitious, friendly, and knowledgeable, true, but Chris is also successful because of his location and his design choices and the employees he hires.

Chris is successful because of all of the choices, both big and small, that he makes for his business.

I'm not in marketing. He'll have to make those choices himself. All I can help him with is making sure he does it all by the book.

I look into the differences between doing his taxes for a business in a few other possible countries and doing his taxes for a business in another state and open up a new document to annotate and highlight the differences between those options.

My phone buzzes and I see the screen flash with Chris' name, so I swipe on it and answer as I read my emails and answer the people whose questions are simple. "Hey, are you on your way?"

"I was just thinking – what if instead of punishing Sarah, we let her work off her debt by working for me for free?"

My head spins at the suggestion. "Yeah, so as your CPA, I would have to advise against that."

"Why?"

"Well, for one, and I'm not a lawyer, but it seems like that could be considered blackmail or extortion or something, right?"

"Then let's ask a lawyer."

I laugh dryly. "Chris, no lawyer is going to tell you hire someone who stole hundreds of thousands of dollars from you and just pay them less this time. She owes you a couple of luxury cars worth of money. Let's just let the authorities take care of it. Okay? Seriously."

"Well, here's what I'm thinking. We'll send her to open the new location. We won't put her in charge of the finances again, of course, she lost that right. But we'll put her in charge of the new location's opening, and we just don't give her a salary."

"The salary that would have been, what, $50,000? It's just not enough to be worth it, Chris," I tell him, utterly confused about his insistence that he do this ridiculous thing.

Quietly, he mutters, "She called me, Hannah. She begged me to do this, said she was sorry about what she'd done and couldn't take the guilt of it."

I feel bile rise in my throat at the idea of Sarah working for him again, getting another chance to betray him and hurt him. I just want him to focus on people that won't let him down and things that fulfill him.

"And you told her yes?"

"I told her I would think about it and talk to you, but I wanted to say yes," he corrects me, his voice an embarrassed murmur.

"Well, you can't, Chris. I say that as your CPA, your girlfriend, and the mother of your children. You cannot let this woman do this to you. Why would you even want to?"

I put my phone on speaker and look for what snacks are left in the kitchen. I find a string cheese and peel open the plastic as Chris mans the silence expertly, breathing lightly into the phone.

"Because. I don't know. It just seems like there's no room for bitterness in this new life."

I laugh. "Then forgive her. Don't put her in the driver's seat. Listen, let me tell you what I think is happening. You have a lot of relationships that are tenuous right now, and it's got you thinking of the past. But instead of facing the person that you really need to face, you're forgiving the person who's easier to forgive."

"Who's the person I really need to face then?"

I can't believe he really needs me to say it, but his denial is so thick that I'm not sure he can honestly see it for himself. The name comes out like a heavy sigh: "Julie."

# Chapter Forty Four
## Christopher

I walk through the farmer's market by myself while I try to clear my head.

Even if Hannah is right, I'm not sure I have it in me to face that particular fear. So, I guess by her logic, that means she is right.

I try to imagine calling Julie and telling her how she hurt me, how she affected my relationships and ruined my ability to trust, but when I do I picture her doing that thing where she holds back a superior smile and I want to gag.

A part of me feels like admitting the pain to her would be a failure on my part; that it would be handing her the win and telling her that she got the better of me.

There's that bitterness that Hannah was talking about.

I stop at the booth of the young farmer, and a relieved smile breaks out across his face. "Hey, there! So, are you a papa?"

I throw back my head and laugh. "Oh, man." I lean against his booth, looking at his vegetables and fruits with all the focus of a professional chef. "I am. Well, at least I am going to be, anyway," I admit, looking up at him from underneath my eyebrows.

He slaps his upper thigh. "Hot dog! I knew it."

"Oh, yeah, and get this." I press my fingers and thumbs together in a gesture to show that I'm about to drop a bomb.

"Twins."

His eyes widen, the blue-gray shining as he digests the words. "Oh, aren't you a lucky man?"

"I didn't feel so lucky at first, but truthfully it's growing on me."

"The truth has a way of doing that, doesn't it?"

"Oh, yeah. I'll take a bunch of strawberries, and hey – if your wife hadn't gotten a job out here, do you think you would have stayed in Pennsylvania forever?" I ask him, handing him a crisp $20 bill.

"Maine," he says without even a thought as he hands me my change.

I shake my head at him, jiggling my palm back at him so that he takes it back. "Maine, huh? Why Maine?"

"Oh, the most beautiful state in the country."

"Really?"

"Oh yes, I really believe that. Not a question in my mind about it. And of course, the freshest seafood you've ever had in your life."

He presses his palms together in silent prayer as if recalling both the lobster and God together simultaneously.

"Maine. Okay, then. Hey, thank you for everything. Although I'm not completely sure you didn't manifest that pregnancy."

He laughs out loud, stroking his beard with his hand, tugging on it like a wizard. He hands me the cartons of strawberries. "I threw a couple of extras in there for you."

Wordlessly, I lift up the cartons in a sign of gratitude and walk back toward my car, having decided what I need to do next and where I need to do it.

I swing the bag of strawberries at my side, thinking of dipping them in chocolate and feeding them one by one to Hannah while I tell her all the ways I've solved every little problem we've ever had and she glows like a woman treated right, her freckles golden and her eyes sparkling.

I eat one and it's tart, nearly sour. I eat another and it's sweet and easy, perfectly ripe.

I pull out my phone as I chew on the strawberry, letting the juice fill my mouth with its sweetness.

"Hi, Chris," Sarah answers. "Do you have good news for me?"

I press my tongue into the bottom cheek of my mouth. "No, Sarah, I don't."

I expected to feel bad, guilty even, telling her that I couldn't give her her her job back. Instead, I feel a sense of calm knowing that this is what's best for everyone, even if it hurts right now.

"Ah," she whispers from the other line.

I spit out the top of my strawberry, watching the fuzzy green sail through the air in an arc.

"Sarah, I think I was tempted to have you come back given our long history and the fact that you seemed truly remorseful. But, having thought it through, there's really nothing you could do at this point to make me trust you again. And there's just no way around that. I can't have you working for me if I can't trust you. I hope you can see that."

"You can trust me, Chris. I want to make it up to you." Her voice is begging, something I haven't heard from her in all the years she's worked with me. She's always been so calm and collected. It hurts that she hid her real self from me all this time, only to show some vulnerability when trying to manipulate me.

"Well, you can't make it up to me, Sarah. Instead, I suggest you think about how you plan to make restitution. I won't put my business on the line again, so we won't be having any further conversations. Rest assured, though, you'll be hearing from both my lawyer and law enforcement."

I hang up, breathing a sigh of relief so hard it sucks the air out of my lungs.

I squeeze the grass under my hands and feel the blades tickle between my fingers. I turn my face to the sky and let the sun shine on my eyelids for just a moment before looking for Julie's number in my phone.

I sift through my call history, looking for the number she called me from the other day.

I count myself lucky that I don't have her number in my phone and that it's a search through a slog of numbers instead; that it's a number that doesn't even stand out.

There was a time that knowing I have Julie's number in my phone would have given me heart palpitations, would have been something I thought about every minute of every hour.

I can see myself checking the log over and over and considering touching it, letting it ring with my breath caught, wondering if she'd pick up.

I finally find it and begin to touch the number, so that I can do what Hannah says I need to do and call her, tell her how she's damaged me, how she irreparably changed the course of my life, but my finger hovers over the number for a moment.

Instead, I opt to block it and delete it out of my received call number list. Now, she can't call me, and I can't call her. We are separated by logistics only, though, and if I ever run into her, I'll tell her exactly what I mean by blocking her:

I don't need that closure from her. I never did.

At some point, it might have felt like it, but I realize now that that was a dream of a much younger man.

There is no such thing as closure with people who hurt you purposefully, and I'm done thinking the same person who broke me can put me back together.

The Julie I thought I knew didn't ever exist. I don't think I ever truly knew her, not really.

There's only Hannah.

Just a few weeks ago, it would have been hard to imagine my life's issues being resolved in an afternoon, but now I'm feeling like a man with only answers in front of him; answers that light the way toward the future I've always wanted, whether I understood what that future would look like or not.

As I drive down the busy LA streets, I make my final call of the afternoon, and I make it a good one.

I call Hannah and hear her voice, syrupy but somehow serious, too. If some women have honey voices, Hannah's is biscotti dipped in chocolate.

"Hey, Baby," she says to me, and I can hear her typing in the background, a quick succession of clicks that seems impossibly fast. Myself, I've only ever been able to type with the hunt and peck method.

"Hi there, Hannah Banana." Her name comes out like a sigh or the tail end of a song lyric. "I thought about what you said. I've realized that you were right, so I called Sarah and told her it isn't happening."

"Oh, I'm so proud of you. Wow, and you did it so quickly."

"That's the only thing I do quickly."

She laughs a tinkly little laugh at my joke and says, "Okay, Tiger, well, I'm working on something, so I'm going to let you go, huh?"

"Fine, but listen, I decided on a location for the new gym. Maine."

"Maine, huh? Interesting. Why?"

"I got word that it's the most beautiful state in the country. I'd like a slice of that. If we have a gym there, I'd get to see it on occasion. We could eat lobster rolls, go sailing. Doesn't that sound nice?" I ask her as I pull into the parking lot of the store and step out, closing the car door behind me.

"Kind of the opposite of California, isn't it? Cold, dark Maine?"

"Sure, but variety is the spice of life, isn't it? That's what they say. Can't you just see Lucy in a little sweater, holding a stick under the snow?"

I open up the door of the store and the bell rings above my head. I look up at it and smile at the woman behind the glass case.

She smiles back, and I point at the phone in my hand. She nods at me and waves her hand, granting me permission to continue my conversation. The store is otherwise empty, and I'm not bothering anyone.

"That would be really cute," Hanna acquiesces. "Do you want to wear a little sweater?" I hear her ask Lucy.

I can imagine Lucy wagging her tail at that, looking with a tilted head the way she does that makes her look like she really understands.

"Okay, I've taken two seconds to imagine Lucy in a little sweater, and I'm on board."

I laugh out loud, catching the smiling gaze of the saleslady. "I'll keep that trick in mind next time I want something.

Get...Hannah...to....imagine....Lucy....doing it. Okay, got it." I say it like I'm writing it down for later use.

"When will you be here? What are you doing, anyway?"

"I'll be there soon, just got one more errand to run, okay?"

"Sure, don't be long, though."

"In more ways than one," I tease, and she laughs in a way that tells me she's rolling her eyes.

We hang up, and I walk over to the woman behind the glass case. Her severe brown bob shines under the hanging light that's positioned directly over her, throwing a glare across her lenses.

"So, tell me about the lucky lady," she says warmly, her brown eyes on me as I kneel on one knee to look closer at the different engagement rings.

"Hannah," I tell her, looking up and smiling, my hands pressed against the glass, transferring fingerprints to it.

"She has changed everything about my life. I can't wait to marry her."

# Chapter Forty Five
## Hannah

The fluorescent lights above me blur as the gurney rolls down the sterile hospital corridor as I'm wheeled in for the procedure to remove my IUD.

My heart pounds like a drum in my chest, each beat a reminder of the two little lives growing inside me.

I grip Chris's hand, his calloused fingers strong and steady, a contrast to the whirlwind of emotions churning within me.

"You're going to be okay," he whispers, his voice a soothing balm in the unfriendly, cold-smelling hospital. I glance up at him, his rugged face etched with worry, his usual confidence replaced by a vulnerability that mirrors my own.

"I know," I manage to say, though my voice wavers. "It's just… the twins, Chris. What if something goes wrong?"

He squeezes my hand tighter, his blue eyes locking onto mine with an intensity that sends a shiver down my spine. "Hannah, nothing will happen to them. Or to you. We have a long future ahead of us."

His words bolster me, giving me the courage to face the impending surgery.

But the fear still lingers, a shadow that refuses to dissipate. I try to focus on the rhythmic beeping of the machines around me, the clinical efficiency of the nurses prepping me for the procedure, anything to distract from the gnawing anxiety.

A nurse with kind eyes and a gentle smile approaches. "Hannah, we're ready for you now. Chris, you can wait in the family room. We'll be out to talk to you when we're done."

I look over at Chris and back at the nurse in confusion, scrunching my eyebrows together as I calculate what's happening. "I'm confused, am I not going to an operating room?"

The nurse lets out a sharp laugh of surprise. "Oh! No."

She reaches out and squeezes one of my shoulders, and I almost lean into it, rest my cheek on her hand, out of vulnerability.

"This isn't an actual surgery. It's more of a procedure. We'll give you some anesthetic, and we'll remove the IUD with the aid of an ultrasound." I breathe a sigh of relief.

"Aw, I'm sorry you've been worried this whole time. Poor thing. You're going to be just fine."

Chris leans down, pressing a soft kiss to my forehead. "It's okay to be nervous, Hanny. But I'll be right out there," he promises, his voice a low murmur meant just for me. "I love you."

"I love you, too," I whisper, my voice barely audible over the lump in my throat. He steps back reluctantly, our fingers slowly untangling as the nurse guides me through the double doors.

As he steps back, standing on the sidelines and looking at me with wide-eyed concern, I feel frantic buzzing rising in my chest.

"Wait!" I cry out, shooting my hand towards him, "I can't do this alone, please! I need him to come with me!"

"Okay, okay," the nurse says soothingly, running a hand over my arm. She looks over at Chris and wags her finger at him. "Dad, looks like we need you."

Chris hurries over to me immediately, taking my hand in his and rubbing the back of my hand with his thumb. He leans down and kisses my cheek.

"It's okay, I'm here now," he tells me soothingly. I feel the warmth of his kiss spread across my skin.

The surgery center is a flurry of activity, the sterile environment a stark contrast to the warmth and love at my side and in my belly.

I lie back on the table, the cold metal pressing against my spine, and try to focus on my breathing. In and out, just like Chris and I do on our runs. In and out, just like the ocean tides.

The exam room is cold, the kind of sterile chill that seeps into your bones despite the thin, scratchy hospital gown I'm wearing. I lie back on the exam table, my fingers gripping the edge as I try to calm my racing heart.

The ultrasound machine hums softly beside me, a constant reminder of what's about to happen. A nurse brings a warm hospital blanket over and covers me, helping to calm my anxiety.

Chris sits next to me, his hand warm and reassuring around mine. He hasn't let go since he reached for it in the hallway. His hand feels like a steady anchor in the storm of my emotions.

"How are you doing?" he asks, his voice low and comforting.

"Just nervous," I admit, squeezing his hand. "But I'm glad you're here."

The door opens, and Dr. Meyers walks in, her expression professional but kind.

"Good afternoon, Hannah. Chris." She nods to both of us before turning her attention to me. "Ready?"

"As ready as I'll ever be," I say, trying to muster a smile.

Dr. Meyers returns the smile with one of her own. "You'll do just fine. The local anesthetic will numb the area, and the ultrasound will help us guide the forceps to remove the IUD since the strings are no longer visible. Chris, I need you to stay up by Hannah's head and just hold her hand. This should be over quickly."

I nod, taking a deep breath as she prepares the anesthetic. The pinch of the needle is sharp but brief, a small price to pay for the peace of mind that will come with knowing the IUD is no longer a risk to my babies.

Dr. Meyers sets the syringe aside and reaches for the ultrasound wand. "Take a deep breath for me, Hannah. Good, now let it out slowly."

I let the air out as slowly as I can, like a steady stream, as Dr. Meyers applies the gel to my lower abdomen. She moves the ultrasound wand over my skin, her eyes fixed on the screen.

"OK. There we go," she murmurs. "I can see it. I'm going to have the nurse take over the ultrasound now as I insert the forceps. This way, I can continue to see where the IUD is located and remove it. You might feel some pressure, but it shouldn't be painful."

I nod again, my eyes darting to the screen where the grainy black-and-white image of the IUD comes into focus. It looks so small, yet its presence has loomed so large over us lately.

The pressure is uncomfortable, a deep, insistent push, but not painful, though I get the feeling that if I hadn't had the anesthesia inserted into my cervix that it would be painful. I keep my eyes on Chris, his gaze steady and unwavering, a lifeline in the midst of it all. "Chris…" I trail off, unsure of what I want to say.

"You're okay. I'm watching," he tells me, his eyes above my head as I face him instead of the screen. "It's going well."

"There we go," Dr. Meyers says, her tone light and reassuring. "Got it. Okay, one more time. Breathe in and let it out slowly."

She carefully begins to remove the forceps, the IUD clamped securely between its tips. I feel it traveling through my vagina and emerging, then suddenly nothing.

Relief floods through me, so overwhelming that I feel tears spring to my eyes. "Is it over?" I ask, my voice trembling with a mix of emotions.

"Yes, it's over," Dr. Meyers confirms, her smile warm. "You did great, Hannah. The twins are just fine, and so are you."

Chris squeezes my hand, his own eyes shining with unshed tears. "I told you," he whispers, leaning in to press another kiss to my forehead. "An entire future ahead of us."

I laugh softly, a sound of pure relief and joy. "I feel so dramatic now."

Dr. Meyers finishes up, giving us some final instructions and assurances before leaving the room.

I sit up slowly, feeling a bit unsteady but infinitely lighter. Chris helps me off the table, his arm around my waist, supporting me. "Well, how do you feel?"

"I feel like I need to eat something."

"Not the kind of feelings I meant, but let's get you something, anyway."

"Hunger is a feeling," I object, leaning on him as he lowers me into the passenger seat.

# Chapter Forty Six
## Christopher

We opt for a diner north of Hannah's office.

I asked her if we should go to the beach, but she told me it would be a betrayal to Lucy, who loves the beach and would smell the salty water on her immediately upon our return.

So, instead, we're in a booth across from each other, eating our meals. I pick at a Denver omelet while Hannah eats waffle fries hand over fist, her eyes glued to her plate.

"I haven't really been hungry lately. I guess I didn't realize how anxious I was."

I smile at her, glad that she's getting the right nourishment. Her confession forces me to realize that I need to keep a closer eye on her health, though. I've been leaving her to it, not realizing the burden she's been carrying.

"We should call your mom, huh?"

She shrugs, her shoulders tensing next to her ears. She dips a french fry into honey mustard. "I guess so. She'd want to know."

"What's up with you? Why don't you want to tell her?" I ask her.

Her attitude's confusing me. She should be more excited than she is, and I know Piper has been worried sick.

"I do, I do. I know she worries. I just…let's have this moment just us for today. We've been sharing so much of ourselves, and that's how Tyler was able to take some of our joy."

"Oh, I see, my private Hannah Banana." I grin at her, remembering the way I found her, living in her office with no intention of ever telling anyone.

Her mother told me she put herself through her accreditation without telling anyone, either, just showed up one day as a CPA.

"I wonder what things you'll keep from me."

I reach for one of her fries, and she makes a show of following my hand with her eyes before cutting them back up at my face.

"My fries, to start," she jokes, pulling her plate farther away from me.

Her phone trills just as she puts another fry in her mouth.

She chews the bite quickly, swallowing it and quelling a coughing fit with a swallow of water before answering her phone.

"Hello? Hannah Banana speaking. So sorry, yes, I meant Hannah Jackson…who is this?"

I stifle a snorting laugh at her mistake, and she shoots me a look that could kill before refocusing on her phone conversation.

"Oh, really? That's...wow, that's fast. Are you sure? Okay...well, let me talk to the client about it, and I'll let you know by end of day tomorrow."

She chews on the end of a fry, not quite eating it, just chewing it like a pacifier, before rolling her eyes.

"Yes, I know it will move quickly, thank you. Let me talk to the client, and I will get back to you by end of day tomorrow, as I said."

She hangs up her phone and silences it before setting it face down on the table next to her plate. "Vultures," she mutters.

"Am I your client?" I ask her, rubbing my ankles against hers and batting my eyelashes at her.

She drops her fry and rubs her fingers together to clean off the seasoning.

"Okay, listen, you know how you said you were thinking Maine?"

"Like a week ago?" I laugh, flickering my eyes to her plate and back to her eyes. "Yea, I remember."

She sighs heavily and faces her head to the ceiling. She closes her eyes and breathes in deeply.

"Hannah, what is going on? I feel like I'm lost here."

Hannah's eyes snap open, and she reaches for my hands.

"Sorry, so basically, I started submitting offers to locations in Maine. Just leasing locations, nothing crazy, I didn't take out a loan or anything. But. That was one of the leasing managers calling to approve you for a space in Maine."

She watches my eyes, her chest heaving with breaths as she watches me think it over.

I grip the side of the table with my fingers and chew on the inside of my cheek.

I pictured myself looking for the location, of course, and I pictured myself finding something overlooking the water, something that would fill my nose with the smell of saltwater, where I could walk down a sandy beach and go get lobster from a nearby restaurant.

Without being able to look myself, it's a blank space where I try to picture the gym. I crack my knuckles. "Well, tell me about it."

"Okay!" she chirps, sitting up straighter in her booth, wiggling around to get settled.

She reaches over the table and runs two fingers over my eyes so that my eyelids automatically close.

"Close your eyes. Okay, picture this. A two-story, red cabin structure but with expansive, modern windows that go from floor to ceiling. The natural light fills the space and allows clients to work out while looking out over the rocky water as it crashes on the wooden stilts that the building sits on."

"It sounds beautiful," I admit, opening my eyes and spearing a particularly thick slice of parmesan cheese on my fork. I chase after a thick crouton that continues to avoid the teeth of my utensil.

"Doesn't it? And there's a deck, like a widow's walk, you know? That's what they call them when they're on the roof."

"Rooftop patio, huh? What am I, a DJ?"

"No, you're a gym owner, and you're cool and hip and all that crap."

She waves around her fry at the same time that I'm waving around my fork. She catches my eye and offers me a sly smile that settles itself into the folds of one of her cheeks.

"You can bring some Los Angeles to Portland."

"Portland, Maine?" I ask her, and she smiles before shoving three french fries into her mouth at once.

"I know, kind of ironic, right?"

I look at her as everything around me fades into the background.

I picture uprooting my life and moving it and I can't really see anything there. This is the only life I've ever had. I don't have anything else, and I don't know how to have anything else, either.

It's hard to imagine the simple things like grocery shopping or taking Lucy on a walk. I've pictured all of the fun parts, but the small actions that really make up your life, those are the ones that I can't imagine.

Part of it, I know, is that my new life will have two children in it, something that I've never considered before.

To have two children, a new gym, and be on the other side of the country is a lot of take in. As long as my new life includes Hannah, it's the one I want, though.

I know that. I feel in my pocket for the engagement ring.

I've been carrying it in my pocket ever since that day I realized that I didn't need anything from Julie, that Hannah had healed all of my wounds. I haven't been sure of how to propose or where, only that I have to have Hannah in my future.

I bite by bottom lip and chew on it, tapping the top of the table, the fake marble rimmed with gray.

"Are you okay?" Hannah asks me, tilting her head so that her beautiful copper hair splays out across her neck and collarbone, falling forward over her breast.

I reach out and twirl a few strands of it around my index finger. "I'm more than okay. I have a question to ask you, actually."

"Okay, shoot," she says, looking across the table for a napkin, finding one, and dabbling at her lips with it.

"Getting to know you this year has been the most amazing time of my life. I know you probably already know this, but a lot of what you've brought to me is just the courage and strength to live authentically. You've taught me to stand up for myself and that sharing myself with someone will result in that person sharing herself with me."

Hannah slaps at my elbow. "Why do you sound like you're proposing?" Her grins widens, showing her big teeth and gums, the smile that I love so much.

I smile back, tears brimming at my waterline. I feel unable to breathe until I look at her, and then the oxygen returns to my lungs as though she herself controls my breathing.

"No," she whispers. "You're not serious, Chris."

"I am so completely serious, Hannah. I started thinking about this when you told me that I needed to confront Julie. It made me realize that...well...that I don't.

"Because you are everything to me, and you've healed all my brokenness, even in the places that I thought weren't broken. You taught me how to be myself in a way that was healthy, and I believe I have been good for you as well. I would be honored to live this life with you by my side as my wife."

I take out the ring box, and Hannah's eyes widen, the green bright and sparkling under the light, and she covers her mouth with two hands, her shocked expression peeking out from behind her fingers.

"I know this isn't fancy, and if you want something different or larger we can change it and I'll plan a candlelit boat ride. But Hannah, just now, thinking about what life would be like in Maine, I realized I want nothing more than for my life to be with you and our children. Wherever we are. Geography means nothing to me. You are the map, the key, and the compass."

She laughs through tears, tossing back her head so that her tears momentarily sink back into her eyes. "You are seriously the nerdiest, corniest gym bro," she says endearingly, looking back at me.

"Well, I guess I only have one more step then," I tell her, swallowing hard as I lower down onto one knee on the filthy, diner floor. Something sticks to the knee of my pants, but I stay in position, holding out the ring box for Hannah.

"Chris," she says, my name coming out in one long breath. "Get up, Chris." She pulls up at my elbow.

Reluctantly, confused, I lean against the table to get back up to a sitting position in the chair. "Hannah, um, I just thought…"

"No, I know what you thought," she says, looking down at her fingers while she talks. Her cheeks have a pinkish tinge to them, and her freckles stand out against the blush.

"But…you don't feel the same?"

Bile rushes up my throat, and my vision tunnels. I wipe sweat away from my brow as I struggle to meet her eyes.

She reaches out for me, her facial expression apologetic.

"Chris, I love you, if that's what you mean. It's just…" she flags down a waiter, who bops up to us in all black, nodding already as though he can read her mind.

"Could I get a vanilla milkshake please?" The waiter nods and slinks away, gone just as quickly as he appeared.

"I think we should wait until Tyler is supportive of...us...of...everything. He's my big brother. And your best friend," she whispers the last part as though people in the diner might hear and judge her, already knowing the whole story somehow.

I nod silently and let her continue. "He's important to both of us. Let's just...see if we can't fix things, OK?"

I fold my hands together underneath my chin and lean against them, watching her beautiful mouth move as she talks.

A shiver goes down my spine as I think of her lips wrapped around my cock. I see her tongue press against the back of her lower teeth, and I imagine that tongue licking at the underside of my mushroom head.

I sit up straighter and push the thoughts away so that I can focus on her words.

"I understand, Hannah. You're right. I want it to be the best day of our lives, so if it can't be that without Tyler..." I trail off, thinking of who exactly would be my best man if Tyler weren't. She's right, of course she's right.

"I love you, Chris, and I will love you while you're in Maine. You don't have to propose to me to keep me. We can make a long-distance relationship work while you get everything set up on the east coast."

"You wouldn't want to come with me?" I ask her, pushing my salad away from me with a loud scrape that makes me cringe.

She tilts her head with a serious expression and pushes her own plate away as well.

"I can't, Chris. I'm running a business here. I have clients that I'm still helping. I'm still helping you. You can't really ask me to leave right now. I'm just getting this off the ground here. I mean, I still have over half a year left on my lease."

Seeing my expression, which I'm sure reflects that I feel I've been kicked in the gut, she squeezes my fingers and whispers, "We will be okay, Chris. I will be okay."

I deflate as her words kick in.

I believe her, that she thinks we could make a long-distance relationship work and that we could, but I can't do it to her. I can't leave her here pregnant, and she can't leave here to help me.

She cups my cheek with her palm and murmurs, "Chris. I mean it. I will be okay here, and so will the babies."

Her waiter arrives with her milkshake and drops it off between us, with two straws inserted into the thick liquid. They sit comically bent toward us, seemingly mocking our moment.

I sit on the sticky booth, making eye contact with Hannah in the dark diner. Her shoulders droop, and I sigh deeply, our bodies having a silent conversation of their own.

# Chapter Forty Seven
## Hannah

Weeks pass of waking up next to Chris and going on our runs with Lucy and taking showers together and then falling back asleep cuddled together. It feels like a dream, to know him so well and to be so thoroughly part of his life.

He teaches me how to make something new every day, and we're even raising a sourdough starter together. It grows and bubbles on the windowsill of his apartment. Sometimes I look at it and think of how in another life, I'm not a city girl with a city job but someone with a farm, my kids running barefoot through the grass.

We're preparing the nursery, and we're almost done except for the clothes and the walls. We're not sure about their sex or their names, so it's hard to get the room completed. We're finding out the babies' genders this week.

We also need more diapers, we hear. Always more diapers, according to everyone.

I've reported Sarah to our local DA, and now we just wait to see what happens. So much of our life is a waiting game now. Wait for the gender announcement. Decide on names. Wait to hear from the DA. Wait for Tyler to come around.

Another thing I'm waiting for is the right time to tell Chris that I told the real estate agent in Maine that my client wants the seaside property.

He's been hounding me about Chris signing the paperwork. I already sent him the deposit from my savings account, but I haven't told Chris about what I did, so I walk on eggshells, unsure of when to bring it up.

I wake this morning to find Chris shirtless and sweaty making cupcakes. I laugh out loud at the sight and tell him, "You look like the cover of a book." He tosses his curly hair out of his eyes, and I point, stabbing accusatorily, "See! That right there – that was the move of a book cover guy!"

"I just went on a run," he defends himself, "And I would have worn an apron, but it was hard to get Lucy to come back, so I was tight on time to get them out of the oven. I thought you'd still be sleeping – what are you doing up?"

I check the clock on the oven, and the neon green numbers stare back at me: 9:30 AM. He's right that I've been sleeping in longer on the weekends. I used to be an 8 AM girlie always. Up with the birds and asleep with the birds, I always said.

"I don't know. Maybe the smell of cupcakes woke me up. What are those for?"

"Today is the day we find out the gender of the little plantains, so I thought it was only fitting to make some banana cupcakes."

He points at my stomach, and I rub it instinctively. My instincts feel alien to me now sometimes, like something implanted in me.

I instinctively rub my belly and instinctively clean and instinctively cook and instinctively avoid caffeine. My body seems to know a lot more than I do.

"Is that fitting? They can't eat the cupcakes." I wrap my arms around him while he holds the hot pan above me, shuffling toward the counter to set it down. "Maybe you should have made some banana mash or something."

"Well, that sounds delicious. Man, I really messed up making cupcakes."

He sighs mockingly and sets them down, extricating himself from me to push a toothpick into them. He pulls the toothpick out clean and smiles to himself before throwing it away.

"Satisfied?" I ask, wrapping myself around him again and feeling the sticky skin of his back against my cheek. "Are they masterpieces?"

"They are. After I get the frosting on them, they'll be worthy of you." He unfurls my hands from his body and turns around to face me and cup my cheeks in his hands. His lips seek out mine, and we kiss gently, bathed in sun from the kitchen window and the smell of his pastries wafting all around us.

His lips massage mine as his hands explore the nape of my neck, his fingers slipping into my hair and gripping at it briefly. I gasp against his mouth, and he pushes me into the counter before lifting me up and setting me down onto it.

My hands slide back behind me as he pulls up my shirt to kiss my stomach. His mouth slides down me, his tongue exploring me, until he's at my underwear, pulling it to the side and licking quickly at the exposed parts of me.

I consider briefly telling him what I did, that he has a spot in Maine waiting for him, but I don't know how to tell him in a way that won't sound like I'm getting rid of him or that I've somehow tricked him instead of seeking his agreement first.

I have a feeling no matter how I frame it, he'll feel too indebted to me to leave, despite the fact that I want him to go and live out his dreams.

I hold his head against me, and his tongue dives into my tunnel. He spreads my legs and kneels, lapping at me, until I start to feel my orgasm approaching like a wave of fire.

Lately, every time Chris touches me, I'm already on the edge of cumming. This pregnancy seems to have me ready to go at all times. Let's hear it for the hormones.

Chris stands up and pulls his penis out over the top of his boxers and shorts. Both of us are partially clothed, which is probably a good thing because I know that if I can see people through the window, they can probably see us.

He pulls me forward to the edge of the counter and lowers his body just enough to press himself into me. I feel the gentle pressure of his cock inching itself along inside me, the swollen shaft touching every bit of me from inside as my muscles contract against it.

I groan against him, my abs wobbling with the force it takes to hold myself up on the edge. Just as I register the strength needed, Chris envelops me with his muscled arms, wrapping them around my back as he pulls me off the counter and onto him. I'm held up only by his arms and his cock.

Feeling all of him entering me at once makes a lusty groan release from my diaphragm. I feel completely full, somehow all the way up my stomach to my ribs.

I clutch myself against him, but he holds me backwards, slanted at an angle, so that he can enter me at the exact angle of my tract.

His cock slides into me like butter, fully inside me and slipping around in my juices. He holds my ass with his big, paw-like hands, his strong fingers digging into my flesh as he bounces me on him.

With every bounce, I find myself rolling my eyes back and letting out a squeal of lusty delight. Already, I'm sweating, and he holds my hair away from my neck with his fist, kissing my sweaty lips.

His tongue dances inside my mouth, and I swirl my own tongue around his.

I cry out in pleasure when he pulls back from me and continues to bounce me against him.

My legs slip from around his waist, so he backs me up against the counter again and wraps them around him tighter. He forces my ankles to encircle each other, and I hold them in place when he lets go.

He reaches for his cupcakes and taps them, feeling their temperature, while still inside me. I grind desperately against him, holding his back and trying to wriggle him deeper into me.

He smiles patronizingly at me and kisses the tip of my nose while reaching behind me for a container of frosting and a knife.

He frosts a cupcake as I bounce against his pelvis, holding his forearms so that I can leverage myself enough to lower all the way down on his hard, veiny cock. My pussy's so tight, the muscles contracting wildly, that I can feel every single vein that spans it.

Chris presents me with a cupcake, one hand under it and one hand behind it, showcasing it like a piece of art. He traces a bit of the frosting on top onto my lips, and I lick it off.

Hunched over me, he mutters into my ear, "Don't move. Not even your tongue." He dips the frosting back onto my lips and a little on my earlobe and my neck before kissing me deeply.

The sugar intertwines with our tongues, sweetening our kiss. He sucks on my earlobe until I tip my head back and moan, feeling my chest flush. His tongue finds the spots on my neck, and he licks with just the tip of it, a gentle tease of a lick.

My hands scratch at his back and his ass before finally, he feeds me the cupcake and lets me taste it myself before fucking me almost violently, driving himself deeply into me and pulling out only to thrust himself back in.

Our hips buck against each other, and the sensation of being filled while I eat the most decadent chocolate and banana cupcake I've ever had has me moaning aloud, unable and unwilling to hold it in.

I feel my own orgasm building just as I see his own face scrunch up as sweat rolls down his nose and drops onto my stomach.

"Hannah, you are so beautiful. And you feel so good. I could cum just looking at you."

I snicker a little, taking another bite of the cupcake. I love this part of sex with Chris, when he forgets his dominant personality.

Usually, he likes to hold me down and fuck me the way he wants to feel me, but toward the end, when he's nearly drained, he can't help but praise me.

"So cum," I tell him, trailing my fingers up and down his arms the way he likes. He shivers a little while inside me, and my walls jump at the feeling.

My eyes move without my permission, and I rest my face against his toned shoulders. "Cum inside me. I want to feel it filling me and spraying all over my walls."

I feel him shake when he hears me talking like that, and his fingers grip me even tighter, pulling me against him.

A tiny grunt escapes him, finding its way in my ear, and he groans in a rattling voice, "Fuck." One word, but that one word gets me every time. I cum with him, letting myself ride the wave as it washes over me. I let it go on for as long as I can as he empties himself into me, holding me tight to him and breathing rapidly into my ear.

We both relax into each other's bodies, melting against each other. He lowers me onto the ground and kisses me deeply.

When the kiss ends, he lifts me up and hugs me with my feet off the ground.

I wrap my legs around his waist and think fondly that I've never dated anyone tall enough to pick me up. Our babies are going to be giants. I snuggle into Chris' neck and decide in that exact moment that he is going to Maine.

I'm going to convince him, and I think I know just how to do it.

# Chapter Forty Eight
## Christopher

The waiting room is painted in muted pastels, and the walls are adorned with framed photos of smiling babies. I sit beside Hannah, our hands entwined, and try to keep my excitement from bubbling over. My leg is bouncing uncontrollably, and I take a deep breath to steady myself.

Hannah reaches over and sets her hand on my knee to stabilize it.

She sneaks her fingers up the hem of my shorts and gently rubs my skin. The anticipation is almost unbearable, and her touch is comforting.

I rest my own hand on the back of hers and feel her cool skin against my warm, sweaty palm. Hannah closes her eyes and leans her head back against the chair, her other hand resting protectively over her slight bump.

I watch her, my heart swelling with love and admiration. I still can't believe this incredible woman is carrying our children.

"Hannah Jackson?" a nurse calls from the doorway, a bright smile on her face.

Hannah's eyes flutter open, and she squeezes my hand as we stand up. I help her to her feet, and we follow the nurse down a hallway to the ultrasound room. At this point, it's so familiar to me that I feel like I know it like my own home.

We do all of it all over again.

Hannah puts on a gown alone in the room, then they let me enter, too. Hannah climbs onto the examination table, and eventually the doctor joins us.

She spreads a cool gel on Hannah's belly, and I feel her grip tighten briefly as she reacts. We exchange a glance, and I can see my own excitement mirrored in her eyes.

"Ready to find out if your babies are little men or little women?" the doctor asks, positioning the ultrasound wand on Hannah's stomach.

"Yes! Yes, yes, yes," Hannah chirps, bouncing while on her back. Her smile lights up her face, and I reach over and wipe a strand of hair off her sticky, glossy lips.

Dr. Meyers moves the wand around and laughs when it's almost entirely at Hannah's back before two gray, lumpy forms appear. She looks over at Hannah and raises her eyebrows with a smile. "How's your back feeling these days?"

"Oh, it's sore," Hannah says back, laughing.

Their conversation is background noise for me as I see the forms moving. One of them appears to be sucking its thumb. I can hear the woosh of their heartbeats, two overlapping.

I glance back to Hannah, and she's being very still now, her eyes on the screen.

It's strange to know that we're both looking at something showing us what's inside her. It's completely surreal and hard to wrap my head around.

"There they are," the doctor says softly. "Let's take a closer look, shall we?"

She looks up at us, and we nod in unison, both of us breathless.

"Okay, see right here?" She touches the screen with her pinkie finger, drawing it in a line upward from her starting point. "There. That's the stem of the apple. We've got a boy!"

"A boy," I whisper to her, my voice choked with emotion. Hannah wipes away a tear from her cheek as my heart soars.

Hannah and I look at each other with barely concealed excitement. Hannah bites on her bottom lip, exposing her two front teeth. Quickly, she turns her head back to the screen. The silence is deafening as we wait.

"And this one," the doctor says, moving the wand again, "is a boy, too! Congratulations. You have a very exciting life in front of you."

"Two boys," Hannah echoes, her voice barely a whisper. She looks at me, her eyes shining with happiness. "Chris, we're having two boys."

I can't speak, so I just nod as Dr. Meyers prints out ultrasound images for us.

I help Hannah sit up, still reeling from the news, and keep my eyes on her as she thanks the doctor and listens while she's told what to expect in the coming weeks.

I think I hear the word 'cramping' but it's all background. My mind races as I watch Hannah's lips move, her eyes sparkling and her smile wide even while she talks. I wrap my arms around her and help her dress before walking her back to the car.

It's dusk outside and the moon is visible at the same time as the sun, the sky's blue darkening quietly.

I tuck Hannah into her seat and kiss her forehead. She looks up at me through her blonde eyelashes, and for a moment, I see the eyes of the girl I knew, all the fear and the vulnerability and the innocence.

"You're amazing," I tell her, and she rolls her eyes before I close the door.

It's a quiet drive home, and I let it stay quiet. Both of us are processing and imagining the ways our life will change. It's easier to imagine the future now that I can imagine the children, the dinosaurs and monster trucks materializing in my daydreams.

Clutching the ultrasound pictures in her hand, Hannah says, "Chris, I've been thinking a lot about Maine."

Outside the window, the nighttime has finally overcome the evening, and the darkness seeps into the car. The moon follows us from the dark sky, flanked by stars.

My heart pounds in my chest, feeling the tension in her words and in the energy coming off her.

"Oh yeah?" is all I say, as though I don't feel my heart leaping into my stomach.

She carries on while looking at her hands in her lap. "I know what a dream it is for you, and I want you to go."

"I can't go, Hannah," I tell her firmly, tightening my hands around the steering wheel.

Sweat pools in the lines of my palms and I look over at her and see the sincerity on her face. "There's no point even talking about it."

"Our kids need to know it's okay to chase dreams," she murmurs, picking at one of her fingernails.

"Yes, but, more importantly, our kids need to know their dad is there for them and always will be," I respond without looking at her, my eyes on the road.

"I've let it go. You should, too. There's plenty to focus on here. Maine will still be there when the time is right."

"I think you're going to regret it," Hannah mutters, "And I don't want you to ever have regrets. You deserve to do what you were planning to do. I have family here. I'll be okay."

"I know you'll be okay. But I want to be with you while you're okay. No, I'm not going."

I shake my head as I pull into the parking lot of the apartment complex. I park the car and relax in my seat, finally looking over at her.

She holds up the ultrasound and points at the two little beans on the glossy white paper, their faces gray lumpy shapes that somehow still bring tears to my eyes.

"We can still visit each other. You should have everything set up within 5 months."

"You're not being realistic, Hannah. It would certainly take much longer than that. And, even if it didn't, I'd have to find someone to run it if I come back here. Right now, I have good managers in my other clubs but getting a new one off the ground is a different proposition. How do you see that working? I get it set up and I just come back? I don't oversee anything? You think it would only take 5 months for the construction, purchasing or leasing the equipment, hiring employees, training them, decorating, get a decent clientele, all that? No, Hannah, I'm done talking about it."

I see her lip quiver, and her eyelashes moisten, but I step out of the car and walk over to her side to let her out of the car. I hold out my hand, but she ignores it and braces herself against the car to get up instead.

"Seriously? Lord, you are such a little brat, Hannah Jackson. Come on." I reach for her hand, and she lets me hold her hand limply. I continue to out of spite.

Despite her attitude, or maybe because of it, I can't stop finding her adorable. There's just something about a woman who takes on your dreams as her own.

I squeeze her hand and unlock the front entrance of the building for her. I hold the door as she enters, her jaw still set angrily.

I can hear Lucy inside, shuffling and sniffing at the crack under the door. Hannah smiles and dips her head away from my line of sight so I can't see it.

When I unlock the door, I'm greeted first by Lucy and second by the realization that all of the luggage normally stored in the top shelf of my closet is packed and sitting in the living room.

# Chapter Forty Nine
## Hannah

Trying to conceal the smug excitement on my face, I see confusion transform on Chris'.

It moves into anger and then a tender understanding when he notices the plane ticket balanced on top of one of his bags – a one way to Maine.

He runs a hand through his curly locks and sighs deeply before turning to me. "So when you said you'd been 'thinking' of Maine."

Grinning, I reply, "I meant that I'd been thinking about how I'd prepared for you to go to Maine. You leave in the morning."

"In the morning as in tomorrow morning?"

"The very same."

"That's insane, Hannah. I cannot leave that soon."

"Yes, you can! I didn't want you to change your mind." I let out a little giggle and clear my throat to hold it back.

"I haven't set up any replacements for me at the gyms here. I have long term clients and employees and…bills. Do you know how to pay the rent here? Or the electric? Wifi? I mean, what are you thinking? How would you feel if I just unilaterally took over your business and told you what you were going to do? Would you like that?"

His voice is firm as he smacks one of his hands into the other repeatedly. He looks at me with pure frustration, his eyes cloudy and his mouth set resolutely.

I catch his eyes with mine, barely suppressing a smile, and watch as my smile spreads to him like a contagion.

He rolls his eyes with a grunt and picks me up off my feet, twirling me and peppering my face with pecks. "Are you sure about this?" he asks me.

"Nah, I was hoping you'd say you won't go, that's why I sent a deposit for the building, packed your bags for you, and bought a ticket," I tease him sarcastically, tossing my head back as he twirls me so that the force pulls me away from him.

"You know I'll pay you back. I'll do it right now."

"Not right now, come on. You leave tomorrow. Just...relax."

Laying me down onto the couch, he kisses my neck and growls into the hollow of my throat, "The last thing I can do is relax. If I leave tomorrow, I need to make tonight unforgettable."

My mind starts to wander as I release into the sensation of his mouth on me, but I come back to earth and yelp, "Oh! One more thing."

I stand and fish around in my bag until I find the paperwork that the building manager has been harassing me for. "Here.

Do not forget this." I zip it into the top pouch of his carry on. "I put all the other paperwork you'll need in that pouch, too. Hotel reservations, addresses, stuff like that."

We stare at each other for a moment, and as the look in his eyes becomes more serious, I reach out and stroke his lips.

"We'll visit each other all the time. I want you to follow your dream, Chris. I already have my dream. And now, because of you, I have a new dream, too."

Smiling sadly, he pulls me into his strong arms and asks, "Will you marry me now?"

"Not yet," I whisper back.

He picks me up and carries me into the bedroom. He lays me down gently on my back and holds my face delicately, stroking my jaw with his thumb. His lips find mine and he presses gently against me. His lips are soft and warm, and the pressure of his mouth melts me. I relax back and lay my hands on his shoulder blades, feeling the length of him coming to life and pressing against me.

His pelvis is against my button, and my eyes roll back in my head as he pushes even harder against it, swirling our hips together in a circle. He pulls my shirt up over my head and off me, trapping me at my elbows for a brief moment and using the opportunity to kiss me again, deeply.

Once my shirt is off, his fingers are on my bra clasp and then he takes his own shirt off. As though it's possessed, my hand strokes his chest and pecs, my index finger trailing down the line of his hair that disappears into his waistband.

Chris catches my wrist and smirks. I pull myself free and unbutton his pants, then unzips them to pull his cock out. Chris places his hands on the back of my neck and massages it, pulling in a quiet gasp.

I circle my lips on the head of his penis and gently lick at his shaft underneath the head, tasting the heady flavor of his skin.

He moans gently and places his hands on the back of my head, weaving his fingers into my hair and twirling strands around them to tug at my head. "God, Hannah, please marry me," he murmurs, his fingertips massaging my head.

I laugh with his cock in my mouth and ease it deeper down my throat. "You want to marry me for my mouth?" I ask him, muffled, with my mouth full.

I lower my mouth further down his shaft. "For this?" I ask, flitting my tongue out to lap around his enlarged and veiny member, feeling the shifting of his muscles.

His eyelids flutter as I swallow his dick deeper and feel it push against the back of my throat.

I close my eyes and breathe out of my nose, pushing my body where it hasn't been before, allowing him to overtake me. I try to make him a part of me, to become one with his erection. Finally, I expel his dick with my tongue, drooling onto it.

Chris pushes me back on the bed and pulls my pants and underwear off. I cross my knees over each other, hiding my hole from him, embarrassed of the sticky mess that's pooled into the creases of my thighs.

"Don't you want to marry the man who does this to you, baby?" he asks, running his finger along the fold of my leg like someone looking for dust. When his finger comes back slick, he pops the digit into his mouth and sucks on it.

I shudder, watching his red tongue find my cream and taste it. He opens my legs up and slides between them to insert himself into my canal.

The initial stretch always makes me gasp, and there's a moment when I remember briefly that I won't feel this again for quite a while, that this is the last moment we'll be together for several months.

At that realization, I look into his eyes and wrap my hands over his cheeks, feeling the slight stubble that peppers them. He looks back at me with his baby blues rimmed with the heavy, curled eyelashes that I've always envied.

While we look into each other's eyes, he pumps inside me slowly, his rhythm steady. I look at his hands and see that his wrists are white with the effort it takes to hold himself up.

I push against him so that he'll roll over onto his back and I ride him, my back arched and my eyes still glued to his. I slide along the length of him, up and down, feeling my pussy empty and fill with every inch that I take and release. I hear my juices stir with the motion, and his hands find my hips, steadying me as I move.

"Marry the man who makes you that wet," he whispers to me, leaning up slightly to kiss me.

I kiss him back passionately, locking my arms behind him, feeling our sweat intermingle as I continue to bob on him.

I'm so wet that I can barely feel the actual girth and length of Chris's penis, only that it's inside me.

"You're so wet that I bet I could fit an extra finger or two inside you right now," he murmurs against my mouth. Both of our mouths are open too wide and moaning as we talk, "When you were a virgin, did you think you'd ever be able to take this much inside you?"

This is the position I lost my virginity to Chris in, although it was in a ripped velvet chair in my office. So much has changed, but still so much is the same.

All I know is that I lost my virginity to the man underneath me, and when I feel the rigid muscle of his dick move underneath the smooth skin on top of it, I feel like a virgin again, despite the growing life in my stomach.

Taking all nine inches of him would make anyone feel like a virgin, I think.

I quiver between my legs and bite my lip at the feeling of the heat building up in me. I almost push him back onto the bed but our imminent orgasms make me want to hold him tighter than before.

His fingers dig into my waist, and I'm nearly choking him with the pressure of my arms as I squeeze him and my tunnel does the same to his thick shaft.

Chris lets out a groan as I start uncontrollably squeezing him, the walls of my vagina tightening and loosening around him at a pace I can't change.

My gasps match the same beat and as I go limp, Chris holds me up and does the work for me from below me, driving his hips forward, pushing me to the brink of my orgasm.

I flop atop him, a lusty puppet for his bidding, until I feel its impending power. I grip Chris tighter and he whispers into my ear, "Are you about to cum for me?" I nod, whimpering into his neck. "That's good. Ride that wave with me."

Chris rolls me over so that he's on top of me and fucks me harder and faster, his hands on the small of my back, shoving my body deeper into the mattress.

My mouth is wide open and drooling onto the bed with us, and my breasts are swollen, my nipples engorged against the sheets. Everything on my body feels like it's on fire, like I could alight and explode right there below him.

His fingers slide down between my body and the bed and play with my nipples. He says, "Are you—" and before he can even finish the words, pleasured moans scream out of me and morph into animalistic grunts.

I turn my face to the bed and let out the screams into it so that it dampens the sound.

Chris strokes my hair as I dump my lusty sounds into his mattress. His hands travel down the curve of my spine and back up to my neck, his touch delicate and loving.

"How was that?" he whispers as he pulls out of me, his sticky penis shifting all the juices inside me so that they make a wet noise of suction.

"Mmm," is all I can manage to say back. Every part of my body is sensitive, and I tremble as he slips out of my warm cave.

"Good enough to marry me?" he asks as he lies next to me.

I roll over and relax against his warm, strong body, feeling as safe and protected as I always do with him.

Again, a thought flashes through my mind that I won't be able to feel safe like this once he's in Maine.

I do want to marry him. But now isn't the time, not with things so up in the air between us and Tyler. It just wouldn't feel right. I want it to feel good for everyone.

I kiss his cheek and tell him, "Maybe once you get me up to two orgasms."

"Is that a challenge?" he asks, sitting up on his heels in bed and crawling over to situate himself between my legs again.

He smirks at me and runs his tongue over his bottom teeth, setting his jaw crooked and showing me his dimples.

"Well? You look so good down there. Show me what you can do." I run my fingers over his eyebrows before settling back down onto my back.

He chuckles, and I feel the wet tip of his tongue bury itself between my folds. I sigh and open my legs up to him even further, knowing the man between my legs will be my husband one day.

\*\*\*

Four months have passed since the day that I drove Chris to the airport and sent him off to Maine with a kiss and a promise that I would hold down the fort in Los Angeles for him.

I've gotten word that Sarah is being prosecuted and I've provided all the proof available to me detailing her thefts over the years, although it will be up to detectives to sort through her finances and find the proof of her spending.

I've hired more employees for Chris and told my own clients that I'm on maternity leave.

I'm considering moving the office to a smaller location since I no longer need to live in the office.

It's gotten chillier here in Los Angeles, no longer the sunny spring during which we met.

It's never exactly cold, but it gets dreary and rainy and the damp seems to somehow soak into my bones, making it unpleasant to be walking the beach. If I can't go to the beach, that means it's winter as far as I'm concerned.

While Chris is gone, I've taken the opportunity to paint a baby mural across one wall of the nursery.

I decided on a landscape scene, with the horizon of LA, the tops of buildings and the ocean water shimmering beneath the high sun. I've nearly finished the lavender outline when I feel a pang shoot through my lower abdomen.

I reach to cup the bottom of my stomach. I catch myself doing that a lot lately, as though I'm worried the babies might fall out the bottom. I feel them stirring inside me, just underneath my skin, the strangest feeling that I now find to be normal and comforting.

I stop on top of the ladder, leaning against the wall and waiting for the cramp to pass.

When I think it has, I ease myself off the ladder before feeling another rip through me followed by water spilling onto the ground below me.

Quietly, I step backwards, staring at the puddle on the floor. I'm still 8 weeks early, so there's no way that my water is breaking. Just breathe.

I walk away and close the door, opting to change my pants and worry about it later.

These last couple of weeks I seem to have completely lost the ability to hold in my pee, so it could just as easily be that.

That's what I tell myself as I pull on a pair of jeans, fitting the stretchy elastic over my stomach, and as I fill my water bottle, and as I clip Lucy to her leash, and as I walk down the stairs.

All of my steps and motions followed by the thought It's still early, it's still early, it's still early, it's still early, the words as heavy as my feet on the ground.

I pop Lucy into the car and drive her down to the dog park by my office.

With Chris gone, and being on maternity leave, I haven't gone by that park in a while, so I'm hopeful she'll find it exciting. I rest one hand on her back as her tongue trails out the window, saliva bubbling up on it against the wind.

We reach the park and I sit on a bench, no longer able to maneuver myself onto the ground anymore. For a while, I brought parasols with me everywhere in the heat, but with it cooling down, I can finally feel somewhat normal in a park, although I'm still hotter than everyone around me. Those pesky hormones again, I think.

I watch Lucy run around, tearfully for some reason, though I'm unsure why. As much as I appreciate being able to keep my babies safe inside me, I'm ready to be done with the emotional rollercoaster of pregnancy.

"Hannah?" I hear from in front of me as a figure stands in front of me, gratefully casting a shadow over me.

I sigh in relief as I look up and see Scott. "Scott, hi. It's been a while."

"Apparently longer than I realized," he jokes, gesturing towards my convex stomach, my outie belly button peeking out from beneath my shrinking sweater.

"Oh, this? No, I'm just bloated. I had a lot of rice on the way here." I smile at Scott and move over so that he can sit next to me.

"You look different, too," I say, gesturing to the new handlebar mustache he's sporting. Right as he twirls one end of it, I cry out in pain as another cramp shoots through me.

"Whoah!" Scott reaches out to me like I'm a bomb that might go off any moment, slowly lowering into a seated position beside me.

"False alarm," I tell him as the pain passes, and I relax against the bench, breathing heavily.

"Are you sure about that?" Scott asks, concern etched onto his face. That didn't sound like a false anything, Hannah. I think you might need to go to the hospital."

I shake my head, holding my breath in my cheeks. I release the air slowly as Lucy runs up to me, slobber flying off her face.

She rests her dirty face against my knees, spreading grass and dirt across my jeans, and I pull at her ears gently, rubbing the pink and silky insides of them with my thumbs.

"Hannah?" Scott repeats, trying to look into my eyes.

I stare into the distance, slowing my heartbeat to the rhythm of Lucy's panting.

"No, no, I don't. Because I'm eight weeks early, and Chris is still in Maine."

"Oh, is Chris your...the dad?"

I turn to Scott and see nothing but confusion and concern on his face, like a light in a stormy night. I grab his wrist and nod.

"I think I understand what's happening. Are you scared to give birth without Chris?"

Tears leak down my cheeks, and I whisper, "I need to call my brother."

"Okay, sure. Let's call your brother. What's your brother's name? Give me your phone, I'll find him." Scott sets his hand over mine as it digs into his wrist bone. He pats it comfortingly.

"Tyler," I tell him, tossing him my cell.

Now that I've started to allow myself to acknowledge that I really am having these babies, the pain is excruciating. It snuck up on me and settled deep in my belly and against my spine, and now it's all I can feel.

"Tyler. Okay, sure. And hey, did you drive? How about you give me your keys and I'll take you to the hospital while we call your brother – does that sound good?"

Scott's hand hooks under my elbow, and I lean against the back of the bench, leaning back dramatically to pick myself up before sinking down into a squat again. "I know, I know, but you don't have far to go. You can make it, Hannah, let's go."

He walks me and Lucy to the car, inputs the nearest hospital into his GPS, and calls Tyler on my phone.

Tyler's quiet over speakerphone, a stark difference from when I last saw him about five months ago. He accepts all the information Scott gives him and agrees to meet us at the hospital.

I lie down in the back, Lucy on the floorboard licking at my stomach as I breathe through the pain and try not to think about how devastated Chris will be if I give birth without him.

And the fact that I'm the reason he isn't here.

Then more pain rips through my body, and the thought disappears.

# Chapter Fifty
## Christopher

I'm walking around Adelaide, a new employee I hired a few days ago to man the front desk and sign up new members. She listens intently as I tell her about safety protocols and nods, her eyes on the machinery.

We've been open for only a short time now, and slowly but surely the clientele is building and I'm still hiring employees.

I see people vacationing who realize they've enjoyed one too many lobster rolls and people who've been around the area for years who've decided they want something new to keep them entertained and physically fit, particularly given the approaching winter season.

Every time someone new comes in, I feel a jolt of excitement.

Hannah says my financials are looking good.

I've been sleeping in an apartment I rent on a month-to-month basis. I had briefly considered sleeping in the back office, but I decided the serendipity would be too much to bear.

It doesn't feel any different when I'm in bed missing her and the babies, though.

An empty bed is an empty bed. And I really wanted to be there to experience the whole pregnancy thing with her. I worry constantly, even though she's quick to reassure me whenever we speak.

I feel guilt every day that I'm not there with the babies, but Hannah always tells me that she wants to me to do it for the babies, that I'm setting up for their future, and I know she's right. Sacrifice is love.

This afternoon in December is absolutely freezing, and we're definitely busier than we were in the fall. I hadn't anticipated the impact of the seasons on business. In LA, it sometimes feels like the year is made up of one big, long summer.

I feel my phone buzzing in my pocket, look at the screen, and tell Adelaide, "Sorry, I have to take this. Why don't you go ask Jordan and Teague up front to show you how to sign up a new member?" I point to the front desk and start walking toward my office, my heart buzzing steadily in my chest.

It says Tyler's calling, and I'm not sure why that might be.

I remind myself that this would still be early for Hannah to have the babies. Maybe he's calling to apologize for that night at my house. He acted insanely, but he's still my best friend.

I feel jittery and anxious and breathe out in one long breath before answering. "Hey, Tyler, how are you?" I stretch my legs out in front of me to regulate.

"Chris? You need to get to UCLA Medical Center as soon as you can."

"Tyler, I'm in Maine."

I stand up straighter as his words zap me out of any daydreams I had about rekindling a friendship. I look around for my things and shove my wallet and keys into my pockets.

They weigh my shorts down awkwardly and slap against my thigh as I walk right out the front door and start walking down to my apartment just a few blocks over. "As soon as I can is probably still tomorrow."

"Then get here tomorrow. Hannah's going into labor and she's scared. She needs you."

I put Tyler on speaker phone so that I can look on my phone for the soonest plane tickets I can get.

His voice gets quieter and turns into a murmur as he says, "There was a guy with her. Some dude she was hanging out at the park with. I asked him who the fuck he is and he said 'Scott' and left. I think I scared him off, but still, you should get here quick."

I chuckle a little as I purchase tickets for a few hours from now. I order a car ahead of time for when I land and breathe out a sigh of relief.

I can see my little apartment over a hill. I can pack and be out of here quickly. I can be with Hannah by tonight. I don't wish a long labor on her, but I hope I might be able to get there before she has the babies.

"You think she's cheating on me at 7 months pregnant?"

"I don't know what she's doing, but that guy seemed like he was sniffing around her. I'm just looking out for you, bro."

Rolling my eyes, I get to my door and unlock it, slamming it closed behind me as I rush to my bedroom to pull out a suitcase and shove things in it haphazardly

"Okay, Tyler, I appreciate it. I'm sure you scared him well enough. We'll probably never see him again."

I have no doubt that Hannah isn't doing anything wrong, but it's nice that Tyler's worried about it. Maybe there's still a friendship between us yet.

"Will you put Hannah on video until my car comes? If she wants to."

Some brief rustling in the background happens, followed by unearthly moans coming from Hannah. I hear the beep of the call turning into a video call and finally see the beautiful mother of my children.

Tears stream down her face, and her cheeks are pink. She's lying back on a pillow, her hair a sweaty halo around her. "Chris?" she shrieks. "Chris, I need you!"

Her desperate voice carves out pangs in my chest, and I wish more than anything that I could reach out and touch her.

I want to stroke her hair and her back and tell her that she's safe. "I know, Hannah Banana. It's okay, sweets, I'm on my way to you now. I'm here with you until I get on that plane, okay? And I know Tyler will be there with you until I arrive. I'm so proud of you."

She sighs and closes her eyes, showing me her wet eyelashes. "I'm sorry I sent you there, Chris. I wish you were here."

"Hey, I'll be there soon, don't you worry." I grab toiletries and chargers and pack them into my bag.

I pack the engagement ring, too, just in case.

I have a good feeling.

When I arrive, it's late at night. An Uber takes me directly from the airport to the hospital. It's only about 15 miles so the drive won't take too long at this time of day.

My palms sweat and I stare straight ahead. The driver tries to talk to me, but I can't focus.

Eventually, he gives up and leaves me to stare in silence out the window. The lights of LA and the water rival each other, and I think that their only real nemesis is the color of Hannah's eyes.

I imagine her now, crying out in agony without me, and I can only hope that her parents and Tyler are offering her some relief.

She's been unable to call for the more than 7 hours I've been on a plane, and guilt has made a home in my chest knowing how panicked and stressed she is right now.

Finally, I arrive at the hospital and rush, my luggage in hand, to the front desk and then to the maternity unit.

I skip the elevator and rush up the stairs, holding my bag across my back, the weight not a concern compared to what Hannah's got to be feeling.

A Labor & Delivery nurse tells me where to find her. Busting in the door, I call out, "Hannah, baby, I'm here. I made it, right? Did I make it?"

A nurse sidles up to me. "You're Dad, I'm guessing. We've been waiting for you. You made it. Baby number one is crowning now. I need you to go hold Mom's hand for me and help her breathe through this."

I'm at her side immediately, holding her warm and sweaty hand in mine.

It feels good to feel her again, and she squeezes my fingers with the strength of...someone giving birth to twins.

I let her squeeze them as hard as she wants to and use my other hand to stroke her hair, pulling sweaty strands away from her face. Still, she's ethereal, dewy and glowing. "You've got this, Hanny," I murmur between clenched teeth.

She looks up at me with frozen fear and whispers back, "I don't know if I can do this."

"You can absolutely do this, Hannah!" Dr. Meyers tells her. "It's too late to go back now, Mama. We got you, though; we're gonna get you through it."

I look at the doctor, then turn and hold Hannah's sweaty palms with mine.

I press my forehead against hers so that it's just us and assure her, "You take your time. They'll come at their own pace. They won't stay in there forever. You don't worry what anyone says or thinks. You make the right choice for you."

I pull back away from her and she nods fiercely before breathing in, then out, and it's all a blur of screaming and crying and chatter and movement.

It's like being on a train station but not getting on. Everything around me is chaos and motion, and I'm the thing in the way.

But finally, the doctor's pressing two naked babies up against Hannah's chest and saying, "A girl and a boy, congratulations, Mom."

Hannah drops her head back for a moment and closes her eyes before snapping them open again and asking, "Wait, what did you say? We're having two boys."

"Oh, well, we must have read the ultrasound wrong. It happens. Give them both a quick cuddle and we're off with them to the NICU to get them checked out. They are two months early, which isn't unusual with twins, but they're small and we need to be sure we're on top of any lung or breathing issues. A nurse will stay and help you get cleaned up. Luckily, you didn't even need any stitches since these little guys just slipped right out. I'll be back to check on you in a while."

The nurses clean up Hannah and take us to her own room and away from the craziness of the Labor & Delivery rooms.

I tell Hannah, "I'm going to go tell Tyler and your folks that you're okay and that the babies are here. Maybe they can go down to the NICU and see them briefly."

She nods quietly and seems as if she's about to fall asleep.

At the door, I turn and ask, "Oh, and who's Scott?"

"Hm? Oh. My boyfriend," she teases. "Were we supposed to be exclusive?"

I run my tongue over my teeth. "You're going to pay for that one later," I promise her, looking through my eyebrows at her.

Catching my meaning, a nurse a few feet away calls out, "Not for 4 to 6 weeks, she won't!"

# Chapter Fifty One

## Hannah

Scott and I walk from the park back to the house.

The babies are in their stroller, sleeping soundly in the sun, their perfect eyelids twitching underneath the shaded awning.

They're just at the age when their vocalizing is starting to resemble words, and in their moments of sleep, when their seashell-colored lips are curled and still, I ache for their baby talk.

Scott holds Lucy's leash loosely. She doesn't take much direction at all; I'm constantly amazed by the luck the universe brought me with having Lucy as my children's dog.

Interestingly, or maybe obviously, someone driving you to the hospital in labor creates a bond, and Scott and I have grown to be good friends.

He struck up a relationship with one of the nurses who helped deliver my twins, and so I have her as a built-in friend now, too. Jessie. She's amazing, compassionate and confident, and with the best stories to tell, of course.

Tyler's constantly telling me to be careful around Scott, but Chris knows he has nothing to worry about.

Now that he's home and we're even making enough money to vacation in Maine over the hot LA summers, we're finally living the life we sacrificed for during my pregnancy. The days are good, and the nights are sweet.

Scott and I reach the front door, and I hand him the keys to unlock the door and hold it open for me so that I can struggle with the stroller wheels against the lip of the floor.

Scott and I head upstairs for water and a light fruit salad after our walk.

It's a ritual that I've grown to love. Sometimes Chris joins us too, but not today.

Today, he's been sneaky and reserved, wanting me to stay away while he makes and takes phone calls.

He keeps pushing me out of the house, asking if I'll run this and that errand for him. I have this feeling he's ordering me some sort of present, maybe a new car like we talked about. My old one is dissolving into rust more and more with each passing day.

When I reach the front door, I look over at Scott and see that he's got on a barely-suppressed smile. He sees me looking and points it at the floor.

"What is going on?" I ask him, my key still in the lock, "I can tell something's up. It's not my birthday, though, so what is it?"

Scott shrugs. "What are you talking about?"

"You know what I'm talking about! Chris has been trying to find reasons for me to stay out of the house for practically a week straight, and look at you, you're grinning!" I point at him accusatorily.

He smacks my hand away and demands, "Can you let me in? I'm dying of thirst. Isn't it enough that I walk your dog free of charge? Now you expect me to read Chris' mind? I don't really even know the man."

Keeping my narrowed eyes on him, I turn the handle, my heart pounding with anticipation, and open the door to…nothing different. Nothing out of place. Everything as it usually is.

I stand for a moment in the silence of the living room, just taking in how much I truly believed something was going on. "Well…" I trail off, recovering, "Let me cut up the fruit then."

"Oh, no, I've actually gotta go meet Jessie. She said she wants to have brunch. Could I just get a glass of water? I really am so thirsty."

"Oh, yeah, of course." I pour him a glass of water while he unclips Lucy.

When he walks over to me, I lean against the counter while he drinks it. I fiddle with my hair and toss it behind my back.

"We've gotta get together again, all of us, soon."

"Jessie would love that, you know she would, Hannah. We'll do that soon, okay? Really soon!" He points excitedly at me as he shuffles toward the front door.

Once he's disappeared, I call out for Chris, but he doesn't answer.

I roll the babies, still in their stroller, to the nursery, where I find Chris in the middle of the dimly-lit room on one knee. His smile splits open across his face, and he reaches out his hand for me, waving at me to come closer.

Tentatively, I step toward him, and he grips my fingers and pulls me in so that my waist is at the same height as his face. He hugs around my hips and pulls back so that he can look up at me into my eyes. "Well, you knew this was coming eventually."

I tilt my head back and laugh at the ceiling. So, this is why. "I guess I did," I sigh, raking my fingers through his curls.

"Hannah Jackson, almost a year and a half ago, you told me it wasn't the right time. Since then, well," he gestures with wide open arms at the room, "It seemed like the right time when your brother forgave me and it seemed like the right time when we bought the vacation home and it seemed like the right time when our kids started crawling for the first time. It has never not seemed like the right time when I'm with you."

I lean against his head, unable to look into his frightfully sincere eyes anymore. I hug him and giggle as he continues.

"You are my absolute dream girl, Hannah. You found your way over my walls and into my heart, and now I can't imagine life with you. I never saw myself doing this. I honestly didn't think I was capable of loving so completely and thoroughly.

But when I look at your face, it's like a siren call to be my best self. You are my better angel."

I roll my eyes, and he shakes my hand.

"No, really. You are empathetic, witty, brave, and resourceful. I would be forever honored to be your partner. Will you marry me, Hannah?" He pulls the ring out of his pocket and shows me it finally, after all this time.

It's a simple band of thirty diamonds, three rows of ten small diamonds in a gold setting.

It's exactly me, and that's reassuring in the same way that everything Chris does is reassuring.

He has a way of showing up at the right time and doing exactly the right thing, as though he has a map of my truest desires.

I press my fingers to my cheeks, feeling the streaks of tears on them. "Yes, Chris, I will marry you."

He slips the ring on my finger and holds me across the waist. "Finally," he laughs and then calls out, "She said yes! You can come out now!"

I watch in awe as everyone I love comes spilling out of different spots in my home. I hear the front door open, and Scott comes back inside, a mischievous grin on his face.

My mother and father come out of hiding to hug me and Tyler wraps his arm around Chris' neck.

Everything is as it should be, even if they've all woken up two cranky year-old toddlers.

I watch Chris jostle them out of their stroller, handing one to my mother and holding another up in the air to coo and laugh with.

Tyler comes up to me, smiling, and kisses my cheek. I smile at him and hug him for the brief second that he'll let me. I am so glad my brother is back in our lives. He's the best uncle I could have hoped to give my children.

"Well, it took a while, and things were complicated, but you're finally engaged."

He bumps me with his shoulder when I ignore him. "It did all work out, didn't it?"

It surely did.

Yep.

It surely did.

THE END

# Also By Claire Kirby

Thank you for reading! Care to make my day?

A honest review would be the cherry on top of this author's sundae and most appreciated!

Please click this link to post a review and then

Get ready for your next obsession!

Dive into the spicy, twin-tastic adventures of Taylor and Steve in the best selling

Sweet Twins For My Billionaire Boss

Where the chemistry's electric, the drama's addictive, and the love story will leave you breathless!

Don't miss out on your next favorite couple!

Made in United States
Troutdale, OR
11/15/2024